SWITCHED

SARAH READY

CROWN

PRAISE FOR SARAH READY

PRAISE FOR FRENCH HOLIDAY

"Ready (The Fall in Love Checklist) whisks readers to the South of France for a saucy enemies-to-lovers romance...This is a winner."

— *PUBLISHERS WEEKLY* STARRED
REVIEW ON *FRENCH HOLIDAY*

"Ready has written a tale that deliciously taps into its French trappings...A charming dramedy featuring a promising sleuthing duo."

— *KIRKUS REVIEWS ON FRENCH HOLIDAY*

PRAISE FOR JOSH AND GEMMA MAKE A BABY

"Romance author Ready gives Gemma rich and complex motivations for wanting a baby...An unusual and winning read about a little-discussed topic."

— *KIRKUS REVIEWS*

"A lively, entertaining, romantic comedy by an author and novelist with a genuine flair for originality, humor, and narrative driven storytelling..."

— *MIDWEST BOOK REVIEW*

PRAISE FOR JOSH AND GEMMA THE SECOND TIME AROUND

"In this sequel—which stands well enough on its own—the happily-ever-after moment is merely the starting point...Ready effectively leads readers to wonder if she isn't going to upend every single one of the genre's expectations. It's a testament to her exceptional writing skill that even the most romantic-minded readers won't be sure which outcome they prefer. A charming and disarmingly tough story of the many ways that love can adapt to crises."

— *KIRKUS REVIEWS*

PRAISE FOR CHASING ROMEO

"A fun and sweet love story..."

— *KIRKUS REVIEWS*

PRAISE FOR THE SPACE BETWEEN

"...emotional roller-coaster, but in the end true love prevails. For hopeless romantics, this one's got the goods."

— *PUBLISHERS WEEKLY*

"A touching tale of adult reckonings and reunions with some heart-tugging reversals."

— *KIRKUS REVIEWS*

ALSO BY SARAH READY

Scrooging Christmas

Dear Christmas

Stand Alone Novella:

Love Letters

Find these books and more by Sarah Ready at:

www.sarahready.com/romance-books

LOVE IS COMPLICATED...

For Serena Otaki, free-spirited Californian, life is simple. She loves smashing atoms at The Large Hadron Collider near Geneva, Switzerland. She loves Star Trek, spicy tofu, and her cat, Captain Purrk. She loves her messy (slobfest) apartment, her chaotic brand of organizing, and staying permanently, happily unattached.

Life is perfect. She has one true love—physics.

Loving a man isn't in her future.

For Henry Joule, uptight Brit, life is simple. He loves making analog black holes, drinking piping hot tea, and organizing his pencil tray. He loves his family, red meat, and obsessively cleaning his spotless apartment.

Life is perfect. He has many loves—physics, family, friends. He can't wait to find the woman of his dreams.

Love and marriage are in his future.

One perfect night Serena and Henry meet. Sparks fly, particles collide, the universe comes to a halt, and...

It was a mistake.

They're too different.

It won't work.

Love isn't in their future.

Until an electric storm causes an unexpected event at the particle collider and suddenly—they've switched.

Serena is in Henry's body.

Henry is in Serena's body.

And both life and love are suddenly very, very complicated.

Switched

SARAH READY

W.W. CROWN BOOKS
An imprint of Swift & Lewis Publishing LLC
www.wwcrown.com

Library of Congress Control Number: 2023947278
ISBN: 978-1-954007-65-9 (eBook)
ISBN: 978-1-954007-68-0 (pbk)
ISBN: 978-1-954007-69-7 (large print)
ISBN: 978-1-954007-70-3 (hbk)
ISBN: 978-1-954007-71-0 (audiobook)

"How do you
describe a feeling
that can't be put
into words?"

Switched

Sarah Ready

1

I'VE ALWAYS BELIEVED THAT THINGS ARE ONLY IMPOSSIBLE until they're not. For instance: particle physics, space travel, and sex on a tree branch. Everyone thinks, "My gosh, those are impossible! They can't possibly happen!" But then they do.

They do.

Everyone has instances of the impossible becoming possible in their own lives. I don't mean HUGE things like teleporting or dating an alien—I mean things like winning the state science fair against all odds or having their cancer miraculously disappear. These things happen.

Of course, HUGE impossible things become possible every day. Remember the world's oldest Twinkie? No one thought it could stay fresh for decades, but here it is, deliciously edible since 1976.

Anyway, the impossible is only impossible until it isn't.

Because I'm a physicist and I have a particular affinity

for graphs, lists, charts, and visual aids, I've included a list to show a few of the once impossible things in life that became possible.

Fair warning, life is more fun with:

- Charts
- Graphs
- Tables
- Footnotes[1]
- Bullet points

Okay, here it is.

THE THINGS ONCE THOUGHT IMPOSSIBLE UNTIL THEY BECAME POSSIBLE:

1. 1 million BC—Humans master fire (and have the first hot date with cooked mammoth and kissing).[2]
2. 3500 BC—The wheel (need I say more?).
3. 1876—The telephone (and phone sex).
4. 1901—Wireless transmission across the Atlantic.
5. 1961—Space travel.
6. 1996—I was born, because *impossibly*, both the condom and birth control failed.
7. 2004—I melted Barbie and Ken using only a potato battery and my Easy-Bake Oven.
8. 2010—The first atom was smashed at the Large Hadron Collider *and* I met Spock.

9. 2012—I lost my virginity to Bernie Berger in the kitchen pantry while my parents obliviously watched *Weird Science* in the living room.

10. 2018—I'm awarded a double PhD in Physics and Computer Science at age 22.

11. 2020—I land my dream job at CERN, smashing atoms.

12. 2022—I'm stuck *to* the seat of the wooden pub booth at The Cock and Bull.

13. 2022—Also, the guy at the table across from mine won't stop staring.

14. 2022—No, I mean I'm really, really stuck. As in, my jeans are practically glued to the wooden seat and they won't budge. How is this even *possible*? It's not.

I tug at my thighs, pry at my jeans, and wiggle-jerk from left to right. There's no fixing it. Somehow, impossibly, I'm glued to the wooden seat in the booth at the back of my favorite pub. It's ridiculous, impossible, embarrassing.

Okay, Serena, pull yourself together. You're a scientist —you can get out of any sticky situation life throws at you.

I gather energy, brace my palms on the tacky wooden tabletop, and shove upward as hard as I can, trying to burst free from my unlikely prison. I move all of a quarter inch, then rebound hard back to the wood.

"Umph."

I collapse back against the booth and let out a frustrated breath. Then I surreptitiously glance from the side of my eyes at the small, round table next to mine.

Yup, the man is still staring while pretending not to stare.

I've never seen him here before, which is why I don't call him over and ask him to brace himself against the booth edge and yank me free from my seat. I've seen some odd things in this pub over the years, but if he's new here, he may not be inured to all the pub's oddities.

The Cock and Bull is a tiny, rough stone-walled and thick wooden-raftered homely British pub owned by a short, hairy Italian named Vinny Vincenzo. There's the usual dark wood and plaid décor, British kitsch, and football (a.k.a. soccer) playing over the bar. The lights are low, the TVs flicker over the dull, sticky wood counters and floors, and instead of amplifying the sound, the old stone walls muffle everything to a garbled murmur.

The pub attracts zombie-eyed, post-five o'clock working schlubs from the neighborhood, rowdy students searching for cheap beer, homesick Brits, and the occasional tourist. I don't really fit the mold, but I live around the corner, and Vinny makes the best French fries I've ever tasted.

The pub is a rarity in Geneva since it's not Swiss, French, or moldy cheese-peddling. Plus it has cheap beer and gives out free eight-inch dill pickles with the purchase of a pint. That's why the dim interior always smells like pickle vinegar and hoppy beer sunk into centuries-old gray stone.

I wander in every Tuesday around six o'clock and grab my usual booth in the back. Tuesday night is my *me night*, when I have a date with myself. I order a two euro pilsner, a long, fat pickle that is so sour my lips pucker, a basket of crisp, buttery, steaming-hot golden fries, and then I pull out my notebook and try to break my mind with new theories about everything. Or at least theories about the fundamental laws of nature.

There are very few windows and even fewer tables, which is why I always make a beeline to the back corner, where there's a small, out-of-the-way two-person booth that no one ever notices. It has a scarred, scratched mahogany table with permanently sticky varnish, two hard wooden seats, and a little colored green glass lamp that casts a small pool of light across the tabletop.

It's a really nice spot. A great spot.

Except. I've never not been able to *move*.

I try to stand again, pushing my feet into the wood floor and bracing against the booth.

I grit my teeth and shove, but my thighs won't budge.

The table shakes, and I make a sound of frustration. The stranger sitting at the table across from me raises his eyebrows. Now he's not even trying to hide the fact that he's watching me.

"Excusez-moi," I say, feeling irritable.

At that, the edge of his mouth quirks into an amused half-smile.

"Are you British?" he asks in a proper Oxford accent. "American? Canadian?"

He tilts his head and gives me an expectant, open look.

It's not a hard deduction. We're in Geneva, Switzerland, home of the UN where nationalities collide and bump along every day. Plus, my French accent is terrible and I look a bit like the love child of Daisuke Serizawa (minus the eyepatch) and Lady Godiva (minus the nakedness), which most men find compelling (a.k.a. I feature in a lot of morning wood fantasies). So that means I'm an easy mark to—

Wait. A. Second.

He's been watching me. He was here before I arrived. He has a slight smile hovering at the edge of his mouth.

He . . .

"Did you do this?" I ask the stranger, outrage tinging my voice. I make a spinning circle with my finger, pointing at the booth, my thighs, and the unknown adhesive that's sticking me to the wood.

It's not outside the realm of possibility. He could be a predator, sticking women to restaurant booths like flies to flypaper, so he can "rescue" them. Sadly, I've seen worse pick-up strategies.

The man is a few years older than me and stunningly good-looking.

It's human nature to think attractive men are "good" and unattractive men are "bad." It's also human nature to think attractive men are "bad" and unattractive men are also "bad."

But the reality looks a bit more like this:

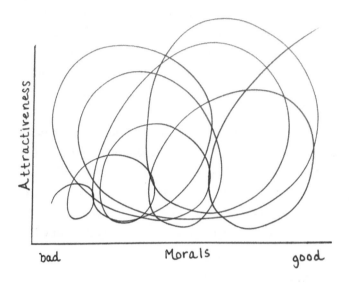

[Here we have a graph with Attractiveness on the Y axis and Morals on the X axis, and a squiggly mess of lines on the graph. And that's it.]

He's at the little two-person table next to my booth, sitting casually in the wooden pub chair, a half-finished pint in front of him and a half-eaten dinner of charred steak, a pickle, and crisp golden fries.

"Do what?" he asks, frowning and looking around the dimly lit pub just to make sure I'm talking to him.

I am.

I take a moment to catalog his features. Blue-gray eyes. Wheat-colored hair that falls just shy of the collar of his navy shirt. There's a light wool jacket slung over the back of his seat, a nod to the early spring chill. He has a nice chin—there's a little dimple there—and his cheekbones are high and sprinkled with a few freckles.

His lips are dark pink, and he looks as if he smiles a lot. His eyes are sharp, intelligent, and I think he's taking me in too. His gaze roves over my face and I feel his searching look as firmly as a touch. An electricity, as tangible as static arcs between us, buzzing and crackling.

He leans forward.

The muscles in his shoulders bunch, and I calculate that he's at least six feet, even though it's hard to tell when he's sitting. He's rangy but muscled. Intelligent, but probably not too intelligent. He's likely a tourist. Maybe he's here for a conference. Or . . . he's a psycho.

"Do this," I say, spinning my finger again. "Glue me in place."

At that he grins—a happy smile that kicks my heart into warp drive—his eyes crinkle at the corners, and he says, "You felt it too?"

2

WHEN I WAS FOUR YEARS OLD I FELL IN LOVE FOR THE FIRST time. It was an epic love, like the sun rising for the first time, spreading its golden light over the fertile ground of my open heart.

It happened one fall night when I was sitting outside in the cool, shaggy grass of our back yard in Northern California. The night-thick scent of cedar and redwood drifting from the old-growth woods just past the edge of our small, grassy lot tickled my nose as much as the grass tickled my bare feet. I could hear my mom washing dishes in the kitchen, my dad humming from the open door of his toolshed, and the raspy droning of cicadas congregating at the edge of the woods. My legs and arms puckered with goose bumps from the chill night wind, so I pulled my sleep shirt over my legs.

Then, I looked up.

I looked up and I was swallowed by the sky.

The Milky Way stitched across the black velvet, the moon full and pregnant with expectation, Mars with its red flickering light, Jupiter bright and strong, and I tumbled headlong into the mysteries of the universe. And then, as I fell, a meteor shot across the sky, streaking a path straight to my heart.

I gasped, swallowing the starlight, and then I jumped up and ran to my dad's toolshed, where he told me the distant stars were unreachable, that everything we saw happened millions of years ago, that some of the stars I saw were long dead, and that none of us, not a single one, could ever reach the stars, and if there were other habitable planets, other beings out there, we'd never know, because it was impossible to reach them too. We could yearn, but we'd never find what we were yearning for.

He said, "Ducky, keep your feet on the ground, and your eyes on what's possible."

But I was in love with the stars, with the universe, and so I decided right then and there that I loved this universe I'd found myself in and I was going to unlock its secrets. I was going to make the impossible possible.

That was the day I fell in love with science without knowing what science was.

But that feeling? That tumbling, rolling, diving through the stars to be swallowed whole by the wonderment of the night sky? Yes. That's a feeling I'd recognize anywhere.

I also avoid it. I flee from it as fast as a proton shooting at the speed of light. I don't have room to love anything else but science. It's my passion. It's my purpose. Plus, I know what happens when you fall for a man. You cease to be you.

You become this new creature, half-yourself, half-someone else. Your tastes change, your passions change, your priorities change. You literally lose yourself in the object of your desire. It's like the anglerfish—one of the most dysfunctional, toxic relationships in the animal kingdom. The clingy, jealous, controlling male anglerfish finds a female and then attaches himself to her. Not with his teeth or his fins or his reproductive organ,[1] but with his whole self. He mates with her and then their skin tissue fuses together, their circulatory systems combine, and they share all nutrients, blood, oxygen, *everything*, until the day they die.

This is basically what happens when two people fall in love.

Everyone knows this. We've all seen it.

Those couples who wear matching his-and-her outfits? *Khakis, white shirt, Converse! We're one person!*

The couples who combine their name? *We're Nathangela! Elizabert! Kerbob!*

The couples who speak as if they are *one* person with *one* opinion? *"We only eat local, organic, gluten-free sausage." "Our favorite color is ecru." "We like to be spanked."*

It's all out there for everyone to see. Fall in love, lose yourself.

Fall in love, have your organs fused, your brain hijacked, and your personality wiped.

So, when the stunningly attractive man with the dimpled smile, the sky-gray eyes, and the rumbly voice that makes my heart pound asks if I *feel* it too, I take a moment to laze in what I'm feeling.

Tingling skin. Thumping heart. Shortness of breath. A pull tugging me toward him even while I'm glued to my seat.

Is it love?

Or is it lust?

Is it stardust raining over me, or is it "yes please, let's get it on tonight and then never speak again"?

My mouth goes dry at the unexpected visual—me with my legs wrapped around him, his hands gripping my bare thighs, his mouth devouring mine. Suddenly I wish Vinny had brought out my pilsner and pickle, but unfortunately no one has come by yet.

The soft rumble of the pub, muted by the stone, folds around us. The dark of the far corner, the shadow of the low-beamed ceiling, blankets us in intimacy. The spice of vinegar and beer pinches my nose.

The man leans closer as he tilts his head, waiting for my answer. I feel that static again, the warm electric pull running through me, lighting up my insides, tugging me toward him.

Lust.

It has to be lust.

Us humans, we're made up of electrical impulses. Our hearts run on electricity. Our neurons are jumping with it. So it's not surprising that I'd find a man who makes me feel as if I'm sitting next to a generator, plugged in and buzzing with delicious, stroking energy.

So. Do I feel it?

"Maybe . . ." I say in a careful voice, and the man grins as if I just shouted "yes" from the top of Mount Blanc for all of Geneva to hear.

At his grin, I can't help it. I grin back.

His eyes widen and he stands, pushing his chair back. It scrapes across the wood floor. Now that he's upright I can see that he's exactly as tall as I thought, a little over six feet. He dwarfs the low-ceilinged pub with its homey plaid, cozy wood, and crowded tables.

I trace my gaze over him. His shoulders are wide and

solid, he's built like a footballer, lean but muscled. He stands with confidence, his shoulders back, his eyes direct, and he takes two long strides to stand next to my sticky-topped table.

As soon as he does, the cool, vinegary air of the pub is swept aside and replaced by viscous warmth and his subtle scent—clean, fresh mountain air, cedar, and . . . can someone smell like starlight? Oh yes, he smells like starlight.

No. That doesn't make sense. People don't smell like starlight.

I blink at him as he holds out his hand. "I'm Henry Joule, from Oxford."

I pause, wondering if this is one of those moments that should come with a warning label. For example: "Proposition 65 Warning for California Residents: This man may contain chemicals[2] known to cause reproductive harm from repeated sex, masturbation, and uncontrollable desire."

Or perhaps the warning is that his last name is Joule, the same as James Joule, the famed English physicist who discovered the relationship between the amount of heat produced and the current flowing through a conductor. The man who the Joule[3] is named after.

I hold my hand out to him and say, "Ducky, from Northern California."

3
_____

You may be wondering why I introduced myself as Ducky. You may also be wondering why I'm addressing you and breaking the fourth wall.

Look, I'm a theoretical particle physicist. I _know_ (okay, theorize) there are more dimensions than the one I'm living in. I _know_ (fine, theorize) that people are watching our lives, reading our lives. I _know_ (alright, theorize) you are there. There's the first dimension, the second and third dimensions, and then there's the fourth wall dimension.

If you ever want to get a kick out of life, go about your day and then stop, look at the sky, and say in a serious voice, "Little did she know, her ordinary life was about to change."

Or if you're having sex, you can pause and say, "Stop watching me! Pervert!" Then your partner will ask, "What? Why?" And then you can say, "I'm not talking to you. I'm talking to _them_." Then you can get back to it, having made your point. Because trust me on this, someone out there, somewhere, is (theoretically) watching the story of your life too.

I smile at Henry as he enfolds my hand in his and says in his crisp accent, "It's a pleasure."

And although he hasn't asked, I can tell he has the same question you do: why Ducky? Am I named after the lame friend from that cult classic *Sixteen Candles*? Or is it a childhood nickname? No. Neither.

"Nice to meet you," I agree, smiling at him with something that probably looks like a foolish grin.

I can't help it. His hand is warm, strong. His lean fingers hold mine and the heat of his touch sends a thrill through my blood, lighting me from the inside out. My mind momentarily goes blank as I bask in the warmth working its way over my skin. His touch feels as if we are pressed together, heart-to-heart, his mouth nuzzling the hollow of my neck, his hands stroking over me. The cells in my body realign and point toward him.

The Large Hadron Collider at CERN has seven-ton superconducting magnets—huge mothers, strong. They don't have anything on the pull I'm feeling.

Lust.

This has to be lust.

The strongest I've ever felt, but nothing more.

Slowly, I pull my hand from his, tensing at the loss of the coursing warmth. Then I wiggle, still stuck in place, and say, "What I meant was, I'm stuck to my seat, and . . ." —I lift a shoulder—"I thought for a moment you may have put down an adhesive."

"An adhesive?" He frowns, glancing down at my stuck-tight thighs.

"Uh-huh." I demonstrate by tugging at my leg and attempting—and failing—to stand.

Henry flashes a grin at my predicament, his dimples deepening. "Well, yes. I did once glue Ms. Treacletee's favorite teacup to a mismatched saucer. It drove her mad—"

"Nanny?"

"Headmistress."

"Ah," I say. "Well. I'm sure the teacup had it coming."

He nods solemnly and studies me with a grave expression. "It did. The saucer was always complaining. 'You're such a *tea*se.'"

Hmm. I trace my finger across the wooden tabletop, doodle a five-sigma,[1] and look up at him. "I wonder . . . I've never been tea or a tease. However, I'm still—"

Henry glances at my thighs then says, "Stuck?"

I wriggle and try to stand again. No luck. "Like a pig in a blanket."

Instead of responding, Henry leans closer, his starlight scent fanning over me, and pulls a piece of paper off the side of the wooden booth.

"I think . . ." he begins, holding out the sheet to me. It's torn a bit, there's a piece of tape, and in bold handwriting it says in French, "Wet Varnish, Do Not Sit."

"Varnish?" I ask, mentally face-palming.

"Varnish," he confirms. The dimples in his cheeks deepen and his blue-gray eyes brim with humor.

I glance around the pub. It's gotten busier in the few minutes we've been chatting. All the tables are full, energy bounces around the wood and the stone, and post-work laughter mixes with the slosh of beer and the scent of French fries and pickles (and, now that I take the time, varnish).

At the long wooden bar, Vinny Vincenzo, hairy and scowling, is completely occupied by a dozen rowdy students calling for another round of "The Unctuous Uni," which is a vile drink consisting of pale ale, cheap gin, and pickle juice. For some reason the male students love to bet on how many rounds they can chug before someone vomits.

Regardless, with the frenzied students, a few clusters of glassy-eyed tourists, and some post-work commuters catching a break before heading home, Vinny won't be coming by my table for a good ten minutes.

So it seems like there's only one good solution. Well, I wouldn't say good, but expedient. It's expedient.

"So . . ." I smile sweetly at Henry. "I noticed you have a coat."

I'm not ignorant of the salubrious effect[2] my smile has on the male population, and I'm not averse to using it to my advantage.

Henry nods, a twinkle in his eye, like he knows exactly what I'm doing and doesn't mind at all. "Yes, indeed. I do have coat."

I lean toward him and say in a low voice, "Do you think I could, perhaps, borrow your coat? Since we've shaken hands, introduced ourselves, bonded over adhesives."

The edge of his mouth twitches. "Of course. Shall I hold my coat up while you Houdini your jeans?"

Gosh, he's a quick study. "That would be delightful. Thank you."

So he does. Like a gentleman he holds his long wool coat in front of me like a curtain before a show. In this case it's a striptease. Luckily, my favorite booth is in the back corner, dark and out of the way, so no one notices as I kick off my high heels, unbutton my jeans, and use the wooden table as leverage while I wriggle free.

Henry keeps his head turned and his eyes averted.

I jiggle, I wiggle, I kick and push up with my hands, until I've managed to kick free. Then I squat on my jeans, my knees folded up, with my bare legs hidden from view behind Henry's coat. I keep expecting someone to yell, "Hey there! She's nudie!" but luckily everyone seems distracted by the beer-chugging throng of students.

My bare legs pucker with goose bumps at the cool air blowing over them. And me, I frequently don't wear underwear, so *everything* comes out to say hi. Plus my sweater hits well above my hips . . . so.

"Don't look," I say quickly. "I'm free. I'm going to put on your coat now."

"Right," he says, his jaw tensing as he turns his face further toward the cheering/chugging students.

I crouch between the table and the back of the booth and quickly take his coat, shoving my arms through the sleeves concealing my bare butt, thighs, and everything else. With fast fingers I button it closed. The warmth of the coat and the fresh air, cedar, and star-studded scent of him wraps around me.

"All set," I say, pulling the coat closed. "Coming out."

Henry steps aside and then turns toward me as I carefully make my way out of the booth. His eyes warm when he sees his gray wool coat wrapped around me. It's so long it nearly hits my knees.

"Well done," he says. He reaches under the table, picks up my black heels, and then holds them out for me.

My heart gives a little flip when he does. I hear myself ask without thinking, "What are you doing tonight?"

He smiles as I take my shoes and then nods to his table. "Dinner. Rescuing you." He shrugs. "After that, it's my first night in Geneva. I thought I might—"

He stops at my wide smile, and I say, "I'll show you around. I'll show you the city at night. I can take your coat on a magical tour, and you can tag along."

I was right. He's a tourist. A lone tourist having dinner in a British pub. Perhaps a tourist hoping for a one-night, no-regret fling with an intriguing—hey, I can be intriguing—woman he met while on holiday.

"That sounds . . . magical," he says, studying me with a familiar warmth that makes me feel as if I'm wrapped snug and comfortable in his arms.

I frown at him, my gaze moving to his bare ring finger. "You're not married, are you?"

I don't do married.

He shakes his head. "No. You?"

"No. Engaged? Dating someone?"

"No." His eyes warm and his golden-wheat hair glints in the pub's low light.

I smile then and bend down to slip on my heels, glad to get my toes off the cold wood floor. I gain three inches from them, putting me about six inches shorter than him. Not terrible. Not terrible at all.

"And you? Engaged? Dating?" he asks, curiosity and maybe a little hope tinging his voice.

"No," I say. "It's just me."

I don't do attachments. I don't do love. But mutually satisfying one-night flings? That I do.

4
———————

HENRY DOESN'T GET A TOUR OF GENEVA. NEITHER DOES HIS
coat.

Instead we're in his hotel room. After he paid for his
dinner, he mentioned he'd forgotten his phone at his
hotel, and could we go grab it because he wanted to take
pictures? I figured he was fabricating an excuse to get us
back to his room, which I was one hundred percent there
for, but when we walked into his hotel room there was his
phone, sitting on the wooden desk near the window.

His hotel is one of those old five-story sandstone regal
palace-like places that look like they belong in a high-
budget historical miniseries about Marie Antoinette. It's
snooty, dignified, and full of marble and self-importance.
I like it immediately.

The hotel spreads its stone-and-ivy terraces out like a
beribboned skirt fluffed over the bank of Lake Geneva.
Strings of outdoor lights line the windows and the stone
walkway where little white boats bob in the mirrorlike
water, ducking their heads to the hotel, the grand lady

above them. The twinkle lights of the hotel and the city along the stone shore all dance and nod in the night water, reflecting magic.

It's five-star, the kind of place where dignitaries and bankers stay, and I wonder for a moment if Henry is either but decide that it doesn't really matter. I've had enough flings to know that small talk—"And what do *you* do?"—gets in the way of really knowing someone. "What do you do?" should probably be the last question you ask someone if you want to find out who they really are.

In my opinion, "What do you *like* to do?" results in much more interesting conversations. For example, I like to search for alternate dimensions, fangirl at *Star Trek* conventions with my best friend Jillian, eat dill pickles with French fries, and swim naked at night. Isn't that interesting?

I spin slowly, my feet sinking into the plush gold carpet, and take in the luxurious hotel room. It smells like orchids and fresh linens, there's a twinkling, gem-studded chandelier, the walls are covered in hand-painted gold wallpaper, and the rich, ivory-colored silk curtains drape from the high ceilings to the floor. The room has French Regency-style wood furnishings, elegant and ornate—a glossy walnut and gold-inlaid armoire, a writing desk with curlicue legs, and a spindly-looking chair that couldn't possibly hold the weight of a six-foot-tall man. And then the bed, a four-poster with a deep mattress covered in a night-blue silk duvet. The headboard is wrapped in navy velvet with a single gold tassel hanging from the center.

Henry quirks a smile at my inspection as he slips his phone in his pocket. "A bit pretentious, isn't it?"

I turn to him, and when I do his wool coat swishes

and the satin lining inside whispers over my bare legs. I'm surprised to find how close he is to me. Close enough to feel the heat of him and the pull of him.

"Maybe a little." I hold my finger and thumb a quarter inch apart.

He nods, considers, then says, "I think ... perhaps ... the tassel ... too much."

I stare at the bed. "You're right. It's the tassel. Way overdone. But still, I like it."

His gaze warms, and as I look into his eyes, bright under the chandelier, I have the strongest urge to stand on my tiptoes, rest my hands on his shoulders, and put my mouth to his.

He must see the need in my eyes. He takes a step closer so that we're nearly touching. The air shifts around us, carrying memories of a starry night, familiar and tempting.

The air pulses, electrified and vibrating with energy. My breath catches in my lungs and my heart beats like raindrops pattering against the windowsill.

Slowly, Henry reaches up, his eyes on mine the entire time. The air crackles, and I lean forward as he gently touches the pads of his fingers to my cheek. His touch is hot, and I light up, my blood magnetized and rushing at the speed of light.

Oh. My. Word.

Thoughts flee.

Words fly away.

I sink into the feel of his fingers, the contact points of each four fingers and thumb, the exact spot he's touching me. The cool of the room vanishes in a rush of heat. The hum of the air-conditioning fades under the rushing in my ears.

Outside the tall, silk drape-lined window, the black night frames the Jet d'Eau. The famous geyser shoots a fountain of frothy water one hundred and forty meters into the starry sky. The water fans out, sprinkling like gold dust across the twinkling lake lit up with city lights.

I hold my breath as Henry shakes his head and says, "I never do this."

He waits, his fingers drawing gently across my cheek, hesitantly touching the corner of my lips—fleeting, needing. There and gone.

At work I play in subatomic distances, spaces smaller than a proton. I pause in nanoseconds, spaces shorter than the blink of an eye, faster than the flutter of a hummingbird's wing.

And I know, from years of capturing once-in-a-lifetime data, "If you don't reach out and capture the moment, you may never find that moment again."

He studies my expression. The room is quiet except for my heartbeat drumming in my ears. I lift my chin. Look solidly into his eyes.

He nods then takes his other hand and places it across the small of my back.

"This is one of those moments? The ones we should capture?" he asks, his gaze direct, questing.

His fingers spread over my spine, firm and strong. A delicious tingle travels over me. My eyelashes flutter and I lean into him. The touch of him holding me, pressing both hands into me, gives a clear answer.

"Yes," I say, giving him a brilliant smile.

He smiles down at me, wry, intelligent, restrained. But all that vanishes when I step back, pluck the buttons free on his wool coat, and then drop it to the floor.

Henry grins at me, his eyes dancing with humor, and

more—a liquid silver heat that might scorch me if I stay too long.

The cool air plucks at my bare legs and thighs and everything else. It's just me, all bare except my cropped sweater and high heels.

"I've never been so jealous of a coat before. I'll never get rid of it," he swears, truth and humor dancing in his eyes. "Lucky, lucky coat."

"Luckier man," I say.

Then I lift my sweater over my head, the wool scraping my skin, and bare my breasts to the cool of the room and the heat of his gaze.

At that, he steps close, the warmth of him curling around me. He cups my cheek, threads his fingers through my hair, and presses his mouth urgently to mine.

5

IN 2010, WHEN THE LARGE HADRON COLLIDER FIRST smashed atoms together, physicists were in a fever pitch of excitement. Even though I was still a kid, I knew the entire world—no, humanity itself—was at a crossroads and nothing would ever be the same again.

We were at a divergence, and what happened at CERN would determine our path forward.

There were some who thought it was Armageddon and the world would end, sucked into a black hole of our own making. Others believed we'd create another dimension and our own dimension would cease to exist. There was no evidence that either of these would or could happen. What could happen was even more incredible. (Yes, yes, I know . . . what is more incredible than a black hole sucking earth to its doom? Well, I'll tell you.)

The LHC is the largest machine humans have ever built. ATLAS, the particle detector where I work, is five stories high, and when you lift your head and stare in awe, you feel as if you're standing inside the mechanism of an intricate, elegant, beautiful, gigantic Swiss watch. The ring that the protons speed around is seventeen miles long, and like I mentioned, the magnets are seven tons. It took years and years and billions of dollars to build.

Thousands of scientists from more than a hundred nations joined together to pursue a theory, a dream. Some of these scientists came from nations that are bitter enemies—with decades of war behind them—yet hate and prejudice has no place in a dream as big as the Large Hadron Collider.

It's beautiful, it's profound, it's a search that began four hundred years ago and has pointed toward this moment for a long, long time. Physicists—philosophers and artists at heart—have spent lifetimes trying to discover the fundamental nature of nature.

Why are we here? What happened in the beginning? What is our place in the universe? Were we created, or are we an anomaly born of chaos?

When the LHC was set to smash its first atoms, physicists around the world held their breath. You could almost hear the world waiting, lungs aching, not daring to breathe, just . . . waiting.

We were looking for the Higgs Boson. Some people call it the god particle, although physicists cringe when they do.

The Higgs was going to tell us whether the universe was created in harmony and symmetry, with beauty and order at its very base . . . or it was going to tell us the universe was a small pocket within a greater universe full of deadly chaos, and that we were on our own in an unstable fragment, set to die, wretchedly alone. It would tell us whether there was more—vive la physics—or that there was no more, nothing else—la mort of physics.

Supersymmetry vs. Multiverse.

Order vs. Chaos.

Life vs. Death.

When we look out at the universe, sometimes we see fragments, dusty bits and pieces of a memory of a reflection of something that, in the beginning, was heartachingly beautiful. We can see the beauty in it, the harmony, and we want—no, we *need*—to know, to discover, to understand.

Some say when you reach the end of physics, you find the beginning of God.

In my small, kidlike way, I prayed that the LHC would point toward symmetry, order, life. I didn't want my search to end before it began.

There are two types of particle physicists. Theoretical physicists (me) and experimental physicists (the other guys).

Theoretical physicists are like the explorers of old, fearlessly wading into uncharted waters, not afraid to take risks. We tumble headlong into unbelievable, unfathomable spaces. We create the theories. We dream.

Experimental physicists are the practical physicists, the builders and doers. They take the theories we create, run experiments, collect data, and tell us theorists whether our theories are true.

It's a marriage. We can't exist without each other.

Well, the LHC smashed its first atoms, and it found the Higgs.

All the seeking, all the yearning, and our answer was found in the moment protons collided and data flowed from the wreckage. The LHC created what happened in the moments after the Big Bang.

It was breathtaking. It was a prayer. It was the best of humanity.

It was like that moment I looked up at the heavens and a meteor shot straight to my heart. I fell in love.

My arms are wrapped around Henry's back, he's slick with sweat and hot to the touch. His muscles bunch under my hands as my fingers stroke the long lines of his spine. He stirs on top of me, pressing me deeper into the silk of the bed, and I'm surrounded by him. Consumed by him.

My legs are still wrapped around his middle, my calves rub across his back. My blood pounds in my ears, my heart thuds wildly against my chest. I'm out of breath, dizzy. My skin tingles, my body thrums with a harmony I recognize. Any physicist would recognize it.

In Supersymmetry every particle has a pair, a match. It's eloquent, really.

And awful.

Because when Henry looks down at me, his thumb brushing over my cheek, his mouth pressing a soft kiss to my lips, I see something in his eyes that I never expected to see.

His blue-gray eyes, they're . . . oh no.

No, no, no.

That's love.

He drops next to me, gently pulls me into his side, and my heart pounds against his chest, foolishly betraying me.

"Ducky?" he asks, brushing at my hair, stroking his hand over my hip.

"Hmm?" I ask, the taste of panic building, because all

I want to do is lie limp against him and let him keep stroking me, kissing me, until we can make star-colliding love again.

"This may be forward, but can I see you tomorrow? And the next day? I feel somewhat idiotic saying this. I've never believed in love at first sight, but I think I've just been proven wrong."

His fingers pause. He holds his breath, waiting for my answer.

And . . .

Holy crap.

Holy ever-loving crap.

Now I know.

I know exactly why Henry smelled like starlight. Why every time I look at him, touch him, breathe him in, I'm reminded of falling.

It wasn't lust.

It wasn't need.

It was just . . . love?

6

I PACE THE HOTEL BATHROOM, THE COLD TILE NUMBING MY feet, the hotel robe chafing my sensitive skin. The fluorescent lights cast me as a pale, ghostly woman with wide, freaked-out eyes and pink, kiss-stung lips.

I'm swallowed by the white terrycloth hotel robe. Even so, the chill in the black-and-gray tile bathroom has me shivering.

After Henry's question I distracted him with a kiss and then told him I needed to clean up. I threw on the robe, grabbed my phone, and headed toward the bathroom.

He asked if I'd like room service. Coffee? Tea? Dinner? That bit of generosity nearly broke my heart. He's a good guy. He's . . . oh gosh.

I can see it now. I fall for him and all of a sudden we're wearing matching outfits, riding a tandem bike in Napa, calling ourselves Denry, Hucky, Hersena (whatever), I'll be pregnant with our fifth child and

Henry will proudly say, "We're pregnant!" even though he (and everyone else) knows *he* bloody (oh no, I'm already using "bloody"!) isn't pregnant, it's me who is pregnant, who is pushing the baby out of my vagina and taking maternity leave and . . . I'll start watching BBC period dramas and unending cricket matches and drinking tepid tea and be British and not Californian, and somehow I'll no longer care about physics, or even work at CERN, because suddenly I'll care more about my husband and babies and breastfeeding and which diaper wipes to use, and my husband's career prospects and his banking/dignitary(?) transfers to Mozambique, and his mom's opinion of my cooking and his friends' opinions of which football team will take the World Cup, and also getting an electric minivan and tax rebates and . . . I'll be gone. I won't be me.

I wonder for a moment what my best friend since childhood, Jillian—she's a relationship columnist in New York—would do. Then I remember she can't talk to men (at all) so she wouldn't even be in this situation. Ever. So that's no help.

I stare into the mirror. The bathroom is large with a modern glass-encased rain shower and little lux toiletries on the black granite countertop. Henry has placed a travel bag of toiletries on the counter. He has a stainless-steel razor, a shaving brush, expensive shaving soap in a metal container—it smells like him—and his toothbrush and toothpaste lined neatly by the sink. Everything is in order. Perfect order.

In fact, I've noticed his hotel room is unbelievably tidy and clean. His suits hang in the closet, pressed neatly, next to crisp white shirts. There are perfectly polished dress shoes—dark brown, light brown, and black—with a shoehorn.

A shoehorn.

Do you know what this means?

Henry is neat. Obsessively neat.

And me? I'm a slob. There's no other way to look at it.

As I stare at myself in the mirror I can see myself fading. If I fall in love, I'll slip away. It'll be unnoticeable at first, until one day I'll wake up and find that I've organized my shoes by color, my spice drawer is alphabetized, and I have a daily planner that I actually follow.

My face pales even further. My eyes are so dark against my skin they almost look black. I take a deep breath, wincing when I pull in the enticing scent of Henry's shaving soap.

I turn on the faucet—a slick modern one where the water falls out of a flat chrome bar, illuminated with a purple LED light. The water is freezing-cold, so I cup it in my hands and then splash my face, pinching my cheeks.

"Pull it together," I hiss at myself. "It's not the end of the world."

Do you remember five minutes ago when I was rhapsodizing about humanity reaching a divergence? A fork in the road?

Supersymmetry vs. Multiverse.

Order vs. Chaos.

Life vs. Death.

Well, this is my fork.

You can't love two things passionately. One will always eclipse the other.

Doesn't the Bible say that you can't serve two masters? You will always love one and hate the other?

This is the same thing.

I fell in love with physics. I made my choice. I can't fall in love with a man too.

I'm not going to anglerfish myself.

I can hear Henry outside the door ordering wine, fruit, coffee, and chocolate cake from room service. His rumbly voice, muffled by the wooden door, falls over me, making my skin tingle as I remember the low sound of his voice in my ear whispering delightful, shocking, delicious things while he was gripping my hips and driving into me.

So.

"Enough of that," I say.

I take my phone from the bathroom counter. I brought it in because I know there's nothing better to settle my tumultuous emotions than a good dose of work emails.

I lean against the cold counter's edge, open up my email, and let the bright vanity lights and cold tile wash away all the lingering heat and need and pull.

I scroll through my emails. Let's see . . . How about some plots from our latest dataset? The z, the nanoseconds, the . . .

The subject of an email catches my eye.

My team has a new project lead. Starting next week.

How didn't I know about this? This is my boss. You'd think I'd have heard something before the announcement. Yet here I am, getting an email at the last hour.

I click it open, smiling because here I am, already distracted. A new boss is a guaranteed distraction. The scent of Henry's shaving soap is barely making a dent in my concentration.

Really.

But then, two worlds collide. They crash together in a nanosecond. And my word, the wreckage is immense.

Because my new boss?

It's Henry Joule, of Oxford.

7

SOME PEOPLE MAY THINK, "OH, THAT'S WONDERFUL! YOUR boss, your fellow physicist, fell in love with you at first sight! You have chemistry! You have magnetism! It's a match made in heaven!"

Every single one of those people and their ejaculatory exclamation points would be wrong.

This is one of those moments that requires a chart to illustrate exactly why Henry and I are not a match made in heaven.

REASONS WHY I SHOULD PURSUE THIS THING WITH HENRY	REASONS WHY I SHOULD PUT THE KIBOSH ON HENRENA
Best sex of my life	It feels like love
That thing he does with his tongue	It feels like love
That bit with his red necktie and my ankles and the lamp	It feels like love
He's funny	It feels like love
He ordered me chocolate cake	It feels like love
He's thoughtful	It feels like love
He gets me	It feels like love
It feels like love	It feels like love x 10^98

That feels like a lame cop-out, I know. However, statistically, the kibosh column has more significance than the pursue column. Also, he's a physicist and my new boss.

I can practically hear you salivating. Oooooh, an office romance! I love office romances! Hot server-room sex. Having a big bang while replicating the Big Bang. Making your parts collide while particles collide. Quickies during coffee break. Paper clip and stapler sex toys.

The answer is no.

A hard no.

It's not happening.

I've been pursuing my dream of contributing to my field, perhaps discovering a new particle or even making a Nobel Prize-worthy discovery, for more than half my life. I'm not going to throw it all away for something that feels a lot like love.

Besides, in office romances it's always the woman who loses. If it goes sour, statistically speaking, it's the woman who leaves her position or is transferred or passed over for promotion—you name it. Dating a male colleague is akin to throwing your career in a raging dumpster fire. Plus, sour or sweet, you're so caught up in the emotion of it all you aren't able to do. Your. Job.

If I'm swept up in a romance with Henry (see the points in the pursue column, esp. row 2), if I take the fork that points toward love, there is only one possible ending. Me, no longer me. Me, without my dream.

On the other hand, if I end things now, definitively, I can continue on my current path. Henry will thank me (someday), I'll thank me (now), and that's that.

Which is why I came up with the best solution possible. Okay, maybe not the *best*, but it's expedient. It's definitely expedient.

Now it's seven o'clock on Wednesday night and I'm in the kitchen of The Cock and Bull.

The vinegary pickle brine stings my eyes, and the loud clatter of ceramic plates hitting the stainless-steel counter and the greasy fryer sizzling bounce around the steaming-hot kitchen.

I wipe at the sweat starting to bead on my brow and then pull my emerald-green silk top away from the stickiness forming between my breasts.

The kitchen is a tight space, dominated by a pyramid of ten-gallon plastic tubs full of dill pickles and a few large metal trays full of steak-and-kidney pies and just-cooked sausage toad resting on the stainless-steel counter.

It's cramped, with grease-covered thirty-year-old appliances, a wheezing refrigerator, a swearing griddle-and-fryer cook with sweat-stained armpits (his name is Giovanni—he's Vinny's cousin on his mother's side), and flypaper taped to the wall above the stove (with many, many flies trapped on the sheet).

I shift in my high heels on the grease-splattered linoleum and take a bolstering breath of the pickle vinegar air.

"Well?" I ask Vinny, keeping my voice steady and my gaze direct. "Will you do it?"

Vinny is the same height as I am when I'm in three-inch heels—five foot seven—except, unlike me, Vinny is bulky and bull-like. He has long, thick black hair that he wears slicked back in a ponytail. His eyebrows are full, his beard glistens, and his chest hair is the stuff of legends. He once told me full chest hair is a sign of virility, then he gave me another pickle.

Vinny strokes his fingers over his beard and pulls his eyebrows down. Then he asks in a slow voice, rich with his Sicilian accent, "You want me to have sex with you?"

His thick eyebrows do an "ooh la la" sort of move.

At the fryer, Giovanni mutters an urgent prayer under the sizzle and pop of frying French fries.

"No," I say, looking up at the flickering fluorescent lights for patience. "I want you to *say* that you and I are having sex. Tonight."

Yes. This is the best plan I could come up with. I know.

After I saw that Henry was my boss, I panicked. I burst out of the bathroom, grabbed my shoes, and told him I'd had a personal emergency and had to go. He said, "Wait, will I see you again?" I stared at him wide-eyed, caught, and he said, "The pub, tomorrow at six." He asked my number and texted me his. Then he gave me his coat, bundled it around me, and sent me on my way with one last firm kiss, where he gripped my hips, and then . . . then . . .

I looked him up.

Henry Joule, of Oxford. Not born in Oxford, but of Oxford University. His resume is impressive. He graduated from Oxford with a PhD in physics, his postdoc positions were at world-renowned institutions—the hub of European particle physics research—and just last year he worked with a team that created an analogue black hole. Yes. Henry Joule created a black hole from sound waves. He wrote an eloquent paper on the

Hawking radiation emitted by the sonic black hole. I won't wax on about it—I'll only say that if I didn't know Henry, his paper would've given me a science hard-on.

But studying him told me one thing I could've already guessed just from spending one evening with him.

Henry doesn't give up. He's intelligent. He's driven. He's passionate.

If I were to sit down with him, have a glass of cabernet, and say in a mature manner, "I'll be working under you. I don't date colleagues,"[1] he might accept this at first or he might have arguments. The problem is, after a while I'd give in. That's my fear. The magnetic pull toward him is too strong. He's that seven-ton superconducting magnet and I don't know if I can resist him. Maybe for a month, two . . . but for six months? A year? Working with him every day? Wanting him every day?

If I tell him I don't date colleagues and he accepts this, he'll still be friendly. He'll be courteous. He'll smile at me and make jokes like he did last night. And sometimes he'll look at me and we'll both remember his red necktie and his tongue and that lamp.

So.

The best way around it, the expedient way, is to make it clear before he even knows who I am that he and I aren't . . . anything. It was meaningless. Nothing.

That way, when he arrives in the office on Monday morning, there won't be anything there.

I'll be able to do what I love.

And so will he.

I won't lose myself for a man. I won't lose myself for love. Not ever.

I focus on Vinny's waggling eyebrows.

"Well?" I ask again.

"My dear mother taught me never to lie," he says, smirking. "I think we should make sweet love and then my dear mother will not be ashamed to have given birth to a liar."

Huh.

I tap my heel on the floor and put my hands on my hips. A bit of sweat runs down my temple. Outside the kitchen, in the pub, the same group of students from last night chants as they chug pints of the Unctuous Uni.

"No," I say.

Vinny holds out his hands with a sad frown and an expression that says, "What can I do?"

Giovanni lifts the wire mesh fry basket from the fryer and the grease drains with a sizzle. He barks over his shoulder, "This British. Is he stalker? Does he bother you? I have uncles in Sicilia. They can—"

"No," I interrupt quickly. I do not need Henry finding a horse's head in his bed. Or worse. "Thanks, no. I just need to make it clear that I'm not interested. That I don't want to be tied to one man. I . . . Look, Vinny, I'll owe you if you just pretend to be my date for the night. In front of the British guy."

Vinny's eyes take on a considering glint. "You'll owe me . . . a kiss?"

"No." I frown at him.

He shrugs like he was throwing it out there just in case I was feeling generous.

"A date?" he asks.

"No."

Giovanni says something in Italian, and Vinny nods.

"You'll have Sunday dinner with me and my mother."

He beams at me, his chest puffing and his chest hair nearly bursting free from his buttoned dress shirt.

I sense a trap. "No."

"What can I do?" He points at the door to the pub. "Outside, there is a man. You want me to lie to this man. You want me to say we are *making love together*."

"It's a little thing," I say.

He sighs, glancing at the trays of sausage toad on the counter. I frown at the fat, glistening brown sausages resting in goopy pudding batter.

I don't know why Vinny has it on the menu. Sausage toad is one of many gross British names for food.

Others gross names include:

- Blood pudding
- Spotted dick
- Mucky dripping
- Bubble and squeak
- Jellied eels

I could go on, but I'm distracted by Vinny poking at a slightly shriveled sausage in the tray.

"There is one thing, one little favor," he says, considering me.

"What?" I ask, trying not to look desperate, because it's five minutes till six and Henry just texted to let me know he's almost here. This morning he texted that he hoped everything was okay (regarding my "emergency"). I didn't text back.

"There is a stray cat." Vinny scowls at the metal door leading to the back alley. "It eats the trash. It makes a mess. It sneaks in and eats my sausages."

"A cat?"

I like cats.

Vinny nods. "You take the cat. I will be your suave Italian lover."

I thrust my hand toward him. "Deal."

8

I SLIDE ONTO A TALL WOODEN BARSTOOL AND PERCH AT THE edge of the seat, feeling like a bird desperate to take flight. The wood is cool against my thighs. My skirt inches up my legs, the fabric scratching my skin.

Usually, I'm comfortable here. There's something soothing about faded plaid curtains, old wood furniture, rough stone walls, and the dingy, worn appearance of an old-town pub. Even the pickle and beer scent is familiar and soothing.

But not tonight.

I glance back at the dark wood of the front door. The students left, their chanting and chugging complete. A small group of Hungarian tourists congregate at a blocky table nearby, arguing over their guidebook and a crumpled city map. An older French-speaking couple hold hands while watching football highlights on the screen over the bar. Two stools down a bald man with bushy ear hair silently nurses a glass of port and a fragrant plate of fish and chips. The pub is quiet. The homey feel wraps around me.

Vinny slides a tall glass of pilsner across the bar, condensation dripping down its sides.

"Thanks," I murmur, gripping the cold glass. I take a long, desperate swallow and let the malty, cold sweetness bite at my tongue.

I'm having second thoughts. I'm changing my mind. I can't do this. I'm not a terrible person, nor a cruel one, I'm just driven and determined. I'll tell Henry I'm not interested and that'll be that. None of this other-man nonsense—that was panic, not logic.

"Vinny," I say, clinking my beer glass to the bar. He's at the other end, pouring the bald man more port. I'll tell him to abort the plan but that I'll still take the cat.

Behind me the door to the pub opens. I feel the cool spring breeze rush through the pub. It strokes over the bare skin of my back and rustles my hair.

Slowly, I turn on my stool and look over my shoulder as the crisp mountain lake breeze blows in. My fingers grip the hard edge of the wooden bar.

The late-evening sun, dipping behind the stone buildings and weaving through the cobblestone streets, fans through the open door, spilling light across the wide-planked wood floor. I blink at the brilliant sunshine, then Henry steps inside and the door shuts behind him, closing out the light.

He pauses at the threshold, blinking into the dim interior, and slowly scans the pub, first looking to the booth where he found me last night and then to the table of Hungarians.

My chest pinches, my heart skips a beat, and then it thumps along again, almost happily. My stomach has the opposite emotion to my heart. It rolls nervously and dips, making me wish I hadn't sipped any of that pilsner.

I forgot the impact of him. How my breath catches, my heart pounds, and my skin tingles. Can you forget the impact of someone in less than twenty-four hours? I did.

His dark golden hair is wind-blown, his cheeks are red, and he's in jeans and a navy cashmere sweater, which makes his eyes appear more blue and less gray. When he doesn't see me right away, his shoulders slump a bit and a little line appears on his forehead.

The pinch in my chest becomes an ache.

I study him in the dim light of the pub, taking in the freckles on his cheeks, the smooth-shaven line of his jaw, and the energy and life radiating off him. I take him in and let myself imagine an alternate dimension where we . . . Never mind. There's no point in imagining something that doesn't exist.

Vinny shouts an order of bangers and mash back to the kitchen, and at the noise Henry looks toward the bar. My breath hitches. I grip the edge of my stool, suddenly feeling as if it's spinning and I'm going to fall off at any moment.

Wow.

The smile on Henry's face.

When he sees me, the doubt, the worry that he'd been stood up, it fades like a cloud skittering across the sky, and in its place his smile appears, as bright as the sun.

He grins and walks toward me, his gait sure, his gaze direct. There's relief there, and then the relief is wiped away and replaced by pleasure and knowing and a happy light. I can read his expression as easily as I can read my own. And right there in his smile? It's there again. The thing that had me running away last night.

I take a split second to feel it. Starlight and cedar, night breezes and love. This'll be the last time he looks at me like this, and it'll also be the last time he'll have any reason to.

Henry stops next to me, the warmth of him wraps around me, and when he leans down, I catch the fragrance of his shaving soap.

"You're all right?" he asks, his accent crisp, his voice low and concerned. "Your emergency? Everything is okay?"

I nod. "Yeah. I'm good." My voice comes out husky from the tightness in my throat. I clear it, and then before I can say anything Henry takes the barstool next to mine.

He's big, tall, and long-legged. The bar area is so tight that his legs brush against mine, sending sparks up my thighs and to my core. A low heat starts to build between us. The dangerously magnetic pull draws me closer.

"I was worried I'd scared you off," he says, his voice low, the edges of his eyes crinkling with his confession. "I've never said what I did last night. My only excuse is that I—"

"Hey, British," Vinny interrupts. He smacks his hand against the wooden bar and leans on the counter, placing himself in the middle of our conversation.

I discreetly try to convey "abort, abort" by shaking my head and chopping my hand. Vinny notices but misinterprets, because he gives me a subtle thumbs-up.

Henry frowns at Vinny's posturing, his wide-shouldered stance, and his antagonistic expression.

"Um . . ." Henry wrinkles his brow. "I'll have a London Pride, thank you."

Vinny levels a hard stare on Henry and then smooths down his ponytail. I clear my throat and make another cutting motion with my hand.

"I don't care what you have," Vinny says, "as long as it isn't my bella Serena. Not tonight, my friend."

Oh no.

"What?" Henry asks, shaking his head in confusion. "Is that a lager? I'll have a London Pride. That's fine."

I slump down in my seat when I realize Henry doesn't know my full name. He thinks "bella Serena" is a beer. He has no idea Ducky is actually my middle name and Serena is my first name.

"Okay," I say, interrupting what I'm sure will be Vinny's eloquent elucidation, "that's fine. He'll have a London Pride."

Vinny shakes his head. "My bella Serena, why be so coy? Does this man not know your name?"

Henry turns to me and gives me a look like "can you believe this guy?"

Unfortunately, I can. I put this guy up to it.

"Ducky?" Henry says, sensing my discomfort. "Do you want to go somewhere else?"

"Not with you," Vinny says, puffing his chest. "Tonight my bella Serena and I make love. Sweet love, as beautiful as an Italian opera. With heaving breasts and passionate screams."

What?

My cheeks go hot and the rest of me goes cold.

Unfortunately, Vinny has adopted his role of lovesick swain and continues. "Her pussycat is eating my sausage. Always the sausage. Do you see, British? It is my sausage, not yours."

Holy. Freaking. Cow.

The *sausage*?

I'm stunned into immobility.

Henry blinks.

That's it. He blinks.

I think he's wondering if he heard correctly.

Actually, I'm wondering if *I* heard correctly.

Then Henry turns to me slowly and asks, "Ducky? Do you need me to . . .?"

He nods at Vinny like if I ask, he'll punch him in the face or crack a beer bottle over his head.

Henry may have a PhD in physics, but clearly, he's not afraid to get dirty.

This is one of those moments where a multiple-choice question would come in handy. For example:

1. Ducky, would you like me to punch this guy for insulting you?

a) Yes, please knock the crazy man over the head. I'm Ducky, not Serena, and I love you too.

b) Yes, please knock the crazy man over the head. By the way, I'm Serena and I don't want a relationship with you, so please stop smiling at me like that.

c) No, please *do not* knock my friend over the head, he's just doing what I asked. By the way, I'm Serena and I don't want a relationship with you.

Well, as every test wizard out there will tell you, when in doubt, choose C. That's life lesson number one.

So, C it is.

I shake my head no. Then I say to Vinny, "Hey. I'm good here. Okay?"

Vinny crosses his arms. "Okay. You'll come by tonight for the pussycat and my sausage?" He waggles his eyebrows.

Oh gosh.

You know that saying, "You reap what you sow"?

Yeah.

This moment.

I nod yes, because of course I'll come for the cat, but when I do, Henry stiffens.

Vinny swaggers away, tossing a white bar towel over his shoulder.

I can feel Henry's gaze on me. His confused, shocked, probably disturbed gaze. It's like when you're a kid happily digging in the sandbox and you think you've found a neat rock, and then you realize it's actually fossilized cat poo.

Yeah.

He thought he found a woman to love, and instead he found . . . Serena of the sausage.

"Look," I say, shifting on the hard wood of my barstool. I look into Henry's eyes, and when I see the lines on his forehead and the corners of his mouth turned down I quickly look down at my hands gripping the bar's edge. "I'm Serena. Not Ducky."

I'm only Ducky to my family—to the people who love me most. I guess I should've known something was up when I introduced myself as Ducky to Henry.

"And you . . ."—Henry holds out his hands in a "what?" gesture—"are with the bartender?"

"No," I say, not willing to let him think I was cheating last night. "Well, I mean, tonight—"

Henry stands suddenly, thrusting his barstool back.

"Right," he says, stepping back, putting distance between us.

And that look, the one he had when he first saw me, the one that made my heart thump happily in my chest, it's gone. Wiped away.

It hurts, and since it does, I decide to pound a few more nails into the coffin. For my own good.

"Henry," I say, licking my dry lips and forcing myself on. "Yesterday? It was just a bit of fun. That's all."

I smile at him—a wide, vacuous smile—and my stomach clenches at the lie.

"Fun?" he repeats, looking at me as if I'm a theorem he has no idea how to solve.

I nod. "Fun. Don't make something of nothing. It was fun. We had fun."

Then that determination, that drive I knew was there, comes out. He steps forward, his blue-gray eyes blazing, and says, "It wasn't just fun. It was once-in-a-lifetime—"

My throat clenches. I almost jump off my stool and into his arms at the expression on his face, but instead I say, "Exactly. Once-in-a-lifetime, meaning you only do it *once*. Otherwise it gets boring."

And that . . .

That moment?

That's when I realize I *am* cruel. But just like any sword, it's double-edged. It hurts.

Henry stands still for a moment, the low rumble of the Hungarians' conversation flowing around him and the light of the TVs flickering over him. He's making theories in his mind—I can see his thoughts racing, throwing in variables, discarding hypotheses, until finally he comes to the only conclusion possible.

"I'm sorry," he says stiffly, his voice cold, absent of emotion. "I mistook the situation."

At that moment, Giovanni bursts from the kitchen, a plate of bangers and mash in his hands. When he sees Henry still standing next to me, he says gruffly, "My Serena. You and me. A date this Friday."

I keep my eyes on Henry and see his jaw clench. At the same time, the bald man down the bar says, "Serena? Isn't that the woman who slept with my football team? It was bad luck! They lost because of her!"

All right.

That one.

That one is partially true.

I slept with all of two guys from Geneva's football club. Different weekends though. And I didn't realize they were on the same team. And it's not my fault one of them always wanted to try sex on a ski lift and then when he fell off and broke his ankle—well, that's not my fault, is it? Also, it's not my fault the other one got all mopey and sad when I told him his favorite planet Pluto wasn't actually a planet. And I'm not superstitious, and I don't believe I had anything to do with their subsequent losing streak. But apparently, locker-room talk says I did.

"The football team?" Henry asks, looking shell-shocked.

I shrug. "Fun," I say lamely, realizing the bald guy is inadvertently helping my cause.

At that Henry nods, his jaw tight, shoulders bunched.

"I'm going to go," he says.

I nod, my throat tight, and then I paste on a smile and say, "Sure thing. By the way, I have your coat—"

"Keep it," he says curtly. Then, with a last dismissive, steel-eyed glance, he turns and strides from the homey interior of The Cock and Bull and doesn't look back.

I sigh and drop my head to the bar, thunking it against the wood.

Well, it worked.

He hates me.

He thinks I'm a sausage-eating, football-devouring, fun-seeking, pants-losing man-eater.

On Monday, when he sees me at work, he won't think what he feels is love. Probably, he'll feel nothing at all except embarrassment, and then even that will fade.

But he won't smile at me, he won't laugh with me, he'll just . . . leave me to pursue my dreams.

My stupid, self-destructive, expedient plan was a success.

Although success has never felt so wrong.

Hours later, I stand in the dark in the narrow cobblestone alley behind the pub. The dumpster is full of half-eaten dinners, French fries, steak, and sausage toad. There are bags of empty beer bottles giving off a bitter scent.

The night breeze barely whispers through the old-town alley, and only the quietest of city noise carries through the thick stone.

I hold the stray cat tightly in my arms and press my face to his matted black fur. He's large-boned but scrawny. One of his ears has been half-bitten off, and his green eyes have a swashbuckling rakish light.

He was skittish at first, but as soon as I fed him a plate of sausage and chicken he let me hold him in my arms. I'm sure he has fleas and probably other injuries from his life of dumpster-diving and alley-fights. Tomorrow I'll take him to the vet and buy him all the kitty delights he can imagine.

I wonder if he'll appreciate me, like me, or even love me. Or if he'll resent me for taking him from his life as a free-roaming, adventuring tomcat and turning him into a pampered house cat.

I look up at the stars, their dull light barely visible through the purple glow of the city sky. Starlight seems farther away than ever. I remember suddenly what my dad once said. "We can yearn, but we'll never find what we're yearning for."

I sigh and the cat wriggles in my arms, meowing plaintively.

"I'll name you James Tiberius Purrk," I tell the black cat, "after one of my heroes. Did you know he reached the stars?"

And someday so will I. Metaphorically, of course.

I take one last look at the sky. It'll be okay. It'll work out. Someday all this will be worth it.

I push the thought of another kind of starlight out of my mind and out of my heart. It's over now. There's no way I'll be swept away by love again. I won't ever have to give up my life for love.

I squeeze Purrk to my chest and then I walk down the alley, onto the old cobblestone street that leads to my centuries-old apartment building.

I walk through the dark with a stupidly aching chest, and I tell myself over and over that sometimes the right thing feels like the wrong thing. And sometimes doing the right thing hurts.

And then, because I'm feeling a little lost and a whole lot down, I look up at the sky and say in a solemn voice, "Little did she know, her ordinary life was about to change."

9

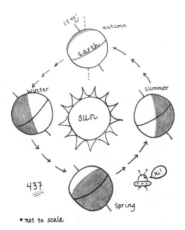

[Here we have a diagram—not to scale—of the earth rotating around the sun with arrows and a little alien spaceship and the number 437. That's how many days have passed.]

Thick gray clouds sit on top of Geneva, a heavy weight, drooping with cold rain and wet winds. The city is surrounded by the Alps and the Jura Mountains, and today the blue-and-green peaks are shrouded in mist and drizzle. The lake is slate-gray and choppy, with a cold mist spraying off it, kicked up by the biting wind.

Geneva is home to the United Nations, the Red Cross, the WHO, and CERN, all bastions of hope, but even so, on a day like today, everyone has their heads down.

The old stone buildings lose their romantic, age-worn sparkle and instead look like dusty gray dresses pulled from a musty trunk in the attic. The little iron terraces with the glass French doors that so commonly line the old apartment buildings don't look charming, instead they look like brittle cages.

The old narrow cobblestone streets fill with dirty, murky puddles. The smell of wet pavement and soaked stone seeps through the rainy byways. The buses shudder with cold as they slide through flooding streets, kicking up sprays of sloshing water. People duck and dodge through a churning sea of bobbing black umbrellas.

All the charm of Geneva—the abundant gardens, the amorous Baroque architecture, the enticing scents of croissants and chocolate, the joyful sparkling lake, and the irrepressible Jet d'Eau—all of it is lost under the heavy shroud of cold, gray rain.

I pull my raincoat tighter, shivering at the wet drizzle sliding down my neck. The wind gusts and yanks at my dress and raincoat, tugging my umbrella so it lifts skyward. I tug it back down and tighten my grip. The rain drums against it, a hollow beating.

I quicken my pace. I'm late. Late, late, late.

Ahead, a few low white metal buildings peek out of

the mist, heralding the outskirts of the *Conseil Européen pour la Recherche Nucléaire* (CERN), also known as the European Laboratory for Particle Physics, also known as the coolest place on the planet, also known as the place where I'm about to get grilled. Again.

When I first came to CERN, back when I was a grad student and thought I might have a chance to do my postdoc here, I was astounded by the sheer size of it all. It wasn't just the confusing maze of hallways, the unending corridors, the underground depths of the LHC, and the height of thousands of minds working together. No, I was overwhelmed by the multitude of buildings perched on swathes of green lawn, the leafy trees sprouting next to windowless metal buildings, tall brick and windowed buildings, modern buildings, postmodern buildings, gleaming statues, colorful murals, snapping country flags, and road after gray road splitting the lush countryside with names like Marie Curie (radioactivity pioneer), Enrico Fermi (father of the nuclear age), and Schroedinger (of the box and the alive/dead cat).

The amazing thing about CERN is that this international hub of scientific research straddling Switzerland and France is surrounded by trees, rolling blue mountains, and farmers' fields (even now, a red tractor chugs through the wet, muddy field that in the height of summer shines with yellows and greens).

The juxtaposition always makes me smile in wonder because when I'm walking into the pinnacle of particle research, a Swiss farmer a half-mile away is plowing his field, kicking up the scent of clover and flax, and fleecy sheep are grazing on sweet-scented grass on a mountainside nearby.

But today, all of that is invisible behind the wall of

rain and cloud. Each building and all the people inside are islands to themselves on a day like today. Even the Globe of Science and Innovation, the eighty-nine-foot-tall slatted timber sphere that sometimes glows like a molten star, is hidden by the rain.

I hurry to the entrance of the ATLAS building, shut my umbrella with a snap, shake off the rain, and then duck into the warm, dry interior. The bright lights blind me for a moment, and I blink and let the cold water drip off my coat and onto the floor in a little puddle. Goose bumps form on my skin as the cold rainwater sluices off and is replaced by dry air. I sniffle a bit and then let out a sneeze.

"You're late," Katerina says, coming through the door right behind me and letting in another gust of wind. She's a postdoc from Greece and works with other Greeks who don't have the same concept of time as my boss does, so she's not late, but I definitely am.

"He won't be happy," she says, shaking off her raincoat.

Well.

He is *never* happy.

That's something I've learned about Henry Joule over the past year and a half. Happiness is another dimension, undiscovered and unexplored, ruled by completely different laws of physics in another pocket of the multiverse. The night we met? It was an anomaly. Possibly another Henry. Because this Henry? He's a demanding, meticulous, evidence-hounding, theory-doubting, experiment-pounding, neat-freak, type-A pain in my ass.

That nightmare boss that pulls sixteen-hour days expecting everyone else to do the same?

Yeah.

That grumpy boss who questions your theories and points out your flawed calculations at team meetings?

Yup.

The boss who keeps his office so neat his pencils are all sharpened to the same height, his keyboard is dusted with a can of compressed air, and there isn't a speck of dust or clutter anywhere . . . and when he comes into your perfectly cozy office with personality and homey clutter and he . . . winces?

Yes, indeed.

The anal boss who only wears white shirts, red ties, and gray suits every day of the week (light gray, medium gray, and dark gray)? The boss who drinks a single cup of English Breakfast tea every morning at precisely 10:15 a.m. in the cafeteria (at a table by himself)? The boss who is the opposite of me in every way?

That's Henry.

When I met him in the pub I thought it felt like love . . . Well, everyone knows love at first sight isn't real. And this is the reason why. You have to get to know someone, don't you?

I know Henry now. I know him as well as anyone here.

And he and I?

Never happening.

I never really had anything to worry about.

"You'd better run," Katerina says, eyeing my wet hair and red cheeks. "Your meeting has already started."

"I'm not going to run," I say, glancing at my watch. "It's only five after eight."

Katerina's eyes dance. We don't know each other well, but sometimes when I'm on break she offers to make me a double shot of espresso from the little machine on her desk, and then she tells me about her research.

"Run."

"Nope."

I give her a wave, and then let's just say I move at a velocity faster than a walk.

10

THE MEETING IS CANCELLED—HENRY HAS YET TO ARRIVE—
which gives the day an early celebratory feeling despite
the continued rain. I decide to treat myself with a flaky
croissant and a double espresso from the cafeteria.

The creamy, rich, chocolatey, bitter flavor of the
espresso warms my insides and chases away the last of
the chill from the damp outside. My small office has the
wonderful scent of espresso and fresh-baked croissant,
and the light rain patters soothingly against the window.

I lean forward in my leather office chair. It squeaks
and then settles. My office is my home away from home.
It's about the size of a small walk-in closet and is filled to
the brim with stacks of paper (a.k.a. data, research, and
theories). Everywhere.

It's pretty much the visual representation of my
brain. (Paper) ideas stacked one on top of another,
overflowing, coming out of drawers, falling off shelves,
mounded beneath the desk, propped on the windowsill
and on top of the chair and under the mini Zen sand

garden Jillian gave me last Christmas that I use as a doorstop, and one small stack in the stapler waiting since last week to be stapled together. My computer sits in the middle of this, and it's the digital representation of my brain too.

It's chaos.

However, as every physicist knows, sometimes when you look at something that appears to be chaos, there is actually order hidden within. You just have to find it.

So, it's chaos with order that only I can see.

The mountains of paper spilling like an avalanche over every surface are incredibly freeing. Working in chaos lets you break free of constraints and push the boundaries of what is known or expected. At least that's how I see it.

For example, as I nibble on my croissant, I'm also writing down ideas in my notepad. It looks like this:

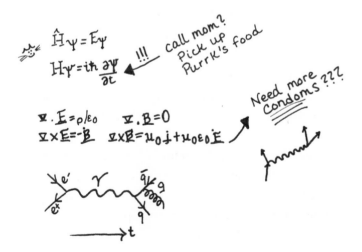

[Here we have physics equations written on notebook paper, with sideline doodles, and a to-do list: Call mom? Pick up Purrk's food. Need more condoms???]

Okay.

Here's the deal. Doodling helps thoughts to flow. And Purrk has a special vet diet for kidney stones. And, fine, the condoms.

I didn't mean to write that down—it just came out, in the free-flowing stream of consciousness thought record.

Why?

Because.

I haven't had sex.

I haven't had sex in nearly TWO YEARS.

The last time I had sex was with Henry freaking Joule.

I haven't been able to do it. I just can't. Before, in the time I call BH (Before Henry), I had a nice thing going. I worked, I had fun, occasionally I had a mutually satisfying one-night fling. Then came Henry, and every time a guy showed interest or I thought about hooking up with someone, my heart stuttered, my eyes got this Bambi's-mother-just-got-shot look, and my mind wailed, "But love love love love, what about love love love?"

He ruined sex for me.

However, it's been a year and a half. It's well past time to get over that little cosmic speedbump called Henry Joule.

I underline the word condom three times, and then the hair on the back of my neck stands on end because someone is behind me, at the door to my tiny office, looking down—I'm sure—at my notepad.

Please let it be Katerina.

Or Fabio—he's cool.

Or Nigel. I like Nigel.

Or Sangeeta. I wouldn't mind it if Sangeeta knew I was hard up for cat food and condoms.

Slowly I turn in my chair. It squeaks beneath me, and the scent of croissant travels with me.

It's Henry.

He stands in the threshold of my office because the clutter repels him like garlic wards off a vampire.

He's in his dove-gray suit today with his white shirt and red tie.[1] The shoulders of his jacket are slightly damp from the rain, and his wheat-colored hair has a few raindrops misting through it. His hair brushes the collar of his jacket. He wears it slightly long and there's a light wave to it.

He fills the doorway. He always fills whatever space he's in. Not because he's tall and confident, but because of that deep, concentrated drive that compels him to search and do and find.

His presence has a weight, a draw, a mass. If we were objects in space, he would be the greatest mass, forcing all other objects to orbit around him.

He hasn't said anything. In fact, he hasn't moved.

He's merely staring at the writing on my open notebook. His eyes are as gray and impenetrable as the rainy sky outside.

My heart gives a slow, painful thud, then jostles itself back into motion.

That happens sometimes. When I see him, I'll forget how color-inside-the-lines and neat-freak and data-rules he is, and instead I'll remember the feeling of his hand cradling my cheek, his fingers trailing over my bottom lip, and his eyes catching mine as he whispered, "I never do this."

When that happens, I'm reminded of the time my

family went on summer vacation to the Mayan ruins in Belize. I'd heard all these stories on the way there— glorious cities, giant pyramids, great ruins. Keyword: ruins.

I stood at the edge of the site and saw crumbled stones and fallen architecture and I knew that thousands of years ago there was a beautiful, perfectly symmetrical wonder of the world. It would've been a sight to see. But now? It was fallen. It was cracked and faded. I could see the beauty that once was—I could hear the echo of it— but . . . that wondrous glory? It was once-in-a-lifetime, and that lifetime had passed.

Slowly I close my notebook, clear my throat, and say, "Hi. Did you need something?"

Henry tears his gaze away from my notebook and looks into my eyes. His expression is perfectly neutral. Neutral like Switzerland, a neutron, or a pH of 7.

I give him a bland smile.

The thing is, he always looks at me with a neutral expression. He has ever since the Monday he started here as our new project lead.

That day I was a mess. I skipped breakfast, chugged three espressos, wore a conservative black sheath dress with high heels and light makeup, and then I schooled my expression into one of pleasant surprise at welcoming him as a new colleague and nothing more. "Welcome. I look forward to working with you," I said, shaking his hand calmly while my heart thundered and my stomach clenched. "Let me know if you need anyone to show you around," I said before I could think better of my offer.

There had been a moment when he first saw me that his eyes flickered, his steps faltered, but then that moment passed, and looking back, I'm not sure if it really happened. It was a nanosecond of emotion. After that it was neutral.

He shook my hand and politely declined my offer. "Thank you. I think I can manage."

And that was that.

I slid into the box for colleagues, not lovers, and I was free to pursue my passion and my dreams unencumbered.

However, as Schrödinger might ask, if you put love in a box and create an event to kill it and don't open the box, is love alive or is it dead? Or is it both and neither?

Regardless, Henry has always treated me in a completely neutral manner. Which is good, except it's odd, because there is nothing neutral about us. There are some things in the world that are neutral (see above: pH 7, etc.), but he and I aren't one of them.

It's like tofu.

No one on earth is neutral about tofu.

You either hate it: "Accck! Tofu is a jiggly, fermented sperm blob that tastes like licking formaldehyde from an embalmer's rubber glove!"

Or, you love it: "Wheee! Tofu is a delicious mouthful of joy that tastes like the tears of a thousand cows thanking us for saving the planet!"

See? Sometimes there is no neutral.

Unless you are Henry.

"Sasha said you had new data from last week," he says, his eyes moving over my mountains of paper and pausing on the dirty Tupperware (lasagna last night) perched precariously on the edge of my desk, the three empty coffee cups stacked next to my computer, and the crumbs from my half-eaten croissant.

I can practically feel the shudder running through

him. I bet he's fantasizing about his can of compressed air and a mop.

"I do," I say. "I plotted it out, plugged it into some theories . . . It completely nullified most everything I've been working on. It's . . . hmmm . . ." I shuffle through the stack of papers nearest me. It's here somewhere. Not in that pile though. Is it under my sand Zen garden?

Henry waits patiently at the threshold to my office, then, after I bend down to look under my desk, he says, "Perhaps you might email it to me."

I sit up quickly, knock my head on the underside of my desk, and then roll out from under it, pressing my hand to the throb in my skull.

"Are you all right?" he asks, his brow wrinkling.

I nod, take a breath, and smell the rain still on him and the hint of cedar and outdoors. I swear he must roll around in the forest every morning.

"I'll get it to you before the end of the day," I tell him. I have to find it first. Sometimes chaos results in unexpected delays.

"Good," he says, nodding at me, and then his eyes flicker to my closed notebook and quickly away, back to me. "Have a pleasant holiday," he says.

I imagine he thinks that holiday is going to include some guy named Purrk that I'm feeding and lots of sex.

"You too," I say. "Enjoy your vacation."

He nods. Leaves without another word. And that is basically the extent of all our conversations. Unless, of course, he's arguing with my theories or debating models or demanding data.

That's okay. Today is the last day before the LHC goes down for three months of maintenance. All the Western Europeans (French, Italian, etc.) are taking a month off to bask in the last lingering rays of summer. They do this every year. Work like the devil's after you all year, and then take a solid four weeks off to do nothing but laze around.

This year Henry is halfway following suit, taking two weeks off. So is the rest of our team. So am I. I get two weeks of unencumbered joy cuddling with Purrk on my couch, eating takeout, and watching *Star Trek* marathons.

Today everyone is wrapping up last-minute tasks, emails, and projects that can't wait a month to complete.

I sigh and grab the rest of my croissant, flip open my notebook, and quickly slash out the word "condoms."

11

THE SOFT VIBRATION OF PURRK'S PURR SEEPS THROUGH MY chest, rumbling soft and warm and fuzzy. I stretch back on my couch, lounging in my underwear and tank top while Purrk kneads his paws into my chest, spins in a circle, and then lies down on me in a tight, fluffy ball.

Now this is luxury.

Purrk keeps one eye open as I fork a mouthful of Kung Pao Tofu from the cardboard to-go carton. The rice and saucy tofu steam, letting out the best eye-wateringly spicy fragrance. See? Tofu. I love it.

"Not for you," I tell Purrk. "Remember what happened last time?"

I get five out of five spice level, the kind that makes you sweat or cry depending on your tolerance. Purrk snuck into the trash once and licked the carton clean. Let's just say I bought a lot of cat litter that week.

He meows disdainfully and then closes his eye, letting his half-bent ear twitch in irritation.

"I do love you. You know that, right?"

He doesn't answer.

So I laze on my old cushy couch, turn up the volume on my TV, and get ready for a night spent with Captain Janeway, kick-butt lady captain of the USS Voyager. I'm going to start with *Threshold*—arguably one of the worst *Star Trek* episodes ever, and thus my favorite.

Sure, I could do that load of dirty dishes in the sink or the laundry spread across my living room (including the push-up bra hanging from my TV) or clean out the month-old takeout in my fridge, but why bother? Tonight is for *Star Trek* and tofu.

I'm going to enjoy my quiet, cozily cluttered apartment in my old building with its two-person death-trap elevator, groaning pipes, cracked walls, and sweet balcony. What's the point in living in a quirky, two-hundred-and-fifty-year-old apartment building if you can't enjoy it?

I stretch out, scratching Purrk behind his ears, and settle in for the night.

Then my phone pings. It's the notification for my work text group. I reach over to my journal-and-magazine-covered coffee table, set my dinner down, and grab my phone.

It's a message from H. Joule: *Did you send the data?*

I sit up and Purrk jumps from my chest, meowing grumpily.

"Shoot. Shoot!"

It's seven o'clock. Henry often works until nine or ten. Sometimes later, emailing in the middle of the night from his home office. At least I assume he's in his home office —I don't know. Maybe he's actually emailing from a woman's silk-clad bed while she entices him to do that thing with his tongue again, or maybe he's emailing from a bench in a lonely park, rubbing a red rose across his lips while he stares forlornly at the Jet d'Eau whispering, "Ducky, my Ducky, why?"

I have no idea what he does in his spare time.

I hit reply, then type: *Took a dinner break. Be back in five.*

It looks like Purrk, tofu, and *Star Trek* will have to wait.

12

I MAKE IT BACK TO WORK. THE LIGHTS IN THE BUILDING ARE dim and most people have left for the day. Everything is shutting down, and the building has a sort of sleepy, blanketed feel. It's almost how I feel when Purrk is purring, curled into my side, and I'm snug under a quilt on a rainy Saturday morning.

The Large Hadron Collider runs at about fifty percent up-time, meaning we're smashing atoms twelve hours a day, seven days a week, six months a year. In a few hours the collider will shut down for the next three months. You can almost feel the slowing inside the building, like a runner having finished their race, their heartbeat steadying during cooldown.

My feet thud in the empty hallway as I hurry toward my office.

I shake out my umbrella as a streak of lightning flashes blue across the sky and thunder booms in response. The chilly late-summer storm has lasted all day and now into the evening.

I hurry down the long corridor, texting Henry: *I'm here. Where are you?*

If I can't find the file on my computer I'll have to give him the paper copy. I remembered where it was on my way here. It's on my bookshelf, a completely illogical place.

My phone pings: *Control room.*

Ah, that makes sense. A day at CERN has a pretty standard flow: arrive at eight or nine, grab an espresso, chat with fellow colleagues, hit the email pile-up, edit computer programs that are running (debug too), and submit jobs to the Grid[1]. Then lunch meetings on detector operation or interesting theoretical discussions (these run for an hour or two). The afternoon is jammed with more meetings—in-person, over video, or in conference—physics, detector and performance, you name it. And then three times a month you have a night shift in the ATLAS control room, where you monitor the detector and make sure it's running correctly and bringing in high-quality data.

And that is a day in the life.

My favorite part of the day has always been lunch—not because of the super high-quality French-Swiss gastronomy, but because of the amazing discussions you can have with physicists from around the world. You'll chat over a warm baguette with figs and honey and discuss the top quark or neutrinos, or the origin of matter-antimatter asymmetry, or what came before the Big Bang, and whether the universe is actually real. Every day at noon you go grab, for instance, a plate of pasta, and suddenly you're discussing spaghettification with a physicist visiting from Trieste, Italy.

And, trust me, if you didn't fear spaghetti before

learning about spaghettification, you will now. I only fear two things in life: love and spaghettification. So.

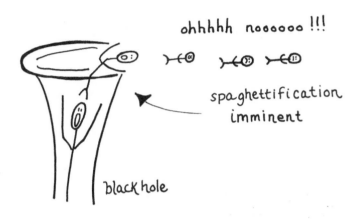

[Here we have a sketch of a stick figure being sucked into a black hole with spaghettification occurring.]

Back when I was a kid my mom used to have to rock me back to sleep after nightmares of spaghetti raining from the sky. She learned to never serve me long pasta—linguine, fettuccine, capellini, bucatini, not to mention the dreaded bigoli.

I don't only pick on the Italians, thanks to my dad, who only eats Japanese noodles like his mom served, I have a healthy fear of udon, somen, hiyamugi, soba, shirataki, and harusame. All banned from my school lunchbox.

Such is life.

I flick on my office lights, duck down to the lowest level of my bookshelf, and grab the sheaf of paper

Henry's after. Then I head to the ATLAS Experiment Control room.

The control room is one of my two favorite places. The first is the cavern where the ATLAS detector lives. It's one hundred meters underground, and the detector is 7,000 tons and twenty-five meters high, and it makes you feel very, very small.

It's the largest particle detector ever built and awe-inspiring to stand beneath. To me, the metal parts look like a mammoth sunflower spreading its petals to the sun. Silly, I know. But it's what I see every time.

The detector investigates everything, from the Higgs Boson to extra-dimensions to dark matter.

It sounds more complex than it is. Basically, we're running a very simple experiment. We're like toddlers taking two LEGO creations, smashing them together, then taking photos of the destruction in real time.

The Large Hadron Collider has a seventeen-mile-long ring (which looks a lot like a subway tunnel) that we send proton beams zooming around using superconducting electromagnets cooled to the frigid temperature of open space. Protons are at the center of every atom. They're very interesting to study, trust me.

So we send them around in two beam pipes at ultrahigh vacuum (think interstellar space), shoot them around the ring multiple times in opposite directions, and let them build up speed like zooming cars in a NASCAR race. Building speed, building speed, until they're near the speed of light. And then—**BAM!**—we collide the two beams.

[Here we have a visual representation of a particle collision.]

At four different locations around this ring, we collect data from the collision by gathering millions of data points for study. The four different points are the four detectors: ATLAS, CMS, ALICE, and LHCB.

We all study different things using different collection methods. For example, ALICE studies quark-gluon plasma. The LHC collision causes temperatures 100,000 times hotter than the core of the sun, and in this, quarks and gluons melt, freeing protons and neutrons. It's very cool.

The LHCB studies a particle called beauty quarks

(isn't that the best name?) where they're trying to determine the difference between matter and antimatter.

I could go on. I won't.

At ATLAS we're looking at the god particle, alternate dimensions, and dark matter, and we do that one hundred meters underground using the ATLAS detector.

We control it all in the control room, my second favorite place. It looks pretty much exactly like you think it would. Imagine one of those Hollywood movies with a NASA control center with lots of big, curved desks full of computer monitors facing a huge wall with data projected on it, and lots of smart people doing smart things behind the computers. If you watch any livestreams for when the LHC is turned on, you'll see the control room.

And I'm here.

The computer monitors glow blue and the wall with the projection screens flashes the last of the data from the end of our latest run. The large digital wall clock with its red numbers flashes to my left.

Henry leans over a computer monitor, his jacket off, sleeves rolled up, forehead wrinkling. He shakes his head at whatever reading he's seeing.

Then something alerts him to my presence. He turns toward me, the computer light falling over him. I lift my hand and wave, holding up the sheaf of papers.

Henry catches my smile and then, slowly, he turns away.

He's neutral. He's never been rude.

Which is when I know something's wrong.

13

"WHAT IS IT?" I ASK.

I step next to Henry and glance at the glowing monitor. On the desk a mug of tea sends out a curl of steam and the hot scent of English Breakfast, milk, and sugar. I wonder how many cups of tea he drinks in a day. Maybe as many shots of espresso as I drink.

I move closer and my arm brushes against Henry's as I lean in to look at the monitor. He's warm. His shirtsleeves are rolled up and the fabric scratches against my bare skin. He doesn't move aside when my arm whispers against his shirt. In fact, I don't think he even notices me.

I ignore the frisson of heat and the electric buzz riding over my skin. Instead I concentrate on the rumble of thunder outside, the drum of rain, and the crack of lightning. The storm is moving directly overhead, growing stronger, shooting down bolts of lightning and growling with booming thunder. I can almost feel the vibration all the way down to my toes.

Henry doesn't look my way. The harsh light of the monitor reflects off his skin as his eyes quickly scan the numbers rolling in front of him. His shoulders tense, his mouth turns down, and his eyes narrow on the screen.

There's a nervous energy in the control room. I glance from Henry to the others at their computers. Heads down, fingers flying, energy crackling.

"Just leave it on the desk," Henry says suddenly, not bothering to look at me. His voice is abrupt, distracted. A lock of hair falls across his forehead, sweeping over his eye. He doesn't bother to brush it back. Instead his mouth tightens, and he shakes his head.

Henry's intense concentration, the low hum of the monitors, and the noise of fans cooling the overworked system all add to my growing unease. It's drumming through me like the rain beating against the building.

Years ago—2008, to be exact—there was an incident at the LHC. A faulty electrical connection between two magnets caused helium to release into the tunnel. You may be thinking, "Oh helium, fun! I love balloons! You can make your voice sound like a chipmunk!" No. The LHC uses liquid helium to cool the air to the coldest temperatures on earth, colder than space. When the faulty connection caused the leak, it vaporized and superconducting electromagnets collided. Imagine a subway tunnel where dozens of train cars collide and the metal smashes, twists, and wrecks. That. The damage was surreal. All because of a faulty electrical connection. So even though this happened years ago, when I was a kid, I'm still twitchy about it.

"What's wrong?" I ask again, more insistent.

"I'm busy," Henry snaps, tapping in a command.

"I can help—"

"You cannot—"

I *can*. I slap the papers onto the desk and accidently hit the glass cup of steaming-hot tea. It slides to the edge of the desk, teeters, and almost in slow motion I reach out and try to stop it—but then it flips over, falls, and smacks the floor. The glass cracks, shatters, and scalding tea and sharp fragments punch my legs. I flinch at the heat lashing my bare skin and the glass cutting my legs.

Henry jerks from the desk and jumps back, trying to avoid the explosion of steaming English Breakfast tea and glass.

It's a mess. Milky tea seeps across the floor and glistening shards of glass litter the ground. The bottom of the mug still holds a lump of sugar not quite melted by the hot liquid. The tea spreads fast, moving toward the hardware.

"Shoot," I say. I don't think—I grab the papers off the desk and drop to my knees to sop up the liquid.

"Don't—" Henry says, holding out his hand.

Too late my knee hits a glass shard, and I flinch as it slices into my skin. The pain is hot, and I hiss at the sudden welling of blood. I'm afraid to move, fearing that if I do I'll lance another shard of glass through my leg. The tea is hot and sticky against my skin. I let go of the papers, hoping they'll soak it up.

Henry kneels down next to me, pulling me up from the broken glass. He gently takes my knee, his warm fingers probing my skin. His eyes darken at the half-inch-long, glistening shard of glass sticking out of my knee. He grips it between his fingers and tugs. The glass cuts his skin—I see blood welling from his pointer finger and thumb—and then the sharp teeth biting at my knee cut loose as he slides the glass free.

He brushes at my legs, his hands moving efficiently over me, until he finds another shard in my calf. He tugs that free too and then presses the well of blood.

Maybe ten seconds have passed, but I'm immobile. The sting of the glass is still sharp. It felt like scalding bullet rain. It's not the pain that stunned me though. It's how quickly Henry dropped down next to me and pulled the glass free, cutting himself in the process.

"You all right over there?" Steven calls from the back of the control room.

I jerk away from watching Henry brush his hands over my legs, scanning them for more glass. A warm shiver slides over me and I shake it off.

"Fine," I call.

Then I turn back to Henry. He presses the cut on my calf with one hand and the cut on my knee with his other.

"Thank you," I say gratefully.

His face is turned away from mine. He's kneeling next to me, looking down at my bare legs covered in tea and a little bit of blood.

I'm feeling almost warm toward him.

Then he looks up, his eyes angry and hard, and I jerk back in surprise. He keeps a tight hold on my leg, pressing his fingers into my skin.

"What is wrong with you?" he asks in a low growl, his voice sharp and cutting. He jerks his chin toward the shattered remains of his teacup. "Do you ever stop to consider the consequences of your actions?"

I flinch—this seems like a gross exaggeration—and

try to pull my leg away, but he doesn't notice and his fingers curl over my calf, holding me in place.

"It's just tea," I whisper, my gratitude flipping to irritation. "There were no consequences."

Minus the shattered mug, the ruined papers, the spilled drink, and the bloody cuts.

"It's not just tea," he says, echoing my thoughts. "And there are always consequences. Cause and effect."

"My gosh. Life doesn't have to be so serious. Lighten up." I tug my leg free from his grip. When I do, I totter a bit on my heels, and Henry reaches out, grabs my hand, and steadies me.

Outside, a slice of lightning streaks across the sky. A spark travels down my arm and jolts my heart into rapid-fire beats.

Henry's grip tightens and his eyes darken from blue to steely gray. "I will not lighten up. Life is not all fun and games."

I blink at him, confused at the whiplike slash of his voice.

"Are you angry because I broke your mug? I'm sorry, jeez. I'll get you another. Heck, I'll superglue it for you."

At the mention of superglue, he drops my hand like I've burned him and I fall backward onto a lukewarm tea-soaked piece of paper, my hips smacking into the floor. Luckily, there wasn't any glass under the paper.

I rub my hip. Henry stares at me as if he's appalled by my predicament.

But then I realize he's just appalled with me, because he says, "An adhesive is the last thing I would ask for. No, thank you."

Oh. Okay. I see where this is going. This is the argument we never had a year and a half ago. Fine.

"Why not?" I ask. "Glue is useful. It fixes things. It's *fun*."

His eyes narrow. He leans closer and then deliberately pronounces each word slowly. "I. Dislike. Fun."

Yeah. Me too.

In fact, I've disliked the word "fun" since I callously threw it out there at The Cock and Bull.

However, Henry needs some actual fun in his life.

I scan my eyes over his flawless gray suit, his crisply ironed white shirt, his red tie, and his unsmiling features. I wonder what he's done with himself for the past year and half. I know what he does here: he works, he works, and he works. He drinks tea at 10:15 a.m. exactly, he dusts his keyboard, he sorts his files alphabetically, and he sharpens his pencils to exactly 177 millimeters. But what does he do when he isn't working? Somehow I think whatever it is, it isn't fun.

I'm not talking about sex. I'm just talking about good, wholesome, old-fashioned fun.

"It's too bad," I tell him. Then I say honestly, "You could use a little fun in your life."

His mouth twists in a disgusted "I can't believe you just said that" sort of way.

He shakes his head. "No, thank you."

And that "no, thank you" isn't directed toward fun as much as it's directed at me. In fact, I've never had someone look at me with such undiluted loathing in my entire life. It's rolling off him like the thunder rolling over the building.

So I was right. Henry isn't and has never been neutral toward me. Our relationship is tofu, not a neutron. There is no neutral.

But then he zips up all that dislike curling his lip,

lighting his eyes, and rolling off him in waves, and goes back to that pH of 7.

I feel a tiny spurt of disappointment. Funny enough, I think I prefer this show of utter dislike over the constant apathy.

Henry glances back at his computer monitor, his jaw muscles ticking, then he gestures at the sodden papers on the floor. "If you could replace the data before leaving for the night, I have to—"

He waves this away, then starts to stand, as he does he reaches out for me, takes my hand in a tight grip to help me up.

My hand slips into his warm one, wet with tea and blood. Behind him, the red numbers on the clock glow. *7:31 p.m.*

He frowns at me then—at the lightning striking outside and the sparks coalescing where our palms touch. His eyes darken. When I smile at him, he flinches.

"I don't understand you," he says, and it almost sounds angry and accusatory.

I shrug, my chest pinching. "Funny. We have symmetry then, because I don't understand you, and I doubt I ever will."

"Do you want to?" he asks, frowning down at me.

My hand is still in his, a growing, sparking, almost painful current flowing between us.

I shake my head. "No," I lie. "Understand the universe, yes. Understand you? No, thanks. We're too dissimilar."

I smile at him to let him know this is all in good fun—even though we both know it isn't.

But he nods as if I've confirmed a theory he's always

had. "That is one thing we'll always agree on," he says. "We are too dissimilar to be anything but—"

Loathed coworkers?

Misunderstood opposites?

Tolerated colleagues?

A regret?

"A mistake," I finish for him. Then I add, "Fun, but a mistake."

Henry swallows, the line of his throat moving painfully as his eyes burn into mine.

This is it, isn't it? Maybe after this I can truly move on. It's apparent, it's blatantly obvious, that Henry dislikes me. A lot. Perhaps his (now apparent) dislike can let me snip away the last threads of connection that have stubbornly held on even though I've tried to snip them again and again.

I move to pull my hand from his.

Outside a loud shout of thunder shakes the building and lightning slices the sky in half. There's a shrieking— a loud, high-pitched screaming sound. I flinch. It's the long, metallic whirring of a drill caving into a skull. An electronic whining that burrows and shrieks. It's the noise of the equipment when the LHC cools down or speeds up. A sound we never hear in the control room, but here it is, ratcheting through my head.

"ATLAS has gone off—!" someone shouts.

"The alarms!" another yells.

The projection wall lights up red, flashing.

Henry whirls around, spinning me with him because he's forgotten he's holding me, and I hit the desk. Stumble. Fall into him. His cedar starlight scent wraps around me.

There's a cracking boom and then the power trips and

the control room bleeds into darkness. Blessed silence. We have a generator—the power should be back on in a millisecond. In fact, there shouldn't be any interruption in power at all.

Yet . . . yet . . .

The LHC . . . Did something happen? Is this another faulty electrical connection? Did the storm disrupt something? Is there another wreckage happening below us at this very moment?

While proton beams collide, while multiple dimensions form and collapse, while particles are torn apart and new particles are born, we wait in endless darkness.

I stand against Henry, my cheek pressed to his chest, and hear the bang of his heart echo and then move in time with mine. I close my eyes, feeling the magnetic pull of him rushing through me. The control room bleeds with an eerie dark silence.

"Henry?" I whisper.

He grips my hand tightly and his other presses into the curve of my back, pulling me close.

Then the room starts to spin like a tilt-a-whirl and a strange high-pitched roar sounds around us, and then I'm shooting, shooting, spinning, faster, faster, faster, until I feel as if I'm being pulled apart—as if my cells, my particles, are shredding, sliced through by darkness— and I'm moving at lightspeed, around and around and around, and I grip Henry's hand because I'm certain if I let go I won't exist anymore, I won't be, so I bury myself against him as I spin and spin until I can't breathe, I can't see, I can't hear—I'm torn into a thousand pieces of myself—and I rush toward something, something pulling me in, pulling me close, something I can't resist, I only know I have to fly, and then—**BAM!**—I collide, I hit with a shattering boom, I break apart—the wreckage is profound—and in that wreckage—*Henry?*—that trillionth of a second, everything in me breaks and then realigns, coalesces, and becomes—

14

A COLD, RAIN-TINGED BREEZE DRIFTS OVER MY SKIN, penetrating the darkness. The smell of rain-soaked stone and cedar pulls insistently at my sleep-shrouded mind. I burrow in the warm nest of my blankets, turn my cheek into the softness of my pillow, and resist the call to *wake up*.

My bedroom window is open, and the cool breeze rustles the curtains, the sound like the soft whooshing of a cotton dress flapping against my legs on a windy day. My room is bathed in the blank slate of night, only the faintest tinge of warm yellow light falls through the window from the street outside. It's too dark to see. It's the middle of the night then. The only sound is the gentle rustle of the curtain, the rumpled whoosh of the covers as I pull them tight, and my long, sleep-filled sigh.

Outside, Geneva is sleep-soothed and peaceful, muffled-quiet after a day of rain and thunder. I love Geneva after the rain. Right now, strangely, I can almost put a taste to the feeling—strong black tea with milk and a plate of buttery shortbread eaten next to a crackling fire. Strange. It feels like a memory, but it isn't. I don't like tea, and I've never cared for shortbread, but right now, in the vestiges of sleep, I swear that's what rain means to me.

I sink lower into my warm, soft bed, wondering where Purrk is since he usually sleeps curled on top of my head like a bulky fur hat. Maybe he's gotten into the trash again, or maybe he's watching the bats swoop between the old Romanesque church spires, or perhaps . . .

I start to drift back into the gentle arms of sleep, cradled by cedar and tea and starlight when I remember the dream.

I was in the control room, something went terribly, horribly wrong, there was a screaming noise, a thunderous boom, spinning, flying, I felt as if I was being pulled apart, Henry was there and . . . gosh, I need to stop eating Kung Pao Tofu "make your unborn grandchildren weep from the heat that lasts generations" Level Five spice. It gives me the weirdest dreams.

"Purrk?" I call.

Holy crap.

Did you hear that?

That voice wasn't mine. It was deep. Mellow, like whiskey and tumbled rocks. It practically rumbled out of me.

I reach up and clutch my throat. Then I shoot upright when my fingers hit not smooth skin, but . . . stubble? Rough, prickly, whiskery *stubble*?

And . . . and . . . and . . . an Adam's apple?

I jab at the protrusion and then wince when my sharp prodding hurts. It's there. It's an Adam's apple covered in beard stubble.

I kick my feet, shove back the bed covers, and as I

struggle to escape my bed I ram into a wooden headboard. The bed shakes and cracks against the wall. I scramble away from the headboard, as startled as a hare under the shadow of a hunting raptor. Because—I don't have a wooden headboard, I have a brass French-style headboard with curlies and knobs and—

I let out a whimper and then slap my hand to my mouth.

It was a growly, low, deep whimper.

Even worse, my hand rubs over my face and there is stubble everywhere. I practically have a morning beard. A five-o' clock shadow, long, long past five-o' clock.

I reach up with my other hand and send my fingers searching, feeling stubble, a sharp, pointed nose, high, hard-planed cheekbones, deep-set eyes, long, feathering eyelashes, thick eyebrows, and my hair—it's not long, straight, and silky. It's short, barely reaching past my ears, soft, and wavy.

"I'm dreaming," I say into the thick, black silence of the room. I make another small noise at the shocking sound of my deep voice.

I have to admit it. It's a man's voice. I'm speaking with a man's voice. An oddly familiar, "I've heard this somewhere before" man's voice. I have stubble. I have an Adam's apple.

Which means . . .

My hands—my large hands, connected to arms that have much more arm hair than I've ever had in my life, connected to biceps that are very, very muscular—okay, my hands quest downward. I reach my chest. There's a dusting of hair, flat muscles, no breasts—my breasts are gone—the rapid pounding of my heart, kicking against my ribs—settle down, don't freak out, it's a dream—down to my abdomen, flat and muscled, down—oh gosh, oh gosh, why am I freaking out, it's just a dream, I don't sleep naked, obviously I'm dreaming, who sleeps naked? I jump back again, hitting the headboard when my hand slips lower, down my flat, hair-dusted abdomen, down lower, and touches—

I bolt out of the bed, hit the cold wood floor with a hard thud, and rush toward where I think the bedroom door and light switch is. I ram my shin into a wooden dresser, stubbing my toe.

"Crap!"

I grope my way across the pitch-dark room, hop on one foot, and stumble into a bookshelf. Something falls. Shatters when it hits the floor.

"Dang it!" I shout, my voice as deep as a freaking ravine.

I find the wall—a cool, smooth plaster surface—and grope along it, following it through the darkness, my breath short, my heart booming.

If I turn on the light I'll wake up. I'll definitely wake up. Besides, I have to pee. I hate those dreams where you have to pee in real life and you're running around desperately searching for a toilet when all you really need to do is *wake up*.

There!

Found it.

I hit the electric switch, flooding the room in bright, brilliant light that hurts my eyes.

And—

I don't wake up.

Instead, I blink.

The light hurts.

I can barely see a thing. My vision is blurry. Frankly,

it's terrible. In real life I have 20/20 vision, but right now, what is this, 200/20? Is that a thing? I rub my eyes, trying to wipe away the fuzzy blur. I hold my hand in front of my face and pull it out and then back in, trying to focus.

I frown. My hands are big, with tanned skin, large, blue-tinged veins on the back, and square-tipped fingers.

Man hands.

I drop them and instead inspect the room. I've never been here before—not in waking life. It's a tidy room (except for the shattered photo frame on the floor), there's a king-size wood-framed bed with navy covers and sheets, a bookshelf full of books (the titles are too blurry to read), a nightstand on either side of the bed with matching silver lamps, a wooden dresser, and a matching armoire. On the wall, hanging over the bed, is a large painting of (I think, but I can't see clearly enough to be sure) a starry sky over the Alps. There's the window —light gray curtains blowing in the breeze, the dark night beyond. The room still smells of cedar, tea, and outside. It's clean, neat. The books are grouped by color and there aren't any clothes on the floor or papers lying about. The temperature is cool, but even so, I'm warm enough that the night air drifting over me doesn't make me shiver.

Finally, on the back of the door to the bedroom, there's a mirror.

I wonder, can you look in mirrors in dreams?

You can't read in dreams (at least I've never been able to), which might be the actual reason I can't see the book titles.

Slowly I walk toward the door and the silver-framed mirror.

My heart beats nervously. My pulse pounds rapidly in

my throat. I curl my fingers into my palms and try to steady my breathing.

It's just a dream after all, even if it feels like real life.

My feet whisper over the wood floor, the cold sinking into the soles of my feet as I stop in front of my reflection.

I don't understand what I'm seeing at first.

My image is too fuzzy, too confusing.

I lean closer, just to be sure.

Tall, broad-shouldered. Square-face, solid jaw. Stubble. Wheat-colored wavy hair. Blue-gray eyes. A few freckles sprinkled here and there. Back to the eyes.

I know those eyes.

They've looked at me with humor, love, passion, disdain, neutrality, and loathing. I've seen all the shades of emotion in these eyes. And now they're looking back at me.

I reach out and press my hand to the smooth, cold glass.

Me—I reach out and touch the reflection of Henry Joule.

15

THE DAMP COLD GRIPS ME AS I RUN UP THE GRAVEL DRIVE. My feet pound the crushed stone, sending loud crunching noises through the oppressively quiet night. It mixes with the wind whistling through the needles of the pine trees populating this side of the mountain. The air is thinner, colder here than down below in Geneva proper. The still wet evergreens send out mossy pine scents as they stand tall and fuzzy in the dark, clouded night. No moon and no stars to be seen.

My breathing is jagged and the piney air pinches my lungs. It was three miles up this mountain. My legs burn from the twisting climb up the little mountain road. Sweat drips down my back, the heat of my skin chilling in the night air.

Dang it!

What the heck is going on?

Frankly, I have no idea. I only know I pulled on the first thing I found in Henry's chest of drawers—a pair of jeans and a white t-shirt—and then by the door I found a pair of well-worn running shoes. I refused to go to the bathroom because, as everyone knows, if you go to the bathroom in a dream you pee the bed, so ... yeah.

Every jarring step running up this dang mountain made me want to wet myself. However, I've persevered. I'm not going to the bathroom until I wake up.

However, in case this isn't a dream, I'm ... look, I'm going to find out, aren't I?

And my first (coherent) thought was, if I'm Henry, is Henry *me*?

I ran a mile through the deserted cobblestone streets to my apartment and pounded on the door. No one answered, although I could hear Purrk meowing behind the thick wood. My neighbors—a couple who fervently believe all wars will stop once humanity embraces veganism—poked their heads out of their apartment and glared at me. Their faces were fuzzy and out-of-focus, but I think when they saw my (somewhat) crazed expression, my towering height, and my fist pounding the door, they decided I must eat a lot of steak, pork chops, and burgers and therefore embrace senseless violence, and they promptly shut and bolted their door.

Regardless, I/Henry/Serena-Henry wasn't home. The door stayed shut.

So then I ran down the stairs, not trusting my death-trap elevator, back onto the dark, stony streets of Geneva, and asked myself, what do you do when you need help desperately?

What do you do?

Easy. You go find your best friend since childhood, your fellow trekker, your soul-mate-sister, your best friend in the whole wide world.

Jillian lives with her husband Daniel above Geneva in

a modern, trendy exhibitionist's dream house where almost the entire wall overlooking the city is made of glass. I'm pretty sure Daniel likes to do it full-tilt against the floor-to-ceiling windows—at least, every time I joke about it Jillian blushes—but hey, you can't really blame the guy. It's a gorgeous view.

Regardless, Jillian's here. If it's a dream, she'll wake me up. If it's not a dream . . .

I stop at the front door, hit the unlock code (474747, which any *Star Trek* fan would immediately guess, and I keep telling Jillian this, but she doesn't listen) and the electronic lock clicks free.

It's three in the morning now. The house is dark except for the under-cupboard lights shining in the kitchen. It smells like chocolate chip cookies and vanilla, and the wood floors creak under my feet as I slowly and quietly close the door.

Daniel's in Rome this week at a big fashion event—I know because I spent Monday and Tuesday night here watching a *Deep Space Nine* marathon while eating dozens of Fran's (Jillian's surrogate mother) cookies and buckets of her homemade caramel ice cream while Jillian complained pregnancy was making her ankles swell, and would I massage her feet like Daniel does? Which I did, obviously.

I tiptoe through the house, not wanting to wake Fran, a sweet sixty-year-old Long Islander who is very partial to animal prints and loves Jillian to pieces. I don't think she'd understand my predicament even in a dream, so . . .

The shadows of the hallway lengthen as I leave the sparse light of the kitchen behind. My heart rate has slowed, the thuds evening to a steady beat. I lick my dry lips, the taste of salt and sweat heavy. The floor creaks again and I pause, listening to my own breathing.

No sounds greet me.

No one wakes.

A shiver of uncertainty scrapes over me, trailing goose bumps over my skin. There have been plenty of nights that I've slept next to Jillian—slumber parties, sleepovers, shared rooms at conventions—so there isn't anything unusual about me waking her up in the middle of the night. I've done it a thousand times to discuss a theory I can't get out of my head or to talk about childhood/adulthood/peoplehood.

But—

No. I shake my head. No buts.

I grip the cold metal knob of her bedroom door and twist.

"Jillian?" I whisper, stepping into the cool of her bedroom. It's a large, open space with a wall of windows and minimalist furniture. "Jillian, wake up. It's me, Serena."

Then, suddenly, I realize the faint pocket of light falling across the bed shows a pile of blankets, but no Jillian.

I frown and turn back to the door, only to find the glint of an aluminum bat crashing toward my skull.

"Get out!" Jillian yells.

I throw up my hands, ducking as the bat whizzes over my head.

Jeez! "Jillian, it's me. Serena!"

She's blurry, but I can tell she's in a *Star Fleet* T-shirt and sleep shorts. Her curly dark hair is wild, and she looks like a warrior as she charges at me, swinging again.

The air whooshes over my head as the bat almost connects with my skull.

Crap!

I duck, dodge, and roll across the bed, frantically avoiding the swinging bat. When I come to my feet, I hold out my hands.

"It's me. Serena," I say, my voice deep and raspy with the adrenaline crashing through me. "Serena, your best friend! Jillian, stop!"

She lunges at me, swinging the bat. I jump across the bed again, landing on the other side. I back toward the door as she stalks around the bed.

"What did you do to Serena?" she hisses, gripping the bat. "What did you do, you raving psychopath? Tell me!"

"No," I say, holding up my hands. I keep the bed between us, edging away as Jillian stalks closer. "Jillian."

"I'll kill you!"

Jeez, dream Jillian is fierce. Then again, I seem to remember her saying she took a swing at Daniel when she first met him too. But this—this is not going at all like I anticipated.

Jillian lunges across the bedroom swinging like the slugger I know her dad always wanted her to be, and instead of dodging, I grab the bat midair.

I flinch at the cracking sting of the cold metal. *Crap, that hurt.*

Things don't hurt so much in a dream, do they?

Your heart doesn't pound so much, does it?

You can't smell cookies or evergreen, can you?

Jillian's face is red, her hands trembling as she tries to wrest the bat from my grip. She's scared. She's scared of me, and she's scared for me.

Suddenly I'm scared too because it's patently,

abundantly clear that no matter how much I wish otherwise, this is not a dream.

My stance relaxes, my grip loosens on the bat, and shock flushes through me, cold and icy.

Then Jillian does something completely unexpected. She lets go of the bat, grabs my shirt, tugs me close, and knees me. Right in Henry's balls.

Fiery, wrenching pain shoots through me, radiating out and branching through every nerve ending in my entire body. Red sparks bust in my vision, my lungs seize, and I drop to the floor.

Holy. Ever. Loving. All that is holy. Why didn't anyone ever say how much this freaking hurts! I thought men were just exaggerating, being babies.

I roll to my side, hitting my fist against the wood floor. *Not a dream, not a dream,* definitely *not a dream.*

My balls are screaming and I have to pee. I have to pee so freaking bad the pain is excruciating and I can't breathe and—

Jillian sprints across the room, grabs something off the dresser, and heaves it at me. A sharp metal object hits me in the chest, and as it rebounds loudly against the wood, I see a flash of pewter and know exactly what it is.

"Jillian! Not your Franklin Mint Enterprise! What the heck is wrong with you? Why are you always throwing it? Jeez!"

She's grabbed something else. Her arm is back, ready to throw, but she stops half-cocked. "What did you say?"

I slide upright, eyeing her warily, rub my chest, and pull my legs up to protect a certain sensitive area. I give my best friend a hurt look. "I said stop throwing your Enterprise. It was bad enough you threw it at Daniel—do you have to throw it at me too?"

"Did Serena tell you that?" She looks toward the bat lying on the floor.

I look at it too.

"I *am* Serena," I say, and when she starts to scoff and lunge toward the bat I say as quickly as I can, "We met as kids at a *Star Trek* convention where we got Wil Wheaton's autograph. My favorite number is 437. I lost my virginity to Bernie Berger and you told me I should've waited until I found someone named Horatio Hotdog because then I maybe would've orgasmed."

Jillian edges closer to the bat so I talk faster.

"I have a cat named Purrk. You couldn't talk to men until you met Daniel, he was a ghost—"

"Who told you that?" she asks, stopping midstride.

"You did. You tell me everything. Well, you still haven't told me whether or not you do it against the windows, but everything else." I hold my hand up in the "live long and prosper" sign.

Jillian shakes her head, her voice trembling, "What did you do to Serena to make her tell you these things?"

For crying out loud.

It looks like I'm going to have to pull out the big guns.

"You remember when we snuck into the Anaheim *Star Trek* Convention for my fourteenth birthday? I didn't want to come—I was prepping for my Quantum Mechanics exam. And you cursed 'qaStaH nuq jay'[1] and then you raised your fist in the air and shouted, 'tlhIngan maH!'[2]"

Jillian's eyes widen. No one knows this story. Just us. There isn't any reason for a stranger to know it.

"And then you said—"

"'qoSlIj DatIvjaj,'"[3] we say together, her voice high and shaking, mine low and insistent.

"Then I closed my textbook, certain I'd fail but okay with it since you were there, and I said, 'Heghlu'meH QaQ jajvam.'"

Today is a good day to die.

That is what we always say to each other when we're in a fix and taking the less-traveled route.

"Serena?" Jillian asks tentatively, her eyes widening. She stares at me as if she doesn't want to believe the conclusion she's come to, but she can't deny it any longer.

Guess what? Neither can I.

"Yeah, it's me," I say, slowly standing, the pain of the ball kick finally passed.

Then the door to the bedroom bursts open, slams against the wall, and I hear a shout of rage. I turn and throw my hands up, but not in time.

Fran leaps into the room and—hardcore, street-smart Long Islander that she is (I'm taking away that sweet, kindly sixty-year-old bit)—she slams her fist into my eye, knocking me back. I trip and fall onto the bed, clutching a hand over my throbbing, sure-to-be-swelling-soon eye. Man, she's got a killer right hook.

"Got 'em, Jilly!" Fran shouts proudly. "I called the police! This psycho's going to jail!"

16

I PRESS THE ICE PACK TO MY RIGHT EYE, LETTING THE ICY bite numb the throbbing and the ache. My eye has swollen partially shut. It's tender and a bright reddish, purply blue.

I lean my elbow on the kitchen table and the wooden chair creaks under my weight. Jillian sits across from me, tapping her finger on the birchwood tabletop and frowning as she takes in my appearance. We haven't had a moment alone or a moment to talk.

I went to pee finally. *That* was an experience. We won't be talking about it. Sorry.

The police came and went with our apologies for the confusion. Jillian explained to Fran that I was an old friend from college and . . . look, it was convoluted and not very convincing, but Fran finally decided that even though I was a big, strange man who'd appeared in Jillian's house in the middle of the night, I was also essentially harmless.

Out of my one good eye I watch as she bustles around

the kitchen, whipping up a fresh batch of chocolate chip cookies—"It'll just take a minute!"—and a pot of strong black coffee. The comforting scent of melting chocolate and freshly ground French roast rolls over me.

Yet . . .

"Is there any tea?" I ask Fran. "Black with milk and sugar?"

"Of course," Fran says, rummaging through a cupboard and pulling out a metal tea tin.

Jillian makes a disbelieving sound, and then I cough, realizing what I just said.

I don't *like* tea.

"You don't like tea," Jillian whispers, giving Fran a quick glance to make sure she isn't listening. She's not—she's pulling out a tea bag and dropping it into a mug.

"I hate tea," I whisper back, leaning forward and dropping the ice pack on the table.

Jillian nods.

"Henry likes tea."

She nods again.

I like espresso/coffee/real caffeine. Tea is tepid water grossly flavored, with milk added as an insult. Not to mention the fact that I'm lactose intolerant.

"I won't drink it," I say confidently.

Fran slides the mug to the table in front of me, her zebra-striped robe swishing as she moves busily. "There you go, dear."

She pats my shoulder, having decided that since I'm Jillian's "old friend" then I'm automatically a dear. Fran is a mom, one hundred percent, and if you're a friend of Jillian, she'll be a mom to you too.

"Thank you," I say, smiling at her, determined not to drink it. Why would I? I hate tea.

Then I take in the mellow scent of tea leaves and sugary, milky cream. Steam curls from the mug. I lean forward, take in the scent, and my mouth starts to water. I feel warm and cozy and suddenly calm and—oh, screw it. I grab the mug and take a slow sip.

I close my eyes. The heat from the tea rushes over me and the warm drink tastes like caramel and milk and a crackling fire and family crowded together telling stories and laughing while rain patters against a windowpane. It's probably the most perfect thing I've ever tasted.

One sip and I feel more centered. No wonder Henry drinks tea every day—it's a wonder drug.

I open my eyes to find a blurry Jillian giving me a look of horror.

I drop the mug and it clatters on the table.

Holy crap. Holy ever-loving crap.

It's my worst nightmare. I've been anglerfished. I'm not me anymore.

I mean, obviously I'm in Henry's body (and I hope he's in mine, because if not, what happened to my body, and what happened to me?), but I'm not just in his body. I have the tastes of his body.

Have you ever heard those stories where someone gets an organ transplant and all of a sudden they're craving Big Macs and have a new love of Scrabble, and then—surprise!—they find out the organ donor ate McDonalds every day and played tournament Scrabble?

This happens.

Organs carry memories. So do bodies.

I'm . . . oh no, I'm a tepid tea-drinking, prudishly uptight, umbrella-carrying, anal neat-freak of a British man.

This is my worst nightmare.

My hand shakes as I push the tea away from me. Fran slides a plate of just-out-of-the-oven chocolate chip cookies between Jillian and me and gives Jillian a mug of decaf coffee (because of the baby).

"I'm off to bed," she says cheerily. She pats my shoulder. "Nice meeting you, Henry. I'm terribly sorry about the black eye."

My chest pinches painfully when she calls me Henry. But I smile at Fran in her zebra-striped robe and night cream mask and say, "It's all right. I'm sorry I startled you."

"Night, Fran," Jillian says, wrapping her hands around her mug of coffee.

Jillian and I watch as Fran disappears down the hallway. We listen to her footsteps fade then wait for the click of her bedroom door, and then, after a tense five seconds, Jillian leans forward, pokes my arm, and whispers, "What the heck! What have you done?"

It takes all of ten minutes to tell Jillian everything I can remember about the incident in the control room. The blackout, the alarms, the screaming noise, the spinning, and then waking up as Henry.

On the birchwood kitchen table between us, the plate of cookies is empty except for crumbs and melted chocolate. Jillian refilled her coffee, and my mug of tea is empty. What can I say? I'm a weak, weak human and tea is horrendously, agonizingly delicious.

Jillian frowns at me, rubbing her hand over her rounded stomach and appearing deep in thought. "So ..."

"What?" I ask, concerned at the look on her face.

She shakes her head then waves her hand at me. "This is what your boss looks like?"

"Yes."

"The boss who's always riding you and sending emails in the middle of the night?"

"Yes."

Although I'm not sure "riding" is the appropriate word to use here.

"The boss you said wants to sleep with you?"

I cough, beat my chest with my fist, and wish for a bit more tea to wash my surprise down. I never told Jillian about me and Henry having sex, or Henry saying it was love at first sight. It was just . . . too much. I was barely able to process it. Plus I was ashamed of how I handled it.

"What did you say?" I ask.

Jillian waves my surprise away. "When Daniel first appeared, we were on the phone, and your boss texted, and you were upset, and you said he was probably such a hard-ass because he wanted to have sex with you or something like that."

"Oh," I say, nodding. "Right. I said that."

"You're very tall," she says, looking from Henry's feet all the way to his head.

I wait for her to say something else, but she doesn't.

"That's it?"

She nods.

"I'm tall."

She nods again. "Isn't it weird, growing eight or nine inches in one night?"

Eight or nine inches? I'm tall?

"Jillian! I'm in a man's body! I have a beard growing in. I have a deep voice and an Adam's apple. I have testicles and a penis! A penis! And you think the strangest thing is that I'm tall?"

She considers me for a moment, tilts her head, runs her gaze over me, and then says, "Mmm...yes?"

I burst out laughing. "Jerk."

She flashes me a smile. "You're freaking out, aren't you?"

"You could say that."

"Me too."

We sit there for a moment letting the quiet of the house fall around us and watching the dark of the night bleed against the yellow glow of the kitchen lights. Then Jillian stands, walks to the counter, and grabs the tea tin. She slips a tea bag in a new mug and starts to make me another cup.

I hate to admit it, but I get a happy little blip as she pours hot water from the kettle into the mug. The sound of water splashing against ceramic is oddly satisfying.

After she adds milk and sugar, she drops the mug in front of me and asks, "What are you going to do?"

"I don't know," I say, shaking my head. "I have to find Henry. He wasn't at my apartment. The only other place I can think he'll be is at the ATLAS building in the morning. I think he'll go there . . ." I pause, then say, "If he's still alive."

"If he's not—" Jillian stops.

I nod. "Yeah. Then my body is—"

"Dead."

There's a quick tightness in my chest. I wave it away. "No. That's a slippery slope of dark thoughts I'm not going down. Insufficient facts always invite fear."

"I thought it was danger," Jillian says, referencing the famous Spock quote.

"Well, this time they invite fear, and fear makes people stupid."

Jillian pulls a chair next to mine, grabs my hand, and squeezes. Her hands are cold compared to mine, small, which makes me freak out, because before, our hands were roughly the same size.

"Henry is alive," I say firmly, projecting confidence, "and he'll be at work, and as soon as I find him we'll switch back. Easy."

Jillian leans against me. "Serena?"

"Hmm?"

"How will you switch back?"

I don't know. I have no clue. I don't know how we switched (if we switched), and if I don't know how it was done, I don't know how to undo it.

"It'll be super easy," I tell Jillian with false confidence. "Henry and I are physicists. We'll figure it out." Then I add half-jokingly, "For science."

Jillian knows me too well even when I'm not me, because she says, "If you don't figure it out, I'm still your best friend, even if you do look like a blond Captain Kirk and have bad taste in hot beverages."

I hug her to me. "Thanks, Jilly."

She sighs, squeezes my arm, then says, "Remember when you told me there are things in the universe that aren't perceivable and are therefore inconceivable?"

"Sure." I'm always going off on one tangent or another about the mysteries of the universe.

"Well, if science doesn't have the answers, maybe . . ." She pauses, and I pull away to look down at her.

"Maybe what?"

"Maybe this happened because of . . . love?" She gives

me a wide-eyed, innocent "don't shoot the messenger" kind of look.

"Love," I say flatly.

Jillian has always been a romantic. While I never had a problem enjoying one-night flings and accepting that people can enjoy each other without commitment, Jillian was on a years-long quest for her one true love. She's always wanted love while I've always avoided it.

"Here," she says, picking up her phone and hitting a video call. "I have an idea."

I hope she's not calling Daniel, because I do not want to explain to him that yes, indeed, I may look like a six-foot-tall man who broke into his pregnant wife's bedroom at three in the morning, but I'm actually her best friend Serena.

Luckily, it's not Daniel who picks up.

"What?" A stick-thin middle-aged woman with a heavily wrinkled face, short, spiky hair, and slit-thin eyes glares at Jillian. "What do you want?"

"Hi Zelda, it's Jillian. Remember me? I had that . . . um . . . annoying spirit hanging around me?"

Aha. So this is the cranky psychic Jillian told me about. The one who could see Daniel when he was a ghost.

She's in a poufy white and baby-blue lace nightgown and she has a takeout bucket of barbeque chicken in her lap. She takes a tooth-barring bite of the chicken and then says, with a mouth full of barbeque, "I repeat. What do you want? I'm busy."

"Okay," Jillian says, not at all deterred by Zelda's abruptness or the barbeque massacre happening on the lady's face. "My friend . . . Wait, can you see energy over the phone? Or do we need to be there?"

Zelda waves her hand, a dripping drumstick her conducting wand. "Show me."

Jillian turns the phone toward me, and I sit still and uncomfortable as Zelda scrapes her gaze over me. Her wrinkles deepen, her skin—or maybe her sense of humor —as parched as Death Valley. I hold still, resisting the urge to squirm.

The feeling reminds me of getting the evil eye from a headmistress even though I imagine—darn him—it's Henry who got this evil-eye treatment. Probably because he was always gluing teacups to saucers.

"Well?" Jillian asks after a good minute of Zelda raking me with her gaze and me feeling as if she's shuffling through the underwear drawer of my mind.

Zelda shrugs and rips another chunk of chicken from her drumstick. "You're screwed," she says, pointing a bony finger at me. "That'll be two hundred twelve dollars."

I'm screwed?

My heart thuds—a hard, pitiful thunk.

"What?" I say in a deep, stunned voice. I rub my chest.

"What do you mean, exactly, when you say 'screwed'?" Jillian asks, shooting me a nervous look.

"Screwed," Zelda says. "Effed, out of luck, balls-deep in muck and mire, bent over backward and slapped with a dead trout—"

Jillian looks stunned. "What—?"

"Excuse me," I say, interrupting the lengthy list of synonyms. "Why am I screwed? And how can you tell by looking at me?"

Not to mention, I'm not paying $212 for a woman I don't know to stare at me for a minute and pronounce that I'm screwed.

Zelda's mouth turns down, stretching her skin into a mask of extreme annoyance. She drops the drumstick bone into her bucket of chicken and takes her time choosing another piece. Her fingers are coated in barbeque sauce, her lips are tinged orangey-red, and there's a bit of chicken meat on her shoulder. Behind her, there's a pile of empty takeout boxes, dirty laundry on the floor, and a stack of wrinkled magazines.

And I hate—absolutely hate—to admit this, but the mess is making me itchy. My hands are literally twitching to teleport me through the phone so I can tidy up this lady's apartment. It's a compulsion, and it's freaking me out.

I'm not a neat freak—that's Henry. I'm as much of a slob as this woman. The twitchy compulsion is awful.

So I demand, "Well? How do you know I'm screwed?"

Zelda grunts then grabs a chicken wing. She pinches it between her fingers and says, "Because you're not in the body you belong in. Obviously."

An icy chill runs through my veins. I lean forward, my eyes on Zelda. She ignores me as she nibbles on the chicken wing and then cackles at something on the television across her living room.

"And?" I ask, drawing her attention back to me.

She rolls her eyes. "Ugh. Why are you people always annoying me? You bother me at all hours of the day. I'm eating. I'm watching my show. I'm resting. Don't you have any decency?"

"Your website literally says 24/7 readings," Jillian mutters.

"I'll pay double," I say quickly.

Zelda puts down her chicken wing, wipes her hands

on her lacy nightgown—leaving a smear of sauce—and then turns off her TV.

Aha.

Money talks.

Jillian raises her eyebrows and gives me a thumbs-up. The kitchen takes on a more hopeful, warm glow. I grip my steaming cup of tea and wait for Zelda to continue.

"All right," she says in a no-nonsense tone, "here's what I see. Your energy isn't attached to this body. It's like a cloak that doesn't quite fit—"

"Yes, exactly! I don't fit. This isn't me," I say excitedly, leaning forward. My wooden chair creaks, the sound loud, echoing off the wood and stone of the kitchen.

"As I was saying . . ." Zelda narrows her eyes at my interruption. "I've seen this energy pattern once before."

I nod but don't speak.

"After a while the energy settled, merged, and that was the end of that."

Merged? Settled? I tense, all my muscles going rigid, the wood of the chair hard beneath me. "What do you mean, that was the end of that?"

"Are you dense?" Zelda asks.

I stare at her. No one in my entire life has asked me that question.

"I mean, if you don't fix this,"—she jabs her finger at me, and I flinch even though she's thousands of miles away, across the Atlantic—"then you'll be like this forever."

Forever?

Forever, forever?

"But—"

Forever?

"I'm assuming you know the other party?" she asks.

I'm stunned. My thoughts are slow, as if I'm trying to walk through—well, balls-deep muck and mire.

The other party?

Henry.

She's asking about Henry.

Jillian answers for me. "She knows him. What do we do?"

Zelda shrugs, looking back down at her bucket of chicken. "Switch back," she drawls, rustling through the bucket.

"How?" I ask, managing that one word.

"Maybe a ceremony," Jillian says, "like with words to chant, or you hold hands—"

Zelda slices her hand through the air. "No. Ugh."

"Then what?" Jillian asks.

Zelda shrugs. "I don't know. Like I said, the only other time I saw a soul swap, it was permanent. It seems to me you don't want this to be permanent."

Permanent.

Forever.

Screwed.

Jillian shifts in her seat. "That's what this is—a soul swap?"

Zelda grunts an affirmative. "Are we done here?"

No. We definitely aren't done.

"Why did it happen?" I ask.

"That's for you to figure out, isn't it?" Zelda says impatiently.

My lips are numb, my body is cold, and goose bumps line the back of my neck. "If I figure it out, we'll swap back?"

Zelda raises one eyebrow, her skin stretching tight. "How would I know?"

"Could it be because they have unfinished business?" Jillian asks. "Or maybe they're supposed to fall in love?"

Zelda scoffs, grabs her remote, and turns the TV back on. "That'll be four hundred twenty-four dollars."

"But . . . love?" Jillian asks.

Zelda looks at the TV, her eyes glued to the screen, and says, "Don't know. The last two this happened to ended up dead." She grimaces at the phone. "Speaking of, I'm texting my bill. Pay it before you die."

Then she hangs up, which is just as well because I don't have anything left to say.

Jillian drops her phone to the table. It hits with a clatter, and then a second later it lets out a little text notification chime. The screen lights up. It's a payment request for $424, plus a three percent processing fee, plus a five percent after-hours fee, plus a two percent international fee, plus . . .

"Jeez."

Jillian nods. "Yeah. That about sums it up."

She swipes her finger across the plate, picking up melted chocolate and cookie crumbs, then glumly pops her finger in her mouth.

"I didn't actually think today was a good day to die," I say, taking a fortifying sip of tea.

I wonder if I'll like more things that Henry likes as time goes on. Will I become more like him the closer I am to . . . never, never, forever?

Jillian's lower lip wobbles. "I'm not crying, I'm just pregnant."

I nod. "Of course. You're a rock."

She lifts her chin stubbornly and demands, "You're not going to die. This isn't forever."

"I know," I promise her.

I just have to figure this out. No problem.

"What now?" Jillian asks.

"Now I find Henry." I look out the wall of windows at the sky over Geneva bleeding from black to dove-gray. The city lights flicker, beckoning me. "Can I borrow your car?"

I'll go to CERN, find Henry, and then we'll switch back right away.

There's no need to worry.

None at all.

It'll be easy.

17

THE GOLDEN-GRAY LIGHT OF THE MORNING TWILIGHT SPILLS over the patchwork farm fields and the leafy countryside sprouting around the myriad research buildings. The dew is heavy and sparkling with rainbow reflections, and the smell of wet grass is heavy and perfumed with clover. A European robin hops through the blades of grass, piping *cheer-io, cheer-io*.

CERN is still and sleepy as I run across the parking lot through shadow and diffused light, past the hopping robin, and into the ATLAS building.

Let him be here. Please let him be here.

If he's not here—Let him be here.

It's not quite 6 a.m.

Henry wasn't at my apartment—I checked again, just in case, knocking loudly—and so I'm praying, *let him be here.*

I run down the long, tunnel-like hall, my feet pounding loudly, past my cluttered office, then Henry's pristine office (both empty, computers off), and turn to the control room. The bright lights reflect off the white of the walls, and my right eye, swollen and blue, throbs with each jarring step.

The hallway is empty. Not many people arrive until after nine, and the quiet is unnerving. It smells like the cleaning solution used overnight. There's the hum of fans and my heavy, nervous breathing. Then, as I near the control room, I hear the clack of typing and the murmur of conversation. I slow my gait to a calm, relaxed walk. Even so, my heart pounds and my hands tremble, so I take a steadying breath and (stupidly) imagine drinking a nice, soothing cup of tea.

It works. I smooth down my T-shirt, run a hand through Henry's windblown, sweat-soaked, and air-dried hair, and then paste that relaxed half-smile on my face that Henry wears whenever he's thinking about Kaluza-Klein states or microscopic black holes.[1]

I step through the doorway, stop, and scan the large open space—where is he, where is he—then scan the curved, circular line of desks—where the heck is he—the flickering monitors, a few people typing, the projection wall glowing with updated info, and—

Thank goodness.

Oh, thank goodness.

He's here.

It's Henry.

My knees go weak and I grab the doorframe. The rush of relief roaring through me is so overwhelming that my vision goes black for a moment. There's a ringing in my ears and I blink, trying to bring Henry into focus. I have one eye with fuzzy blurred vision and another eye that's swollen and only halfway open. But still, it's Henry.

Even if I couldn't see him, I'd know by the pulse of electromagnetism pulling me toward him.

I make a sound in my throat, clutch the doorframe, and shake my head, trying to clear the mind-fuddling tug arching between us.

Henry is across the control room standing rigid at a desk, digging through a stack of papers, throwing some to the side and reading others only to throw them down with disgust, then grabbing more. He's searching for something, and he looks almost . . . frantic.

Okay, he also looks like me.

A frantic me.

The second I see him is one of the most bizarre of my life. There's me, my body, and I'm not in it. You hear about this, for instance, when people have out-of-body experiences and they're floating above their body, looking down on themselves. But their body isn't moving/doing/being, it's dying.

My body is a whirlwind of activity. Henry looks like he had a rough night too. He came here in my thigh-length buttercup-yellow silk negligee, covered with a buttoned jean jacket and a pair of fuzzy pink soft-soled boots I wear as house slippers. My black hair is tangled, staticky, and sticking up on one side. I look . . . my gosh, I look like a deranged squirrel digging for acorns in a pile of leaves.

"Henry!" Someone calls a jovial good morning.

I lift my hand, waving offhandedly.

Henry whirls around and looks across the room, not remembering he isn't *Henry* right now.

It's then that he sees me.

I start across the room, pulled toward him.

Henry's (my) eyes go wide, his mouth falls open, and

the papers in his hand fall to the floor, scattering around his feet. Or should I say, the papers scatter around my feet? Cute, petite, black-haired, brown-eyed, science pinup model-hot Serena Otaki's feet.

I stop in front of him and take in a deep breath. He smells like the mint conditioner I use, and I almost cry at the familiar scent. I look down, surprised by how tall Henry is and how small I was. I never realized how petite I looked, or how Henry had to tilt his chin down to look into my eyes. He lifts his chin and steps forward.

There's a charged silence between us, electric with the implausibility of what has happened—what we're seeing with our very own eyes.

We've switched.

Swapped.

Our gazes connect like two magnets yanked together, and I see in his eyes a reflection of what must be in mine. *Thank goodness you're here. Thank goodness I found you.*

"Serena?" he whispers, his voice shaking.

I nod, swallowing the lump of fear that lodged in my throat at the thought that I might not have found him. "Yeah."

"What took you so long?" he hisses, his pale cheeks flaming red. "Where have you been?"

Okay, so we weren't thinking the same thing. Not at all.

"I was looking for you. You weren't at my apartment," I whisper, glancing around the control room to make sure no one is listening in. It's not as if they wouldn't want to. Henry looks like a crazed lingerie model, and I imagine I look like a ratty bruiser. We aren't behaving like our typical selves at all.

Henry's gaze catches on my swollen eye and he says with a hint of outrage, "Were you mugged?"

It's really odd to hear his proper British accent coming out of my mouth. I imagine it must be just as odd for him to hear my California accent coming out of his.

"No," I say, looking around the room again.

A few people are glancing our way, but Henry hasn't noticed. Probably because I'm so tall I'm blocking his view of practically half the room.

"I've been researching for hours, trying to figure out what happened—"

"The incident," I say, looking at the data projection on the wall. "When the power outage occurred. Did you ask—?"

"It's not in the record. There's no data. No one remembers it. It's as if it never happened."

I frown. Look around the room.

That doesn't make sense. The power went out. The screeching sound was so loud I thought my ears were bleeding.

At the back of the room I spot Steven. He was there last night. He even called out to ask if everything was okay when I broke Henry's mug.

"Steven," I bark. He jerks and looks at me in shock as I stalk across the room. He rolls his chair back from the desk and glances around when I point at him, as if he wonders if anyone else is seeing this.

I try to tone it down. I keep forgetting I'm a big guy with crazy hair, pirate-thick stubble, sweaty armpits, and a swollen black eye.

"Last night," I say slowly.

He nods and looks between me and Henry, who

followed me. Henry has his hands on his silk-clad hips and he's tapping a pink fuzzy slipper impatiently.

"Um, yes?" Steven asks.

"You were here," I say.

"You okay, Henry?" Steven asks, he's from Canada, and an all-around nice guy. Now he's giving me a concerned look. "You don't look so good."

He gestures at my eye.

"I'm fine. About last night. The power went out. Did you get a record of that? It was 7:31—"

"The power never went out," he interrupts, glancing at Henry. "I already told Serena that."

I hold up my hand. "There was an error in the LHC—"

"No." Steven shakes his head.

"There was—"

Henry elbows me. "Stop joking around, *Henry*."

What?

I give Henry an irritated "what the heck?" look. He leans close, stands on his tiptoes, and says between clenched teeth, "He doesn't know anything. Stop making me look deranged."

Oh.

Uh-huh.

He's one to talk.

He's wearing my lacy, backless negligee to work and has oral-sex hair. That's my body. My reputation.

I turn aside and direct a hard stare at Steven. "Last night Serena *accidentally*,"—I glare at Henry—"broke my tea mug. Did that get cleaned up?"

Because if Steven doesn't remember that, then we're dealing with . . . another dimension? An alternate timeline? A break in the space-time continuum?

Steven looks between me and Henry, and I imagine by the uncomfortable look on his face he senses the strong undercurrents and he's not excited to be swimming with us.

"Sure, Henry. Yeah. Your tea." He licks his lips nervously. "Aren't you guys on vacation for the next few weeks?"

In other words: "Leave me alone. You're freaking me out."

I get the point.

"Right. Good talk," I say, and then I slap Steven's shoulder and give it a firm bro-grip.

As we walk away, Henry whispers, "What are you doing?"

"The man slap," I say, looking back at Steven and smiling.

He grimaces at me.

"You know. It's what guys do. They grunt and slap each other on the back. You said I looked deranged, so . . . I'm blending."

He gives me a disbelieving stare.

"I've died," he says, his face woebegone. "I've died and this is hell."

"Buck up," I say, grabbing all his papers from the desk and the floor then hurrying toward the door. "Come on— we'll look at the logs from last night in your office."

But an hour later the only thing the logs show is that nothing exceptional happened last night. No power outage, no incident, nothing.

Just the LHC powering down.

I click through the files. The trouble is, every time particle beams collide at the center of ATLAS, six different detecting subsystems record paths, momentum, and the energy of particles coming out of the collision debris. And the amount of data from each collision is mind-blowingly enormous. We have a trigger system that allows the computer to accept or ignore data, but it's still a colossal amount of information. Henry and I are searching through it, narrowing the data readings down to 7:25-7:35pm. But . . . that whole "needle in a haystack" thing? Try a needle in a universe of haystacks.

"What's your theory?" Henry asks, leaning forward in his seat and brushing his long, messy hair back.

Okay, this is weird. I have to acknowledge it. When I talk about Henry, it's Henry in *my* body. So Henry has long black hair, big brown eyes, full pink lips, B-cup size breasts and a vagina.

Hopefully sooner rather than later, Henry will no longer have my breasts and my vagina, and I'll have them back. He's welcome to his own body.

"I'm not sure," I say, frowning at the data flicking across the computer screen.

Henry lifts his eyebrows. I never knew how well I could do that—they go really high.

Huh.

"You're a theoretical particle physicist—your job is to make theories." He gives me an expectant look. "In all the hours we've been switched you haven't made a single theory?"

"Well . . ." I look at the cup full of perfectly sharpened yellow pencils, tap the pink eraser of one, and then admit, "No."

He shakes his head and purses his lips. "I've gone

through the data. I've done my job. If we figure out what happened, we can switch back—"

"I talked to a psychic."

Henry stops. Stares at me blankly.

I tap my finger nervously on the desk. "She said she's seen this once before. If we don't switch back soon, our souls will settle and we'll be stuck like this forever, and also, the last people she knew like this . . . died."

He's silent.

Outside his office window, the sky has turned a cheerful blue and the breeze ruffles the boughs of the nearby pine trees. A hawk wheels past, its wings spread.

Inside I wait, but Henry doesn't say anything.

He just stares.

The computer fan hums at the amount of data we're driving through the processor. I'm hot—Henry, I've come to realize, runs hot—and I'm craving tea, toast, and sausage.

I ran four miles in the middle of the night and those cookies have long burned away.

I'm getting the worst case of hangry I've ever had.

"Well?" I ask him when he hasn't said anything for a good thirty seconds. "She said we could be like this forever or we might die."

Finally, Henry flutters his long eyelashes, then he blinks. He leans forward, pointing a finger at me. "I've been pulling data, working on theories, and you . . . talked to a charlatan who scams gullibles for a living?"

Charlatan?

"It wasn't a scam—"

"How much did you pay?"

I close my mouth.

He lifts an eyebrow. Gosh, I never realized how annoying I look when I do that.

"How much?" his voice is high-pitched and tense.

"Four hundred twenty-four dollars," I mumble.

"Four hundred!"

"With fees . . ." I shrug.

Henry stands, rubs his eyes in exasperation, and says, "We have to figure this out today."

I nod. "I completely agree."

He paces the length of his office, the silk of my negligee swishing as he moves—five steps forward, turn, five steps back.

"I'm not staying in this body." He looks at me. "No offense."

"None taken." I wave my hand. Then I frown. "Why not? What's wrong with my body?"

It's a lot better than his body.

He gives me a flat look. "You're short."

Oh brother. He's just like Jillian.

"Big deal. At least I can see. I bet a cyclops has better vision than you."

Henry swings around and says, "I have to take two steps for every one of yours. I can't reach the top of my bookshelf." He points to his perfectly organized bookshelf, the journals and books stacked alphabetically.

"It's never bothered me," I say.

"Not to mention," he says, his accent becoming more pronounced, "these." He points to my breasts. "I tried to run here, and they bounced everywhere, and they *hurt*." He sounds offended by that fact.

"You don't like my breasts?" I ask, then I realize exactly how that sounds and add, "Never mind."

I narrow my eyes. "Besides, breasts bouncing is

nothing compared to—" I point down at my zipper. "I don't like it. I don't want it."

You can ignore breasts. You can't ignore a penis. It's obtrusive.

He lifts his eyebrow again. "Really?"

"Really." I cross my arms over my chest. "And another thing, I hate tea. And all this body wants is tea, tea, tea. And sausage. I'm a vegetarian—I don't eat sausage—yet here I am craving a meat lover's breakfast special. So yeah. I'd like my body back before you make everyone around here think I'm a deranged, pajama-wearing, suddenly British maniac."

Henry steps closer, the fragrance of mint coming off him. He tilts his chin up and says crisply, "Your complaint is having testicles and tea?"

I nod. "That's right." Then I add, "Liking tea, and tidiness, and"—I wave my hands at his office—"you. It's my worst nightmare."

Becoming Henry. Merging into Henry.

Losing myself in a man, especially Henry, is my worst nightmare.

He takes a step back as if I've struck him. The diffused light from the window falls across his pale face and I notice for the first time the tired blue smudges under his eyes.

"Your worst nightmare is *liking* me?" he asks, a strange light in his eyes.

"Something like that," I say, not willing to admit it's because I'm terrified of loving him, much less liking him.

The hum of the computer fills the silence as we stare at each other, the charge between us growing, sparking.

"All right then," he finally says. "Let's try it."

He gestures at me and steps forward.

"Try what?"

"Switching back. Let's try it. Do exactly what we did last night."

I frown, thinking back to the moment of the blackout.

"The LHC is shut down," I begin.

Henry shakes his head. "If it had to do with the LHC, then we have to wait." Three months at least. He swallows, his eyes large and suddenly nervous, but then he straightens and says, "But if it didn't, then we can switch back now. We just have to replicate our actions from last night."

I nod. It's worth a try.

"We were both bleeding," I say.

"Right."

"And there was spilled tea on my hands."

He nods. "I said I didn't understand you."

"And I said . . ." I can't remember what I said. I frown.

"You said we had symmetry, because you didn't understand me either."

Henry and I give each other a stunned look.

"Was that it?" I ask. "Was this some cosmic wish gone awry?"

Maybe.

"I don't know," he admits.

Right now, it's the only thing we have to go on.

So five minutes later we have a spilled cup of tea, a shattered mug, a pricked knee, and two pricked fingers with bright red drops of blood.

"Ready?" I ask, my fingers burning from where I sliced them enough to bleed.

Henry nods. "Ready."

His hand is wet with hot tea. His knee has crimson blood trailing down it.

My heart pounds. Outside the sky is cerulean blue. There isn't a cloud in sight and the sun shines through the window and falls over us, a persistent, happy glow.

Henry steps close to me. The warmth of him settles in the pit of my stomach. The silk negligee whispers against my jeans.

He holds out his tea-wet hand. I grip it in mine.

"I don't understand you," he says, looking into my eyes.

"Then we have symmetry," I say, my voice deep and rolling like the thunder of last night. "I don't understand you either, and I doubt I ever will."

Henry clenches my hand tightly and the cuts on my fingers burn. "Do you want to?" he asks, his eyes glowing in the light.

I shake my head, and I mean it this time—with all my heart. "No. Understand the universe, yes. You? No." Then I remember what else I said and add, "We're too dissimilar."

He nods and steps closer. I tug him to me, pressing my hand to the base of his spine. He rests his head against my chest. I can feel my heart booming underneath his cheek.

If I leaned forward I could rest my chin on Henry's head.

He presses closer, making certain we're touching everywhere possible. His bare legs tangle up with mine, the silk of the negligee falling against my jeans, his breasts (my breasts— the ones he finds annoying) settle against my chest, and his cheek rests against me. His long hair whispers over my arms, and Henry's scent—not my minty scent, but the one of starlight—curls around me.

I feel it. Something's happening. I feel as if I'm in a

tunnel and I'm being propelled around and around by a magnet, compelled closer and closer.

My hand burns on the silk separating Henry and me.

"That is one thing we agree on," Henry says, and he sounds out of breath. I realize he's still playing out last night. "We're too dissimilar to be anything but . . ."

He looks up at me.

I focus on his eyes because the room is spinning and he's the only thing that can hold me in place.

"A mistake," I finish. "Fun, but a mistake."

My throat tightens, my mouth goes dry, and I pull Henry even closer—as close as humanly possible.

Please work, I pray. *Please work.*

The room grows hotter. It spins. There's a breathless tightness in my chest. I stare down into Henry's eyes. I can see him there even though it's my face I'm looking at, my eyes I'm looking into. He's still so quintessentially Henry that there isn't any mistaking who I'm looking at.

He grips my hand. Drops his head back to my chest. Takes a deep, shuddering breath that I feel to my toes.

And then . . .

Then . . .

Then . . .

Nothing.

Henry steps back. I drop my hand from the curve of his spine. He pulls his hand free from mine.

I look around the small, square, tidy office and then down at my long legs, my muscular arms, my—Henry's —hands.

Then I look at Henry, buttercup negligee and all.

We failed.

18

<hr />

IF AT FIRST YOU DON'T SUCCEED, HAVE A CUP OF TEA AND try again. At least, that's Henry's philosophy. For which I am very, very thankful.

In fact, I'm feeling warm and fuzzy toward Henry right now. Somehow he knew exactly how hangry I was, because after our attempt to switch back failed, he sent us both a ream of data from last night to comb through later, and then we drove back to the city.

We're back at Henry's apartment, sitting at the small round wooden table in his modern kitchen. The morning sun shines through the kitchen window, lighting the black marble countertops and pale birch cabinets. Shining copper pots hang from a pot rack and sparkle in the sunlight. The countertops glisten, there isn't a crumb to be seen, and all the dishes are stacked beautifully—I can see them through the smudge-free glass doors of the cabinets.

Henry's refrigerator is tidily organized and full of fresh vegetables, fruits, meats, and cheeses. He has a fresh loaf of bread in a bread box. And—I was right—his spice cupboard is organized alphabetically.

It is the cleanest, most well-organized kitchen I have ever been in, and it smells amazing.

In fifteen minutes flat Henry whips up an entire full English breakfast and a pot of tea. The only time he needs help is when he's hopping up and down trying unsuccessfully to reach a mug on the top shelf of his cupboard. When I grab it for him, he gives me a look that says, "See what I'm talking about, shorty?"

While he throws beans and eggs and sausages into pans and tomatoes into the oven, I slice the bread, set the table, and throw out ideas for what possibly could be going on.

The conversation goes like this . . .

Me: We may have entered a mirror dimension and switched bodies—

Henry: I don't think so.

Me: Maybe the collision resulted in a new particle that causes soul transmutation—

Henry: No new particles were on the readings.

Me: A mini black hole—

Henry: Not a chance. It wasn't in the data.

Me: There was an accident last night, a major incident, and now we're all in a shared reality, except in actual fact we're already dead—

Henry: Do you want tomatoes?

Me: Two, please.

That is basically the extent of the conversation. Me tossing out ideas and Henry rebuffing them.

I scrape my fork over my plate, gathering up the last of the baked beans, broiled tomato, and . . . I stare at the Cumberland sausage I pushed to the edge of the plate. It's as big as a ballpark frank, golden-brown, and flecked with pepper and herbs. It has a crisp, spicy, peppery aroma, and my mouth starts to water every time I smell it or glance at it.

"You're going to want to eat that," Henry says, nodding at the offending meat.

He has a bowl of porridge drizzled with honey and sprinkled with currants that he's nearly finished eating.

"I'm vegetarian," I say firmly, imagining the spicy, herby flavor and the crisp skin of the sausage. My stomach growls because apparently baked beans, tomatoes, eggs, and bread weren't enough to fill me up.

"But I'm not," he says, "and my body isn't either."

He rakes his gaze over me, and my eyes flick to the sausage again. He scoffs.

"Serena. In less than twelve hours you've managed to turn me from a normal, clean-cut human into an unkempt, grizzled, black-eyed—" He waves his hands, clearly at a loss for words, then he gives up and says, "Eat the sausage. I don't want to be anemic when I get my body back. I want my body to be in as good of condition as when I left it." He ponders this for a moment. "It's like a rental contract. Normal wear-and-tear is acceptable, but nothing more. A black eye, not acceptable. Anemia from not eating meat, not acceptable."

I take the last bite of the baked beans, enjoying their sweet tomato-sauce flavor, and ignore the delicious-smelling sausage. "Beans have iron."

"Eat the sausage. It's my body."

And clearly his body wants the sausage. But—

"It's my moral conscience."

We stare at each other, locked in a battle of wills. The

scent of peppery sausage and broiled tomato rises between us.

"Then I'll eat it," he says, taking his fork and aiming it toward my plate.

"Hey!" I pull my plate away from him. "That's my body. Keep it free of meat!"

Henry lifts his eyebrow, gives me a meaningful stare, and then sets the fork down.

Fine. He has a point.

"All right, I'll eat meat, but I want it noted that it doesn't count and I'm still vegetarian, because you"—I point at his bowl of oatmeal—"won't be eating meat while you're me."

He nods. "That's fair."

"Good." I pick up my knife and fork and poke at the sausage. I cut into it and a puff of steam drifts out, sending the peppery scent my way. Gosh, that smells amazing. I tentatively put a forkful in my mouth and chew. My eyes drift halfway shut at the delicious flavor.

Henry must really, really like Cumberland sausages.

My lips curve into a smile, and I suddenly feel as if I'm sitting at a crowded breakfast table. There's chaos and laughter and elbows hitting elbows and a dog waiting for a dropped bite—

I open my eyes and snap out of the feeling, back to the bright sun of Henry's kitchen.

"You have a good point," I say, swallowing a sip of tea. "We need rules. A rental contract. I want my body back in perfect condition, and I expect you do too."

He nods. "Agreed."

I scan his messy hair, the wrinkles on my silk negligee, my blue-bagged eyes, and I know I look worse. So.

"First, grooming. You have to dress like I do. You have to shower, wash your hair, condition, shave, wear makeup. Do my nightly facial care routine. Basically, maintain my normal appearance." Then I add—because Henry wearing face masks and putting on makeup is a stretch—"To the best of your ability."

He lifts a hand to the rat's nest on top of his head and then nods. "Fine. Same. You have to wear the clothing I would wear. You have to shower, shave every day. You must eat a protein-rich diet and exercise five days a week. That's a three-mile run minimum, and you lift weights for an hour."

I frown at him. "I don't really like weightlifting . . ."

He picks up his fork and threateningly reaches for the sausage.

"Fine," I say. I yank the plate back then jab a piece of sausage and shove it in my mouth.

It's devilishly good.

"What else?" I ask after I've swallowed.

"We maintain good behavior. We don't act out of character. We respect each other's lives, careers, and relationships and don't do anything to sabotage them."

"Obviously," I say.

Henry stares at my black eye.

"It was an accident."

I finish the sausage then stare forlornly at my empty plate, disappointment curling in my stomach that there isn't another.

Henry stands, grabs my plate, walks to the stove, drops another sausage onto it, and then sets it back down in front of me. He slides his chair out and sits, giving me a little half-smile that is one hundred percent him.

"You know yourself well," I say. "Your appetite is bottomless."

He flashes a smile my way and I give him a stunned look. Gosh, I'm cute when I smile.

No wonder guys like me so much.

Speaking of.

I wrinkle my brow and stare at Henry. He's cute now. He's me. And goodness knows I've been incredibly, incurably horny lately. I practically have carpal tunnel from how much I've been typing on my personal return key all night. And if *I'm* feeling what Henry feels, then Henry is feeling what *I* usually feel.

Which means . . . he'll want to . . .

"No sex," I blurt out.

Henry coughs and clears his throat. "Excuse me?"

"No sex with strangers. No sex with friends. No sex, period. No masturbation either. You aren't allowed to fondle, fiddle, or explore. No touching my erogenous zones except when strictly necessary."

He drops his spoon in his bowl and wipes his hand on his napkin. Then he gives me a *look*.

I scoff. *Yeah, right.*

"Don't tell me that when you woke up, you didn't touch my breasts and my vagina and—"

"Did you?" he interrupts.

I purse my lips tight.

His eyes light with outrage. "You did, didn't you? You took me for a bloody test drive and now you're concerned I did the same!"

"I did not!"

"Really? Then why are you blushing? I know how I wake up."

Ready. He wakes up ready to go.

"Well, what am I supposed to do? I have to touch it to pee."

"Do?" He crosses his arms over my breasts. "You don't take test drives."

"I didn't," I say. "I barely touched it."

He stares at me for a moment, then I guess he decides to believe me because he says, "I barely touched you either. I was confused. It won't happen again. I'll respect your body."

"And I'll respect yours," I say.

He shifts in his chair, looking around the kitchen at the mess of pots and the sun sprinkling across the counter. His cheeks are red, but when he looks back at me his eyes are calm again.

"All right. Good. No sex. No masturbation. No fiddling, fondling, or exploring."

"Right," I say, my voice deep and firm.

"That's settled." Then Henry waves his hand at my plate. "You should eat."

Gosh, he's concerned about his diet. I sigh in pretend annoyance and then happily dig in. As I'm enjoying the spicy flavor and considering another piece of bread, I say, "I think we need to stick together."

"I agree." Henry nods.

And as much as it makes me nervous to think of spending every waking and sleeping second with Henry, I continue.

"I mean it. I think from now on we need to stay with each other every minute of every day. I don't want anything to happen to my body, and I don't want to get separated either. We don't know when the opportunity will arise to switch back, so we need to stay together. Full stop."

"Right." He crosses his legs and looks over the kitchen. "We can stay here."

I shake my head. Purrk would never want to live somewhere so neat. "No, we'll stay at my place. Purrk wouldn't understand the change."

Henry turns back to me when I say this. "Is Purrk your boyfriend?"

His voice is tight and there's a flash of something in his eyes. I remember when he saw my notebook with my doodle "get Purrk food" and "buy condoms."

"He's my cat."

I stand and gather my plate and Henry's bowl. I've finished, it was delicious, and now I'm going to do the dishes. In fact, I feel almost compelled to tidy up and do the dishes. No wonder Henry's place is so neat.

"Your cat? You mean that fuzzy demon that was suffocating me when I woke up?"

I grin at him and drop the dishes in the sink. "He likes to sleep on my head."

Henry shudders. "He was the most terrifying part of waking up. It wasn't that I was you, it was that I had a massive furry monster yowling and clawing at my face."

Huh. "He probably realized you weren't me."

"Oh. That isn't his usual charming personality?"

I narrow my eyes, remembering the fragment of memory involving a childhood kitchen and a dog. "Are you a dog person?"

"Guilty."

"Figures." I flip on the water and start a whirlwind scrub-down of the kitchen and the dishes.

While I'm cleaning, Henry leans against the counter, looks at me out of the corner of his eye, then starts to tap his finger nervously against the marble.

It's funny. Whenever he's nervous he taps his foot or his fingers. Henry never did that as himself, so I'm guessing it's something I do. It must be an unconscious tic, because I don't remember doing it all that much.

"Do I tap my fingers a lot?" I ask, scrubbing out his porridge bowl.

"Sometimes. When you're thinking or irritated or nervous—" Henry cuts himself off, looks at his tapping finger, and stops.

"I didn't know that," I say, wondering what else Henry has noticed about me over the past year and a half.

He looks away from me, apparently lost in thought.

The sound of the water running over the dishes is soothing, and steam rises around us. I scrub at my plate and let the soap suds swish over my hands. There's a soothing pattern to washing dishes that I never noticed before. The water gurgles, the pans clank, the steam is warm, and the lingering smell of breakfast is homey and comforting. It's even nice having Henry stand next to me, quiet and preoccupied with his own thoughts.

If I weren't stuck in his body, losing my own tastes and likes and identity, I'd almost think this was nice.

"I have a problem," Henry says, turning to me, his expression cautious.

I stop washing and pull my hands from the dishwater. Suds drip from my hands back into the sink.

"What?" I ask. The look on his face has my stomach clenching. "A bigger problem than switching bodies?"

He gives a small nod then taps his finger on the countertop. "See . . . I'm taking holiday time because . . ." he pauses, looking at me.

"Why?"

The *look* on his face.

Oh no.

"Are you dying? Are you scheduled for surgery? Wait. Are you getting married?"

Maybe he's dating someone. Maybe he has a fiancée. How would I know? I wouldn't. Am I about to marry someone I've never met?

"My brother is."

"What?"

I'm confused.

He nods. "My brother is. He's getting married this weekend."

Relief washes through me. That's an unforeseen complication, but it's fixable.

"All right. Maybe you could miss it? Tell him you're sick and send an ugly crystal vase as an apology present?"

Henry shakes his head slowly, his chin tilted stubbornly, gaze firm. "No. I won't miss it."

I tilt my head. "Why not?"

Then he says exactly what I was afraid of. "Because I'm the best man."

19

Ah, England.

Land of double-decker buses, pea-soupers, fish and chips, the stiff upper-lip, and all that Victorian prudishness that paved the way for the modern sexual revolution.

Outside the car window the jewel-green countryside rolls past. The deeper Henry drives into the country—through yellow sun-dappled woods, past dry stone wall-lined farms with fluffy sheep grazing like drifting clouds in a green sky, and down the tiny hedgerow lanes so twisty and narrow the hedges close like the pages of a book around you—the more it feels as if we've been transported into a fairy tale. My window is rolled down and the scent of grass and crisp green apples tinges the cool breeze rustling over me. I lift my face to the late-afternoon sun and listen to the distant bleating of sheep, the rumbling of a tractor far beyond the hedges, and the piping notes of a songbird.

A few miles back we drove through a tiny storybook

village. There was an intersection with a cluster of thatched-roof stone houses. Some of the houses were built from local beige-and-gold stone, some were wattle-and-daub and washed white, some were blanketed in ivy and wisteria vining and flowering, yet they all looked as if they were wearing nicely rounded, thick straw hats instead of roofs. They were like nodding garden gnomes standing cheerfully along the roadside.

Each house had a postage stamp-size garden with pink, yellow, and white flowers spilling exuberantly over short dry stone walls. The road through the village was only wide enough for one-way traffic, so when another car or farm truck came along, Henry stopped in a pull-off and lifted a hand as they passed.

It was probably the cutest village I've ever seen. We stopped for tea and coffee to-go from the little pub/inn near the edge of the village. I sip my tea now, a builder's tea, and smile at the tannic strength of the tea leaves and the rich cream of the milk.

"Tea is better in England," I say.

Henry makes a noncommittal noise and takes a sip of his coffee—black. "Coffee is not."

He's salty because firstly, he now craves coffee and not tea, and second, he found out I'm lactose intolerant and milk and clotted cream are off the menu. Apparently, Henry loves milk, and when he eats a scone, he wants it with jam *and* clotted cream. I told him he could eat clotted cream, he just wouldn't enjoy the consequences.

He passed on the dairy.

We've been driving for more than two hours since landing at Terminal Five. After Henry dropped the bomb that I'd have to be best man at his brother's wedding, he mentioned he had a ticket to London Heathrow for early afternoon.

I hurriedly showered while Henry packed a suitcase, then I shaved his caveman stubble, only nicking myself three times. Henry handed me a pair of glasses and suddenly I could see again (at least out of one eye). Then we hurried to my apartment, where we repeated the process. Henry showered, I packed, and then we dropped Purrk off at Jillian's. I reassured her I was fine, Henry was fine, and we were going to figure everything out, we just needed to run to England for the weekend, and thank you very much for watching Purrk.

Now we're curving along the tiny byways of England and everything feels cozy and homely and familiar, and I can feel my muscles relaxing and something in my chest easing. I think Henry must really love his home. The further we drive into the country, the happier I feel.

We passed Stonehenge and Avebury, where I suggested, only half-jokingly, that we might try circling our arms around a standing stone at Avebury and wishing ourselves back into our own bodies. Henry kept driving.

While I'm becoming more relaxed the further we drive, the tenser Henry appears. He's tapping his fingers on the steering wheel, furrowing his brow, and biting his lip. He keeps shooting nervous looks in my direction.

"What?" I ask, trying to stretch my legs out. Small sedans were not built for men over six feet.

"This isn't going to work," he says, shaking his head.

I frown at him. "Of course it is," I say with confidence.

I look like Henry. I can act like Henry. No one will know the difference. Right now I'm dressed in worn-in jeans, a soft gray Henley, and leather boots. It's Henry-casual—a look I've never seen, but which he assures me is how he dresses when he's not at work. Plus, my hair is styled just like Henry styles it, I did an okay job shaving, and I remember everything he told me about his family. It'll be fine (probably).

"You have an American accent," he says, drumming his fingers nervously on the steering wheel.

I wave that away. "Please. I can do British—that's easy."

Henry takes his eyes off the road for a moment—we're passing through another adorable village—and lifts an eyebrow.

"It'll be easy," I repeat.

"All right, do it. Show me."

Okay.

Well.

Now that I'm on the spot . . . hmm. I shift in my seat then clear my throat.

"How about . . . I'll just pretend I'm meeting your family?"

Henry waves his hand for me to proceed.

I paste on his quirky smile, put my shoulders back, and say in my deep Henry voice, "Hiya, Mum! Dad! I'm well chuffed about this wedding." I grin at him then deliver the British kicker. "Fancy a cuppa? I'm knackered."

Henry gives me a horrified "what is happening?" look, so I continue, trying a bit harder.

"Oh, hullo, lads. John, Niall! Me bruvers. P'raps a chinwag at the pub? I love fish and chips and tea, right-ho!"

I think maybe Henry's choking, because his chest is

shaking and he's making a sort of coughing, wheezing noise that sounds like the rattle of a dying car engine.

I pat his shoulder and ask, "Awright, mate?"

He wheezes again and then turns to me, his face red, eyes wide, and shakes his head, apparently unable to speak.

"Okay?" I ask.

He doesn't respond.

Slowly he pulls the car over into the shaded grass alongside a dry stone wall and a sloping field of grazing sheep. In the distance there's an old stone farmhouse sitting at the top of the hill with smoke piping from its chimney.

Henry takes a breath, puts the car in park, and then finally turns to look at me.

"Serena?"

I nod, smile. "I did good, right?"

"You sounded like a two-penny villain in a Dickens novel!"

I scoff. "I did not! My accent is perfect."

He shakes his head, the hair falling free of the braid I quickly tied for him this morning. "Is that what you think I sound like?"

I think about it for a moment. Hmm. I've never actually heard Henry use any of those phrases. He's very proper.

"Maybe my accent could use some work," I admit.

He agrees. "Come on." He opens his car door and walks to my side, opening mine for me. "We're going to practice."

I stand, stretching my legs and arms. The afternoon sun falls onto my shoulders, and the smell of mud and grass and the sound of sheep bleating gives me a happy little boost.

"Okay. Ready." I roll my shoulders and clear my throat, giving Henry an expectant look.

Henry studies me for a moment, then he puts his hands on his hips and blows back a bit of hair drifting in the wind across his mouth. He's wearing one of my favorite dresses. A short chiffon floral dress that's flirty and cute. He balked at first, saying he wanted to wear nice trousers, but I don't own nice trousers. I own skirts and dresses and jeans and jean shorts and *Star Trek* cosplay, and that's it. Plus, if Henry's family meets his "girlfriend" Serena, then "Serena" is going to look cute and wear dresses to the wedding festivities.

"First," Henry says, "you need to stand like me."

"I am."

Henry points at my hands fisted in my pockets and my casual, slightly slouched stance.

"Like this." He puts back his shoulders, stands straight and tilts his chin slightly.

I mimic him, and he nods in approval.

"Now walk like this." He moves with a firm, no-nonsense sort of stride, his arms stiff by his sides, gaze forward.

He leans against the dry stone wall and watches as I parade in front of him.

"Stop moving so loosely. You're too"—he pauses, waving his hands at me—"loose."

"So you want me to ... unloosen up?" I ask.

He considers this then flashes a grin my way. "I suppose so."

I think about how to move for a moment, then I try again.

"That's it," Henry says in approval. "Perfect."

I smile at him and then lean back against the dry stone wall. A small hatchback drives by—the only traffic we've seen since we stopped. Nearby, a honeybee buzzes at a bit of purple clover. The droning is soothing and sweet.

Henry hops up onto the dry stone wall next to me and then swings his feet. He's wearing black flats. I didn't want to torture him with heels just yet. The breeze rustles the dress and I smile. I knew it was a good choice. It looks perfect in the English countryside.

"We'll start easy," he says, glancing at me out of the corner of his eye.

I lift myself onto the wall. The stone is warm from the sun and rough like dried sand. I scoot closer to Henry so our thighs are pressed against each other. A quiet, gentle, sun-warmed energy flows between us.

"Try this," he says, glancing down at where we're touching. "May I please have a cup of water?"

"May I please have a cup of water?" I repeat.

"Water," he enunciates.

"Water."

"Wart-uh," he says. "Not wat-errrr."

"Wart-uh," I say.

He nods. "Hahhhhve," he says, drawing out the "ahhh," "not have." He says the final "have" with a nasally short A.

I repeat, "Hahhhve. May I please have a cup of water?"

"Perfect." He grins at me.

The wind blows long strands of his hair across his face, and I reach out and brush them back. He blinks.

"Sorry," I say, drawing back. I feel my cheeks heat to a

bright red flush. "I always get annoyed when my hair comes undone. It's habit, I'm sorry."

"It's fine," Henry says. He reaches back, combs his hands through the braid, and then hastily ties his hair back at the base of his neck.

"Here—try something else." He looks at the hedge across the way, at a soft-gray sparrow hopping between the thick green leaves, and then says, "Hello, Mother, Father. This is my girlfriend, Serena Otaki. She's a colleague in Geneva. She's from California, she likes me very well, and I'm especially fond of her." He looks back at me then, a small smile curving his lips, and my chest clenches a bit. His eyes crinkle and he nods. "Go on. Try it."

"Do you think your family will like me?" I ask.

Henry leans close, his nose nearly touching mine. "Serena, you are me, and they love me, so of course they'll like you."

I shake my head. "No, I mean, do you think they'll like . . . you as me?"

He frowns. "They'd bloody well better or I'll know they've only pretended to like me all these years. Imagine, my own family disliking me when I'm you. Ridiculous." His eyes sparkle with the humor of it.

I smile back. Then I repeat the phrase he gave me. "Hello, Mother, Father. This is my wonderful girlfriend, Serena Otaki. She is a brilliant colleague in Geneva. She is much smarter than me and constantly corrects my short-sightedness. I don't know what I would do without her. She likes me very well, and I am in perpetual awe of her."

Henry snorts and nudges me with his knee. "Cheeky." Then he sobers. "That was better. If you avoid slang and stereotypes and don't talk too much, I think it'll be okay."

"All right," I nod and then tilt my face up to capture the warmth of the sun slowly sliding down the sky. The bee buzzes past, wandering to another patch of sweet-scented clover at the base of the dry stone wall.

"I wonder, will you speak American?" I give Henry a sidelong glance.

He nods.

"And?" I ask, wanting to hear.

He smiles and his eyes light up. He leans closer, an eager, puppylike expression on his face. "Like, it isn't hard. Being from California is totally awesome. I love avocado on, like, everything. I even put avocado in my coffee. Because coffee is awesome. And so is avocado. I do a juice cleanse, like, every month, and I do yoga with my cat. He's a certified animal yoga instructor. Like, so cool, right?"

I stare at Henry in mute horror. I'm appalled. I'm horrified.

"Like? Awesome? So cool? Who are you, a made-for-TV Valley Girl from the nineties?"

Then I notice the spark of laughter in his eyes and the twisting of his lips in a barely repressed smile.

"Oh, I see." I nudge him with my elbow and he turns his head, hiding a laugh.

His shoulders shake with suppressed laughter and I grin, smiling up at the bright blue sky, and the fat white clouds lazily drifting overhead.

"Turnabouts fair play, hmm?" I ask.

Henry looks back at me, a grin on his face. "Did I do good? Am I American enough?" he asks in a perfectly neutral west coast accent.

I nod. "You did awright, mate," I say in my terrible Dickens villain voice. Then I perk up. "Hey, if I'm a Dickens villain, can I be Wackford Squeers? No, Uriah Heep. Definitely Uriah Heep."

"Funny," Henry says. His expression thoughtful, he taps his bottom lip, thinking. "If you could choose anyone, I thought you would've gone for Master Charley Bates."

Charley Bates, from Oliver Twist?

"Master Bates?" I ask.

He nods solemnly. "Mm-hmm. That's right."

"Master Bates."

He nods again, radiating pure innocence.

Then I shove at him. "You wretch! You looked in my nightstand, didn't you?"

He looks up at the sky, practically whistling and twiddling his thumbs in mock innocence. Unbelievable. He did! Now he knows (since he's living it) that I'm incurably horny and I have a few[1] items to help me remedy that situation.

"Master Bates, my foot," I grumble. I give Henry a sidelong glance. He grins at me. I snort.

Then Henry gives a mirth-filled, delighted laugh and I smile at him, enjoying the sound. It's not my laugh, it's Henry's—it's full and throaty and it invites you to join him. I remember it from the one night we were friends. He laughed like this that night too.

My chest pinches as I smile back at him. I've missed this side of him. I didn't know how much until this moment. I only had his laughter for one night, and then it was gone. I was so scared that if he was kind to me, if he laughed with me, I'd fall in love with him.

Now here he is, laughing in spite of the fix we're in,

and my heart is drumming at the sound. This time, though, I can't hide, I can't run, and I can't push him away.

I can only move forward and hope we switch back soon before I literally and figuratively lose myself in him.

Finally, Henry's mirth fades to a small smile. His eyes crinkle happily as reaches across and puts his hand over mine. It's a warm, comforting weight holding me in place.

"I didn't say thank you," he says quietly, "for doing this. I love my brother. I love my family. I don't want to hurt them or disappoint them. That you agreed to do this . . ." He shrugs, looking down at his hand on mine. "I . . ." He looks back up at me, searching my expression. "Just . . . thank you."

A lump lodges in my throat the size of a plum pit.

"I think it'll work out," he says, squeezing my hand.

"It'll work out," I agree.

Even though, seeing the trust and gratitude in Henry's eyes, I'm not so sure it will.

20

By the time we wind up the little wooded drive to Henry's childhood home the sky is the color of a ripe plum—deep purple with streaks of shell-pink, dappled with a sprinkling of fairy-light stars. The car headlights cut across the early evening gloaming, illuminating apple trees heavy with fruit, a riotous garden that in the twilight looks like a child finger-painted hundreds of flowers across a green field, and finally, a soft slope that cradles Henry's home like a hand holding a warmly glowing candle.

I step out of the car and breathe in tart apple, wet stone, moss, and fallen leaves. The cool evening air weaves a soft spell over me as I look up and feel a twinge in my chest that sighs "home."

Henry steps beside me, the gravel crunching under his shoes, and glances up, up, up.

To which I say, "You didn't tell me home was a castle."

"It's not a castle." There's a hidden smile on his face, buried under the evening's shadows.

I'm not fooled.

Henry told me everything about his family while we were packing, on the flight over, and during the car ride here. He quizzed me on birth order, names, hobbies, current jobs, likes, dislikes, childhood stories—I know, for instance, that his sister Lizzy is allergic to strawberries, and his other sister Kate was mad for corgis as a kid and now runs a corgi rescue—but he never mentioned his "old, tottering family home" is a six-story-tall, rectangular, blue-gray stone-built, medieval-looking—

"Castle," I say, pointing. "That's a castle."

His family home glows in the dark, the old wavy glass windows bright and welcoming like a string of Christmas lights, beckoning us inside. The walls are thick, the corners of the castle slightly rounded. It's not especially large—maybe the width of a townhouse—but either because of its age or how it's settled happily above the little woods and riotous garden, it feels larger. All glowy and warm.

"Actually," Henry says, pointing past the lights of his home to a shadowy pile of rubble outlined against the trees, "that's the castle." He points back to his home. "That's just the latrines. So you could say I grew up in the latrines."

I look at him swiftly. "The castle is a ruin and that big, beautiful building is the ancient toilets? You grew up in a fancy outhouse?"

He gives me an impish grin. "It reminds us not to take ourselves too seriously."

And here I always thought Henry *only* took himself seriously. He's always so uptight, but how could someone uptight joke about growing up in a latrine? He couldn't.

I study him in the deep plum light. "I thought you said your dad was a retired rally navigator and now your parents run a catering business—weddings and anniversaries and such. But this . . ." I gesture to the glowing tower and castle ruins. "This isn't . . ." I narrow my eyes. "Are you a secret Viscount or something?"

He snorts. "No. And my dad *is* a retired rally navigator, and my mum does run a catering business. Us Joules have always lived here. Charles the First granted this pile to my ancestor, Lady Elizabeth, for services rendered to the crown. The castle was destroyed during the Civil War. Three hundred Cavaliers were stationed here. The latrines came in handy—six stories of toilets." He shrugs. "But no, I'm not anything but a physicist. And my family is—" He glances up then at the large wooden front door bursting open and a pile of at least a dozen people rushing out into the grass. He grins at the noise. "You'll see."

My chest constricts for a moment. I almost can't take in the wealth of unbridled joy washing over me. I've never seen such a greeting, such a rush of noise, and laughter and shouts—*Hullo! What took so long? Driving like a granny? Oi Henry, Lizzy thought you wouldn't make the wedding! Charles, did you turn the kettle on? Henry, tell Niall I won't share a room with him—tell him you will! Uncle Henry, did you bring us sweets? Henry, did you remember your cufflinks? Tell me you did—Oh, never mind. Is that a black eye? What a mouser! Uncle Henry, sit by me for dinner!* —and the barking of at least three nipping corgis, and a swirl of hugs and kisses, and the bright rush of color, and a dozen voices, and the familiar smell of Henry's mom (I think that's his mom)—roses and bergamot—and the hard slap of Henry's dad (I think it's his dad) as he roughly embraces me and grips my arms in happy approval.

All the chaos and joy feels right. It feels familiar. Slowly I fold my arms around Henry's sisters as they come in at the same time for a tight hug.

Then, finally, the swirling rush and the riot of colors and confusion of voices slowly cuts off and rumbles to a stunned silence filled only by a single corgi's bark and the rattling of wind through the apple trees as everyone notices Henry. Or Serena.

"Oh, hello?" Eugenia, Henry's mom, says, glancing between me and Henry, who for all the world looks like a fairy sprite in a ruffled floral dress, with long, tangled black hair blowing in the wind and wide brown eyes.

He's looking at his family with a sort of wistful longing, almost like an abandoned child with his nose pressed against the cold window of a candy shop, wishing silently for just a single taste of something sweet.

I didn't think about how this moment would feel to Henry. I was worried about how I would handle meeting his family, and how I would pull off being Henry for the wedding. But I didn't think about how Henry would want to hug his parents and joke with his siblings and tell his brother and his family that he loves them, and now, since he's me, he won't be able to.

For the first time since we switched, Henry looks lost.

I step closer to him, the gravel crunching under my feet, and take his hand.

A little spark of solidarity flows between us.

His grip is tight, his hand cool in mine, and I give his fingers a firm squeeze. He gives a slight squeeze back, and at that I smile.

Henry's sisters exchange a look. Niall's eyes widen.

John and his fiancée Olivia look pleased since, I suppose, all people getting married want other people to fall in love and get married too. Henry's mom has a curious, expectant look on her softly lined face.

"Everyone," I say, trying my best to sound like Henry, "this is Serena Otaki, my girlfriend—"

I don't get anything else out, because as soon as I say "girlfriend" another mad rush begins. Henry is embraced in a chaotic hugging spree—*How do you do? My, you're lovely! How did Henry fool you into dating him? Girlfriend! Oh rats, that means I have to share a room with Niall. Serena, what a lovely name! Do you like tea? We've just put some on*—and there's more barking, and more joking and laughing. And when Henry's mom hugs him he holds her tight, wrapping his arms around her middle and giving such a squeeze that when he lets go his mom backs up with a sort of stunned expression.

She pats his arm, looking surprised and pleased. "There, there," she says. "That's all right."

"It's lovely to meet you all," Henry says, affecting a perfect American accent. He turns to his brother John, who is a bit shorter and a bit softer-featured than Henry, with curly blond hair and a good-natured, goofy smile, and says to him and Olivia, "Congratulations. I hope it isn't too much trouble that I'm here."

His hand twists nervously in mine. But at his words there's a collective "No, no, of course not!" and then Henry's mom takes charge and pulls Henry away from me, linking her arm through his.

"Come along, you must be tired. I'll make you a cup of tea and you can tell me all about yourself as I make these heathens dinner!"

Henry looks back at me as his mom guides him

toward the glowing front door of his childhood home. There's gratitude in his eyes, but also wariness, because he's leaving me on my own with his family.

I lift up my hand, feigning confidence. Fake it till you make it.

When he turns around, John disengages from Olivia and strolls nonchalantly across the gravel drive. Everyone seems to be watching expectantly.

"Henry," he says. There's a peculiar light in his eyes that makes the space between my shoulder blades itch, but since I don't know John, I'm not sure if his expression is out of the ordinary.

"Yes?"

"About the stag do," he says, coming to a stop in front of me.

I nod. I have no idea what he's talking about. Oh gosh, he expects me to say something, and even though Henry told me not to use stereotypical phrases, I'm nervous and everyone is staring, waiting for . . . something . . . so I say, "Right. Jolly good."

"Jolly good?" John shouts, and the good-natured, affable guy I thought he was disappears as he tucks his shoulder, rushes me, and flips me in the air, executing a perfect rugby-type take-down.

I land on my back. The breath jars from my lungs as I smack the cool grass, and a pointy rock digs into my spine.

Ouch.

Ouch, ouch, ouch.

Around me Henry's family is laughing and cheering, and I swear they're all *mad.* Insane.

I cough and hit my chest, trying to drag in a bit of fresh air as the stars swirl above me.

John bends down, a grin on his face, and holds out his hand. "Jolly good? You arse. Are you taking the piss?"

A corgi rushes over and starts licking my face. I push away his doggy-breath tongue and groan. What is it about being in Henry's body that makes people want to tackle me, punch me, and whack me with aluminum bats? Gosh, I'm amazed Henry's survived as long as he has.

I grip John's hand and sit up. Niall's there—he's the youngest, he's tall and stringy, and has orange-blond hair and thick-rimmed glasses. He's only twenty-one and he's in old jeans and a sweatshirt.

"John's sore because the lake was frigid, Henry. You really should've left him an oar."

"That's not the point, though, is it? It certainly isn't the point," Charles, Henry's dad, says in a philosophical drawl, gazing at us all fondly.

"I thought it was brilliant," Lizzy says, adjusting her green woolly hat and matching sweater and winking at me. "Get John pissed, toss him tied up and naked in a rowboat, and set it out to drift in the lake with no oar. Brilliant, Henry. Absolutely brilliant."

Okay, I was right. This family is insane.

"Don't worry, John," Olivia says, pulling him to her side. "It looks like you can pay Henry back soon at his own stag do."

There are oooohs, and ahhhs, and then everyone starts migrating back to the house, teasing each other about dinner and pre-wedding jitters and pre-wedding-night jitters.

I follow behind, the cool, quiet, woodsy night air blanketing around me, as Henry's family tumbles back into their home. A lone corgi sniffs my boot and looks up at me as if it senses something isn't quite right, but it's not sure what.

"Coming, Henry?" Kate calls from the castle.

I lift my hand in a wave.

I look down when I feel someone tugging on my other hand. It's Maeve, Henry's niece, and Lizzy's four-year-old daughter. Her curly gold hair is in pigtails and she's in a rumpled dress.

"Uncle Henry, will you sit next to me at dinner?" She has a lisp from her front missing teeth, and she smiles when I nod. "Okay. Grandma is making peas, and she says I have to eat them if I want pudding. But 'member, I despise peas, so can I slip them to you under the table like I did last time? Shhhhh," she says, putting her finger to her lips, her eyes wide with the secret pea plot.

I hold back a grin at her mega-cuteness and give a solemn nod. "Yes. Let's."

I put my fingers to my mouth and zip my lips, promising to keep her secret.

Then she drags me, all three-and-a-half feet of full-tilt kiddy enthusiasm, through the front door, and I'm welcomed by a home so foreign yet so familiar that I have whiplash from the knowing but the not-knowing.

The inside walls are stone. Some are covered with plaster, some not. The ceiling is high—ten feet at least—with plaster and long wooden beams. There are mismatched chandeliers and brass sconces on the walls, and paintings and tapestries I'm certain are centuries old. Maeve tugs me through the entry hall, over padded oriental rugs that are faded and worn from years of feet skipping over the same path to-and-fro, through a sitting room full of mismatched furniture, and past a bookshelf overflowing with books, knickknacks, bowls, and vases full of rocks and acorns and dried leaves. She skips through another room—a library of sorts, with two desks, books stacked everywhere, a tea tray, and two cups of tea half-finished on the wooden desk in the corner with clawed feet shaped like lions' heads—and then finally I hear the echo of voices and we burst into the warmth of the kitchen.

I stop at the entry when Maeve drops my hand and skips to one of the corgis settled under the table—already awaiting dinner and potential food gifts that fall magically from the sky. I take in a stunned breath of the savory, herby air. It's the kitchen that I saw in the memory that wasn't a memory.

It's brightly lit in here, with ceiling lights and a large kitchen fire, crackling and warm. Its glow bounces off the white plaster walls and warms the old wooden table and farm chairs to a soft sheen. The table is long, like the lords of old had in their mead halls. It has to seat at least sixteen people, which is just enough. The large kitchen is packed and noisy and chaotic. The table is full of food— steaming rolls, buttery potatoes, peas, glistening carrots, bubbling savory pies, and a roast as big as a small car— and all the china shines and sparkles in the flickering firelight and candles.

One of the corgis—Ralph, maybe?—bumps my leg.

"Henry, pour the wine," Kate calls, pointing to a half-dozen bottles on the counter.

At that Henry looks around the kitchen, searching for me. He's at the butcher-block counter, a chipped teacup in his hand, his mom mixing a salad and asking him a question.

He catches my eyes and lifts his eyebrow at me. *Are you all right?*

I nod. Smile. *I'm okay.*

His shoulders relax and he turns back to his mom, apologizing for missing what she said.

Kate strides over. She's the second-youngest, twenty-four, and the only sibling with brown hair. She has a quick stride, a mismatched skirt and frilly top, and a playful glint in her eye that makes me like her immediately. She hands me two bottles, both Cabernet Sauvignon from California, a small vineyard I've been to before.

"It's been voted. I'm the one to warn you," Kate says under her breath, nodding subtly across the kitchen.

I glance in that direction. Almost everyone has congregated around the island's marble counter, where a silver platter of cheese and crackers is set and a few bottles of whisky have been opened.

I take the wine and shake my head. "What?"

"Lorna," Kate whispers. "When she saw Serena, she wasn't happy." Kate winces and then says apologetically, "'Wasn't happy' is a drastic understatement."

Who the heck is Lorna?

I search my memory, scouring through all the names Henry told me. I learned parents, siblings, nieces, nephews, friends, ushers—dogs, for crying out loud!—but no Lorna.

"Ummm..." I shrug. "I'm sorry?"

Kate scoffs, pats my arm, and then gives me a sympathetic look. "Duly warned. Duty done. I like Serena, by the way. She seems nice."

I give her a helpless smile. "Thank you."

Henry will be happy to hear that. His family likes him even when they don't know it's him.

Kate gives me the sort of fond eye roll that only a

sister can give an older brother, and then she leaves me with the wine.

I stand there for a moment taking in the warmth, wishing for a cup of tea, and then I start to pour the wine. I stop when someone clears their throat delicately at my side. I pull the wine bottle back and turn toward the noise.

It's a tall, willowy woman in a pale coral pantsuit. She's beautiful in an understated way, with thick mahogany hair, violet-blue eyes, a prim, upturned nose, and a small, plump, doll-like mouth. She glances at me with—Well, I'm a woman, so I know it when I see it. She glances at me with a proprietary expression. As if I'm hers and I just haven't realized it yet.

"Henry," she says, her violet eyes shimmering with misty tears that look like dewdrops on a petal. Her pink mouth trembles. She reaches out and lays a hand over my arm. "I've missed you. Henry? Aren't you going to say hello?"

She puts her hands to my shoulders then, stands on her tiptoes, and in a wave of floral perfume offers her rose-petal-pink cheek for me to kiss.

I suppose this must be Lorna.

21

———

THE DINNER IS EXACTLY LIKE I KNEW IT WOULD BE. A crackling warm fire, the scent of apple wood tangling with melted butter, sweet peas, marjoram, and savory roast. Candlelight flickers and catches the ruby sparkle of wine in mismatched glasses (inherited, I'm sure, through the centuries). The wood of my chair is butter-soft, sanded down and worn from decades of Joules sitting in it, the stones under my feet are sloped from treading feet, and a corgi sometimes nudges my ankle, its fur soft and nose wet, hoping to remind me of my duty to share the bounty.

Laughter and good-natured joking are tossed and batted around the table as quick as a flash, the sound echoing off the plaster walls and the conversation bouncing between everyone like a professional ping-pong match. I almost can't keep up with the back-and-forth. It's lightning-quick and hilarious.

The main focus is the wedding and how John must have the dumbest luck to have actually convinced Olivia to marry him. Olivia laughs at all the jokes, joining in and teasing John. She came to England from Jamaica when she was twelve, and she's known the Joules since her family moved into a flat in town and her dad joined Charles as a driver in the rally. Everyone sobers a bit when they toast Olivia's parents, Alden and Barbara, departed but still loved.

Olivia doesn't have any family here. She teaches at the primary school, and I think, she's lucky to have found a family that clearly loves her dearly.

Next to me Maeve stealthily drops another spoonful of peas into the napkin on my lap. They hit like little raindrops kerplopping against a windowpane. No one notices except Henry. He's sitting across from us, and every time Maeve's spoon dips below the table his eyes fill with laughter.

"What's so funny?" Lorna asks, leaning close and pressing her shoulder against mine. Her floral perfume drifts over me and her mahogany hair brushes my shoulder.

I turn to her and notice the daggered look she shoots across the table, narrowing her eyes on Henry. She's been skewering Henry with warning glances all dinner, not realizing that when she glares at the (adorable) woman across the table, she's *actually* glaring at Henry.

It's enough to make you feel sorry for her.

"Hmm?" I frown at her. "Oh. Nothing."

Lorna studies my expression as if she can delve inside me and discover all the mysteries of my mind. She's on the hunt, and boy, is it making me uncomfortable.

Unfortunately, it turns out she's a bridesmaid and one of Olivia's closest friends. And . . . I'm getting the feeling she and Henry have some history. Or . . . it's not history and it's a current event. Except wouldn't someone have said something when I introduced "Serena" as my girlfriend? And wouldn't Henry have mentioned Lorna before telling me to introduce him as my girlfriend?

I go back to my roast, sending my knife through the soft, herby meat. I didn't miss the glance Henry sent my way, nodding at the meat, reminding me of our deal. I noticed he only has salad, vegetables, and a roll on his plate. I'll have to thank him later.

I spear a piece of meat, and then instead of peas hitting my napkin, I feel fingers stroking along my thigh. Up. Up.

Is that . . .?

Up.

My fork and knife clatter to my plate.

"You all right, Henry?" Niall asks, stopping his story about John's irrational fear of bananas.

Up.

Lorna smiles over at me, batting her eyelashes, not letting on that her hand is currently stroking over my thigh, trailing higher and higher toward somewhere she is definitely not welcome to touch.

"Oh, fine. Fine," I say, nodding.

I reach down and bat at Lorna's hand. A pile of peas falls from my napkin and thuds lightly to the stone floor, pattering almost noiselessly. The three dogs simultaneously scramble across the stone, their claws clicking and their tongues licking.

Lizzy laughs at the canine scramble, covering the noise of the dogs, and says, "Isn't it John that's supposed to be nervous? I mean, Olivia, you're nice, you're charming, you're beautiful, you deserve someone splendid, which is why I can't for the life of me understand how you ended up with my brother."

Olivia grins at Lizzy. "Right! It was how terrible he was at maths. I felt he needed me."

"And I will forever thank Mr. Crawley for his iron-fisted hold on Calculus, because it gave me you," says John, dropping a kiss on Olivia's lips.

And they're off again. The table conversation veers toward wedding-night jitters, the honeymoon, and why Charles can't drive the limo (because he drives like he's on a rally course and John doesn't want to frighten the guests).

Lorna twinkles at me. "Remember our anniversary dinner at Il Bacco?" she whispers huskily, her breath tickling my ear. "When I . . ."—her hand slips up my thigh—"did this at the table?"

Before she can reach her final destination and lovingly recreate a "night to remember," I shove my chair back and stand. All the remaining peas tumble to the floor. The kitchen falls silent. Maeve stares at me with wide eyes, and the dogs scramble around my feet, slurping up the buttered peas.

All eyes are on me. Henry's mom gives me a concerned look. Lorna folds her hands primly in front of her and gives me a look that reminds me of a coral-colored python that just swallowed a mouse and is happily digesting it.

"I . . . uh . . ." I clear my throat, shoot Henry a meaningful glance, and then say, "Excuse me for a moment."

I hurry from the kitchen. Silence follows, and then someone says something and the conversation flows again. I push my hand through my hair and roll my shoulders, shaking off the come-ons from Henry's (apparent) ex-girlfriend.

Jeez, she's bold.

Those poor, innocent corgis certainly got an eyeful.

I hurry through the library overflowing with books, past the two desks, the growling clawfoot lions, and the empty tea tray, and into the entry, turning into a small room on the left with a wooden door. The room is dark and smells like wool and stone. I flip on the light and find it's chock-full of wool coats, raincoats, trench coats, rubber boots, umbrellas, and a hat rack full of quirky hats, whimsical hats, and functional hats.

It's crowded, only maybe six feet by six feet, and most of the space is taken up by the coats hanging on the wall and a low wooden bench for putting on boots, but it's big enough and private enough for Henry and me to have a quick chat.

Mostly about his ex. And also about that stag do I got body-slammed for. And also about where we're sleeping tonight. Because I'm not sleeping with Niall.

I leave the door partly open and hope Henry will hurry.

Dropping my head and rubbing my temples, I close my eyes and let out a sigh. It's been so busy, such a rush, that it's hard to believe I've been Henry for almost twenty-four hours. I've barely had a moment to look through the data we pulled, and I haven't pondered any theories to *fix* this.

The door creaks and then clicks shut.

"What took you so—?" I cut off. It's not Henry.

Lorna smiles. A seductive, sultry, sloe-eyed smile. Then she unzips her coral suit jacket, shrugs it off, and drops it to the floor. Quick as a snap she's out of her camisole, and it's joined her jacket on the stone floor in a little clothing party for two.

She isn't wearing a bra.

Her breasts—well, they aren't bad. I mean, I've seen a lot of boobs. I'm a female. I took gym class. I was on the swim team. There was boob. Lots of it.

Every boob is different. Boobs are like snowflakes, unique. And Lorna's? They're all right. If I was in the locker room and I saw her boobs in passing I'd be like, huh, okay, whatever. I wouldn't give them a second glance.

Just another bit of boob.

BUT.

I have never seen boobs as a man. I have never seen boobs while in a man's body.

And I clearly have never seen boobs as Henry, who obviously—very, very obviously—*loves* boobs.

Boobs are the *best thing* that has ever been created. Boobs. Mmm, boobs. I have a flash of an image, a memory of Henry's, stroking my hand lovingly along a silken breast, my lips running over the hot, satiny skin, my heart pounding wildly, my body tight as I graze my teeth over a taut, rosy nipple. It tastes sweet, like mint and apples. I blink. My mouth goes dry.

My word. *My word.* Now I know what it means when someone says they're a breast man.

Lorna smiles at me. The coat-room light shines down on her pearl-dust skin and falls over the sloping edges of her breasts. Her pert, apricot-colored nipples pucker in the cold.

I can't look away.

It's like that kid's game, freeze tag. I've been frozen in

place and I can't move until Lorna tags me, setting me free.

Why?

Well, I'm going to remind you of something I have as a man that I didn't have much of as a woman.

Testosterone.

That delightful hormone that spurs arousal.

I paid attention in health class. I took notes. I drew diagrams. Our instructor, Mrs. Wilinski, used a projector with ink drawings from the 1950s and a Ken doll to show us the region of the (nonexistent) male parts.

Here's what I remember about the science of the male reproductive system from my sex-ed class:

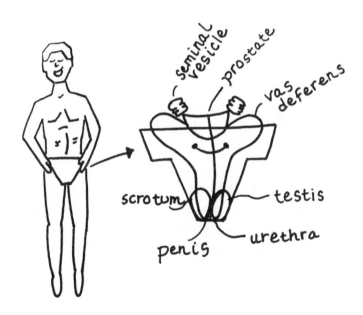

[Here we have a basic, labeled diagram of Ken Doll male anatomy.]

Look, I could get scientific, explain how blood flows to the penis, how it becomes hard, and— I can't, because I'm not quite thinking clearly. I'm a bit lightheaded, actually.

"Henry?" Lorna says, stepping toward me.

My jeans are becoming uncomfortably tight. I almost want to reach down and adjust myself, and that's when I remember who I am, snap out of the boob freeze-beam, and take a quick step back.

"Ack," I say. "No. Get ahold of yourself. What's wrong with you?"

She's a boob bedazzler, a breast beguiler, a titty temptress. It's horrible. I wave my hand in front of my face, blocking my view of her breasts.

Lorna reaches for me and I stumble back, knocking over the hat rack. It's a long, wooden, tree-like hatstand with limbs extending from the trunk and two dozen hats hanging like leaves. I catch the wobbling stand and hold it between us. I use it like a shield, waving the fuzzy and quirky and practical felt hats menacingly.

Lorna tries to step around it, but I shove it in her way.

"Back off, and for goodness' sake, put your shirt on," I say, thrusting the woolly hats at her.

She swats them away. "Henry!"

My word, she's persistent.

"I'm with Serena. Don't you have any self-respect? Who does this? Honestly. Haven't you heard of the sacred law of sisterhood? Don't poach! And respect yourself! Jeez!"

"Henry!" Lorna grabs the hat rack and begins to grapple with me, attempting to wrest the hats from my hands. "Why do you sound like an American? What's wrong with *you*?"

What's wrong with me? I'm being accosted by a horny ex-girlfriend.

Not to mention this isn't my body and I just got freeze-rayed for the first time by a plucky pair of B-cup British breasts.

A big, Kool-Aid-purple felt hat with yellow ostrich feathers tickles her boobs, and another, a brown bowler hat, keeps punching me in the jaw every time she yanks on the hatstand.

"I sound American because I *like* Serena. My girlfriend. I'm with Serena," I say forcefully, even though I'm not quite sure how Henry would actually want me to handle this situation. He did say we shouldn't ruin relationships, but . . .

"But you can't be with Serena! You and I are getting married!" Lorna wails, dropping the hat rack.

And because this is a shocker that I absolutely did not expect, I also drop the hat rack. It clatters noisily to the stone floor, throwing hats everywhere.

I stare stunned at half-naked Lorna, my mouth falling open in shock, and that is exactly how Henry and his mom find us when he yanks open the coat-room door.

22

TEA IS THE MOST USEFUL BEVERAGE EVER INVENTED. I realize this now. I spurned it before. I scoffed. I was an unbeliever. But now I know. There are many, many situations in which tea is the correct (the only) answer.

For example:

1. When your grandma drops by unexpectedly for a chat—tea.
2. When you're having a bad day at work—tea.
3. When it's cold and rainy—tea.
4. When the Nazis are bombing the coastal cities and the situation is desperate and you must keep calm and carry on—tea.
5. When you need a quick pick-me-up—tea.
6. When your mom and girlfriend find you in the coat closet with a giant boner and a flushed, bare-boobed woman—tea.

See? Isn't tea incredible? It isn't just a beverage, it's a mindset.

I think when I'm me again I just might give tea a chance. Or at least I won't begrudge Henry his 10:15 a.m. daily cup in the cafeteria. I didn't understand before. Now I do.

As soon as Henry flung open the door, Lorna let out a shriek and grabbed her camisole (thank goodness). Henry's mom, Eugenia, stared at us for a moment like a pigeon that just smacked into a window and was stunned stupid. Then she shook her head clear, blinked, and said, "I'll put the kettle on for tea. That's just the thing."

Bless her.

She hurried off, her dyed blonde hair frazzled and her long beige cotton dress flapping behind her. Lorna shot me a daggered look and then ran after her, her coral jacket clutched to her chest, calling, "Eugenia, wait! I'll plate the lemon biscuits!"

When they'd gone I whirled on Henry, thrusting my finger at him. "She stripteased! She manhandled me in front of the corgis! She . . ." I ran out of steam at Henry's appalled look, but then I remembered what Lorna said and I hissed, "She said you're getting married!"

"What!" Henry's voice was high, and frankly, he sounded as stunned as I felt. He gave me a dazed, appalled look. "Did you say—?"

"Married."

"No." He gave a firm shake of his head. "No."

So I think it's safe to say the HenLorna/Lorenry/Horeny pairing is off.

Thank goodness.

Then Maeve ran into the coat room and said, "Grandma says the tea is ready!"

So we followed her to the bustling, noisy kitchen.

Which is how I find myself happily sipping a cup of piping-hot tea (loose leaf), with just the right amount of milk (from a dairy in Devon), and a single lump of sugar. The kitchen fire crackles, casting an orange-embered glow over the blue-gray stone floors and white plaster walls, and a wonderful woodsmoke smell wraps around me. I lean toward the curling heat of the fire, close my eyes, and take a sip, letting the creamy tea settle into me.

Better.

Dinner is done and the kitchen is a flurry of activity, with everyone clearing and cleaning and washing and drying. The dogs are happily catching scraps accidentally —or, in the case of Lizzy's kids, Maeve, Martin, and Michael, purposely dropped. Eugenia orchestrates the chaotic clean-up, directing the dance of scrubbing and washing so efficiently I'm sure this scene has played out hundreds of times before.

Instead of joining the after-dinner work, Henry and I were shooed to the little round breakfast table in the nook near the fire with the order to drink our tea and rest after our long day of travel. Lorna left after a quick word with Eugenia, a hug for Olivia, a meaningful glance at me, and a promise to see everyone tomorrow at the wedding.

I'm not going to lie and say I was sorry to see her go.

Henry nudges me with his foot under the table. I open one eye and peer at him, looking over the rim of my purple pansy-patterned teacup. The cup is tiny in my hands—the delicate porcelain looks like a cup for a doll's tea party—and it would be laughable if I weren't enjoying it so much.

"What?" I ask, opening my other eye.

I take off my glasses and wipe them on my shirt. The lens was all fogged up from me shoving my face so far into the deliciously steaming tea. I put them back on and study Henry.

The firelight bounces off his skin, making him glow, and his thick black hair swallows the light of the fire, gleaming as dark as the darkest night. I never understood why my dad called my hair color night-light, but now I do. It's as if the black of it has gobbled up all the light and now it glows from within.

My favorite floral dress has wrinkled and sagged from the day's travels, and the left strap falls down Henry's shoulder. I itch to reach over and slip it back into place, but I don't. Instead I wrap my hands around my teacup. The heat sinks into me, scalding my fingers.

Henry has a ceramic mug of instant coffee in front of him. Black. Apparently, as me, he's craving coffee even if it is poured from a packet and stirred into hot water. I imagine it tastes like bitter plastic shavings. Poor guy.

"You all right?" He leans forward and the strap falls further down his shoulder.

I nod and take another sip of tea.

He sits primly, poker-stiff, which reminds me a bit of the way he sits during meetings when there are maintenance issues, budget issues, or I'm throwing out theories he disagrees with. It makes me smile because I never thought I'd see me, fun-loving Serena Otaki, look so prim and proper.

Across the kitchen his mom sends us a worried look. She's been shooting covert glances our way ever since we walked back in.

"Your mom's worried," I whisper, dropping another lump of sugar into my cup and stirring it in. A little whirlpool forms in the golden-brown liquid and a curl of steam drifts toward me.

"It's because she likes me," Henry says. He sweeps his hair behind his shoulder, still not noticing the loose strap, then absently drums his fingers on the wood of the table. I'm really going to have to curtail that nervous tic when—if—no, when—we switch back.

"Mum said she feels there's something about me," he says, frowning when I scoff. "Well, she did. She said she likes me very much and she hopes all the chaos won't scare me off. She promised me it isn't always so chaotic, although it is,"—he smiles at that—"and that she hopes I'm not overwhelmed. Then she sang my—Henry's—praises, telling about my science projects and how I rescued a wren with a broken wing when I was seven, and how as a boy I was the most quiet and sweet-natured of all her children." His eyes crinkle. "This was before we found you in the coat room."

Eugenia bustles over then, a rag in her hands.

"Henry," she says crisply, a hint of disapproval around the corner of her eyes. I shift in my seat although *I* haven't done anything wrong.

She tsks then peers at my cup to make certain I've finished my tea. "I made your room up. You and Serena can share, unless . . . " She looks between Henry and me and wow, it's awkward. She turns a motherly gaze on Henry. "Unless dear, you'd like to stay in a separate room. Or at an inn. Anything you need. Anything at all."

Oh gosh. She thinks her son is a horny cheat and a mega a-hole and she's trying desperately to be a good hostess. All while her second-eldest son is getting married in the morning.

Henry looks up at his mom and seems to come to the

same realization as me. She thinks her son is a big douche and she feels terrible about it.

So he does something I think is more for his mom than for anyone else. He reaches over and puts his hand in mine, threading our fingers tightly together. Then he gives his mom a brilliant smile and says, "The coffee was delicious, thank you. And of course I want to stay here with Henry. Earlier . . ." He pauses, taps a finger in thought, then says, "It was nothing. It was a misunderstanding. Please don't worry. There isn't anywhere I'd rather be—not in the whole world. I love your family. They are truly wonderful."

The worry wrinkles around his mom's eyes soften and her shoulders loosen as she smiles. She pats Henry's arm. "You're a dear."

Then she turns on me and her eyes narrow. "And you . . ." She purses her lips.

I give her Henry's quirky half-smile. "Thanks for the tea, Mum."

She gives me a surprised look and then lets out a huff. "Go on, you. It's an early morning. Everyone is off to bed."

It's true. They already waved Olivia out the door. John stood at the entry like a lovesick teen about to be parted from his true love for twelve long years instead of just twelve hours. Lizzy and her husband (James, I think? His is the only name I forgot) and all their kids tumbled up the stairs for baths and toothbrushing after the dishes were done. Henry's dad Charles has gone outside for a puff on his pipe and a goodnight stroll with the dogs. Kate and Niall are arguing over who gets to sleep on the bed and who is on the couch in his tower bedroom. Everything is wrapping up.

"I'll get the luggage," Henry says, standing and making for the kitchen doorway.

"Nonsense," Eugenia says, shooting a censorious look my way. "Henry!" She flaps her hand in a "shoo" gesture. "Get the luggage! Go! I'll take Serena upstairs."

I stare at Eugenia a moment, realizing belatedly that she's mortified because my petite, frilly dress-wearing, one-hundred-pound-wet girlfriend offered to lug in two suitcases while I—six feet, muscled, Henry—sat there and nibbled on a lemon biscuit.

Luckily, she didn't see us when Henry held the door open for me at the pub/inn where we got our tea and coffee. Or when Henry opened my car door for me. I admit, I didn't really think it was odd until we started getting strange looks. And I bet if his mom saw it happen, her ears would shoot out steam like a hot kettle and she'd explode.

"Sorry," I say, quickly standing and wiping the lemon biscuit crumbs from my hands.

Henry widens his eyes at me, although I'm not sure what he's trying to tell me. Maybe it's directions to his room, because I have no idea where to go once I've retrieved the suitcases.

"I'll help you," John says from across the kitchen, looking up from his phone.

"You'd better not be texting Olivia," Kate calls, interrupting her argument with Niall on sleeping arrangements. "Not seeing the bride before the wedding includes not texting the bride before the wedding!"

John waves that away, slaps me on the back, and steers me out of the kitchen. I shoot Henry one last look, a bit worried because John was the brother who tackled me less than two hours ago.

But when we make it outside and the cool evening air nips at us, John merely shoves his hands in his pockets and hunches his shoulders. We crunch across the gravel, down the path toward the car. The stars twinkle in the night sky and there's a hint of tobacco smoke hanging in the air. Far across the grass, past the smudge of the castle ruins, I can see the orange spark of a lit tobacco pipe moving steadily toward the woods. A yip and a bark echo over the stones, and John smiles.

"Dad ought to stop smoking." He shakes his head then looks over at me consideringly and says, "But I suppose we all do things we ought not to. Right, Henry?"

I freeze up. John is casting a grave look my way and I have no idea what he's asking.

We come to a stop next to the rental car. The warm lights of the house barely reach us, and shadows fall close. The car is dark, the suitcases two lumps in the backseat. The smell of tobacco smoke has faded, although the dogs still yip happily in the distance and I can see the orange light of Charles's pipe bobbing as he walks around the ruins.

"Sorry," I say, hoping I'm not about to get tackled again.

But no, John looks too solemn for that.

In fact, I think I've stepped into some deep, murky quagmire Henry knows about but I don't. I have no idea how to answer John's question. Of course we all do things we shouldn't—that's what makes us human. But what *exactly* is John referring to? I don't know.

He nods, though, and leans against the car, stretching his legs out and tilting his chin to stare at the dim, flickering stars lighting the sky.

Since it seems like something Henry would do, I lean

against the car too and look out over the stain of dark trees lining the hill, and the night sky casting deep, blanketed silence over us. The cold of the metal sinks into my back and the wind rustles the leaves in the woods. I take a deep breath of the cool, mossy night air.

"Is she the one?" John asks suddenly, breaking the quiet.

I look over at him, raising an eyebrow. Is he asking about Olivia? How would I know if she's the one? He's marrying her, isn't he?

John scoffs and shakes his head at my silence. "You're taking 'stoic and serious' to a whole new level, Henry. What's wrong with you? I'm concerned, that's all."

"About what?" I ask, trying my best to keep a proper British accent. Henry was right. My accent is subpar at best.

John bends down then, picking up a pebble from the gravel drive and rolling it in his hand. Then he throws it toward the woods. Three seconds later, there's the distinctive plink of rock hitting metal.

"Got it," he says, grinning.

I bend down then and search out a pebble, finding one the size of a penny, sharp-edged and cold. I aim in the same direction as John then let it fly. I count to three, then four, but nothing sounds.

John snorts. "You never could hit it. That plane has been teasing you for decades."

Plane?

They have a plane here?

How did I miss that?

Well, I admit, I was distracted by the castle, but you'd think I would've noticed an airplane (rusting?) in the woods.

"Do you remember when we used to pretend we were RAF?"

I nod, but John doesn't need my ascent. It was a rhetorical question, and he's off.

"You always had to be pilot, flying missions. I didn't mind being gunner though, since I have the better aim." He grins over at me. "Although Lizzy hated that you were pilot and always wanted that damn surly dog Crispin to be in the captain's seat."

I laugh, imagining a corgi in a Royal Air Force uniform flying a World War II fighter plane, a Union Jack painted on the side.

John's lips twist into a smile and he chuckles, leaning back again and letting out a relaxed sigh. The wind slips past, tugging at my shirt and leaving a cool chill on my skin. I tuck my hands in my pockets and breathe in the woodsy, mossy scent, marveling at the feeling of home. Even the kindred feeling I have with this man, who looks so much like Henry, leaning against the car next to me.

"I remember when you first went to Geneva," he says, staring out at the ruins, where three dog-shaped shadows hop over mounded stones and his dad's pipe bobs along. "Mum was worried you wouldn't eat well. Dad was worried and pretending not to be. I couldn't be bothered because I was enthralled with Olivia." He notices my wry smile and scoffs. "Sod off. You know how it was."

"Right," I say, because it seems he expects me to say something.

He nods then digs his foot into the pebbles, scraping them back and forth. "But I wasn't so enthralled that I don't remember the phone call. I asked, 'How's Geneva?' and you said with pure conviction, 'I met a girl, John. She's the one. I'm in love. I'm going to marry her—you'll see.' I laughed. I thought you were mad." He sighs, kicks at the gravel again. "Next day, I ask you about her—Serena, that was her name—and you said, 'Don't you ever say her name again. Don't you mention her again. I was a bloody fool. A bloody stupid fool.'" He shrugs. "I never did say her name, just like you asked. But . . ." He looks over at me, his eyes narrowed, the wind turning chill, the night falling dark, and says, "But now I'm going to say, as a man about to be married and endlessly happy with 'the one,' you be careful. I don't want you hurt. I don't think you're meant to be doubly a fool. We all do things we shouldn't, but we shouldn't do them twice. Yeah?"

Holy.

Holy ever-loving crap.

My heart thumps, a hollow drum in my chest.

Henry . . . That night . . .

When I was snug in his arms he said he thought he was falling in love. He said it felt like love at first sight. He wasn't just saying it. He thought he was going to *marry me*. He told his brother I was the one.

And now Henry's brother is warning me away from . . . me.

What can I say? *Don't worry, John. I'm actually Serena, and Serena is your brother. You have absolutely nothing to worry about. We aren't even dating. Henry will never fall for me again, and I'll never want to get married. You can relax. Henry won't get hurt, because this time his emotions aren't involved.*

Well, I can't say that to him, so instead I clap my hand on his shoulder in the man-slap that annoyed Henry so much.

"Thank you," I say, gripping his shoulder, touched by

how much he cares about Henry—enough to watch out for his happiness. "You're a good brother."

John gives me a strange look—the same one Henry gave me when I claimed in a lunch meeting one day that *Star Trek* is the greatest fictional universe ever created—then he shakes his head. "You've gone funny in the head. I told everyone that particle accelerator would addle your brain, and now I've been proven right."

I laugh and John shoves at me, jokingly punching my arm.

"I'm getting married in the morning," he says, and he sounds incredibly, enthusiastically happy about it.

The funny thing is, as Henry in Henry's tea-loving, dishes-doing, romantic-hearted body, the thought of marriage doesn't frighten me at all. In fact, it sounds . . . wonderful. Like sitting by a cozy fire, a dog at your feet, with a cup of hot tea and a lovely book, and when you look up to share a quote the person next to you is the person you love the most in the world—the one you want to see every day for the rest of your life.

That thought isn't scary at all. In fact, it feels like the most natural thing in the world. Wanting that moment, that day-to-day, feels as natural as breathing.

Which is why my chest clenches, my throat tightens, and I have to consciously drag in a breath.

I'm not Henry.

I'm *not* Henry.

I don't do marriage.

I don't do love.

I'm me.

I'm *me*.

"Don't forget the rings tomorrow, or I'll have to kill you," John jokes, oblivious to the war raging inside me.

"Why . . .?" My voice cracks, so I clear my throat and try again. "Why do you want to get married? Aren't you worried you'll lose your independence? Or yourself?"

John peers at me from under his brow. He tilts his head, giving me a curious stare. So I avoid his speculation by unlocking the car, grabbing a suitcase, and dropping it to the ground. I grab the next. Shut the car door.

John looks down at the suitcases. Black for Henry, red for me. Then he says in a slow, musing voice, "I'm not worried about leg shackling or any rubbish like that. I'll be me with Olivia or without her. But I like the me I am when I'm with her. We work. I stop thinking so much about myself and what I want and I think about other people. She stops worrying so much about what others think and just enjoys life. We do that for each other. Besides, you can be independent and be married. I'll keep watching football and eating too many biscuits. She'll keep terrifying me with threats of banana custard and keep teaching year three and volunteering at Lizzy's rescue, and . . . what?" He frowns at me, looking closer at my expression. "What?" he asks again.

"But your tastes will become the same. You'll start to look alike and talk in 'we' and 'us' instead of 'I' or 'me,' and you won't be *you* anymore."

John snorts and punches me on the arm. "Daft. Daft idiot. Where'd you get that rubbish from?" He picks up the red suitcase and walks back up the drive.

I grab Henry's black suitcase and hurry after him.

In the distance the corgis yip. They're making their way back toward the house too. I glance at Henry's dad, still too far off to be anything more than a dark shadow in the night.

"Aren't Mum and Dad like that?" I ask.

John laughs. "Dad still smokes his pipe and drives ninety miles-per-hour down country lanes and Mum still moon-bathes naked on summer solstice, God help us all. Two more independent-minded people I've never found. What's happened? You don't sound like yourself."

I clear my throat. We've made it back to the front door. "Just . . . stressed. Work." I shrug.

John nods. "Right. Leaving ATLAS. The big job change. I forgot."

With that he hauls the suitcase inside and leaves me open-mouthed, staring after him.

23

HENRY'S ROOM IS ON THE THIRD FLOOR OF THE latrine/tower/castle. The stairs are at the back of the house and climb in a spiral up, up, up, six stories total. The steps creak and groan, their old wood dark and polished, as John and I lug the suitcases upstairs. The walls are smooth gray stone, brass sconces light the spiraled steps, and small slit windows glow with a dash of moonlight.

The further we climb, the older the house feels. The thick stone walls muffle sounds, and I can imagine centuries of Joules climbing these stairs, brushing their hands along the cool stone as they climb. There's the smell of wood polish and damp stone and a hint of woodsmoke and tea. It's a familiar smell even though I've never known it until today, and it makes me feel as if I've just finished hugging someone I love.

John leads me down a short hallway with faded oriental rugs laid over wide, uneven wooden floorboards. At the end of the hall light spills across the floor from the open door of a bedroom. I can hear Henry's mom.

"—always was tidy. Even as a boy he'd trail after us, picking up our messes. The boys would knock down blocks and then Henry would stack them. Charles, bless him, would leave his racing journals lying about and three-year-old Henry would sort them by issue date. I never had to get on him about tidying his room. Not that he minds a mess. He once told me he likes a mess because it's homely and—"

"Sounds like Mum's singing your praises," John says, eyeing me over his shoulder. He drops the suitcase in front of the bedroom and the plastic wheels clatter on the wood floor.

Henry's mom cuts off at the noise. "Oh, here they are!"

I step up to the door of the bedroom and try to pretend like I've seen it before. I set the suitcase down at the entry and send Henry a reassuring smile. He's standing in the middle of the large room looking a bit overwhelmed.

Honestly, I feel the same. Henry's childhood room is the stuff of dreams. It's a large, expansive space. The ceilings are high, with plaster and dark wooden beams, and the wall opposite the door has a large, built-in stone window seat with a tall leaded glass window. The panes are separated by thin strips of silver metal, and the glass has that centuries-old wavy appearance that makes the world outside look like a soft dream painted in pastels. In the center of the window are panes of colored glass, red and green and yellow-gold, in the shape of a knight's shield. The entire window is framed by rich burgundy velvet curtains. I have the sudden urge to lounge on that window seat for hours, curled up with a book, a cup of tea, and a corgi.

In fact, I think Henry has done just that thing many, many times over.

The rest of the room is neat, tidy, just like Henry's apartment and his office. Except it's better, because the antique furniture is dark wood polished to a high sheen, with brass hardware that glints in the light. His bed is as neat as a pin, the sheets tucked in at the corners and the white duvet fluffed. There's a row of old library bookshelves, perfectly organized, and a wooden desk with a computer. The computer makes me smile because it looks so incongruent next to—honest to God—the highly polished suit of armor.

I try not to gape. Henry wouldn't gape. Not if this is his bedroom.

"Well, we'll be off then. Good night, Serena. Good night, Henry."

Eugenia hurries to me, wraps me in her arms, and presses a soft, motherly kiss to my cheek. Then her eyes twinkle as she reaches up and wipes her lipstick away. At her thumb rubbing roughly over my jaw, she shakes her head and says, "Shave in the morning, Henry. And perhaps Serena has makeup for that black eye? And—"

"Mum," John interrupts, "I've a button loose on my trousers. I don't want to pop tomorrow. Can you—?"

Eugenia hones in on the emergency of John's pants falling down during the wedding because of a loose button. She grabs his arm, and without another word to Henry or me, she tugs him down the hall, peppering him with wedding-day reminders and questions that she answers for him. While they hurry down the hall John shoots me a final look over his shoulder. I don't have any trouble deciphering it even if I'm not actually his brother. It says, "Be careful. Don't be doubly a fool."

Then they're gone and I'm left alone with Henry.

I close the door. The heavy wood swings shut, scraping over the floor, and closes with a quiet sigh.

I stare at Henry—looking a bit rumpled in my floral dress and a bit dazed from the day—and say, "Henry Joule, you have some explaining to do."

I'm wearing Henry's pajamas—basically cotton boxers and nothing else. When I protested the lack of clothing, he swore that a T-shirt would make me so hot at night it'd be flames-of-hell unbearable. Considering I was completely naked when I woke up as Henry, I'm inclined to believe him.

Henry is in a pair of my sleep shorts and a pink tank top that says, "Schrödinger's Cat: Wanted Dead or Alive." Henry snorted when he saw it, a little hiccup of a laugh, and I grinned back.

Now we're in the great expanse of his four-poster bed, the fluffy down comforter an ocean of feathery comfort below us. We float like two icebergs at opposite poles on the sea of his mattress. He has his knees tucked up, chin resting on them, as he leans against the wooden headboard. I'm perched on the other side of the bed with as much space between us as possible, my Arctic to his Antarctica.

Being in a bed with Henry—well, it's a vivid reminder of the last time we were in a bed together.

Even thinking about that bed, imagining the way Henry reverently ran his hands over my breasts and kissed behind my earlobe and whispered delicious proposals for what we might do to follow up that thing he did with his tongue . . . Well. Let's just say, my boxers are getting tight and blood is flowing, and jeez, do men always have this problem, or is it just me? It's just me, isn't it?

I clear my throat, shift on the bed, discreetly adjust my boxers, and drop a pillow in my lap. There. That's not obvious. Not at all.

"So, questions," I say.

"Right," Henry says, wrapping his arms around his knees and peering at me through the dim light of the nightstand lamp. "Questions. Proceed."

I've dropped my horrible British accent, and Henry has dropped his stellar American accent.

"These are not in order of importance," I say, wanting it known up front.

Henry nods, and I continue.

"Okay. Here goes. Who is Lorna? Why did she stroke my thigh and then strip for me, and why does she think we're getting married? Two, what the heck is a stag do, and why did I get tackled because of it? Three, do you have a plane in your back yard? Four, are you seriously leaving ATLAS, or was John mistaken? Five, do you have memories of mine and cravings that are mine, because I have memories of yours, and I crave all sorts of things like tea and roast and those lemon cookies even though I don't like any of those things. And I constantly want to tidy up. And why would you leave ATLAS? Why? Are you out of your mind? Also, why is there a suit of armor in your bedroom?" I fold my hands in my lap, set them on my pillow, and add as an afterthought, "Finally, why do you get hard every time you look at or think of titties?"

As I progressed through my list Henry straightened and sat up, his eyes growing wider and wider, until finally, at my last question he lets out a choking laugh.

"Excuse me?" he says, another laugh bursting forth.

I scowl at him. "I'm not joking. It's an evolutionary flaw. Every time I get a flash of tit, *whoopsie*, there it goes again. Erect! You have this memory of stroking a breast and kissing it, and every time, it hits me like a lead pipe over the head, and *bam*—rock-hard! What the heck is wrong with you? Who can function like that?"

I look over at Henry, faltering in my tirade, because his face has gone a bit pale and his eyes are dark pools full of something that looks almost like pain.

"Sorry . . ." I say, holding up my hand. "I didn't mean to suggest—"

"I don't get hard every time I see breasts," he says, sitting so straight he looks prim and proper again. His British accent is crisp as he scowls at me. "I believe that is unique to you. I function quite well in life. In fact, I don't think I've gone 'bam—rock-hard' since I was fifteen. To be fair, as a teenager, lying on my back in the grass staring at a cumulus cloud could made me hard in seconds."

I think about this then ask, "Did the cloud happen to look like a pair of breasts?"

Henry loses his disapproving air and flashes a grin my way. "Perhaps."

I lean back into the pillows, moving a bit closer toward the middle of the bed. I'm tired of perching on the edge. As I move, the duvet sends up the scent I always associate with Henry, cedar and starlight.

I suppose it's just my luck that I respond like fifteen-year-old Henry. Although, come to think of it, maybe it wasn't Lorna's breasts that made me hard—maybe it was the memory that did it. That was what did it just now too, that incredibly erotic memory.

"What is that memory of?" I ask. "The one where you're kissing—"

"My first time," Henry says. He wraps his arms around his legs again and glances at me from under his eyelashes.

"Was it good?" Although it must've been if the memory makes me hard all these years later.

Henry gets a faraway look on his face as his lips curve into what I can only describe as a dreamy smile, and he nods. "Life-changing."

There's a pinch in my chest. I think maybe it's . . . jealousy?

Or maybe envy. After all, my first time was with Bernie Berger, and it was a quick, awkward fifteen seconds in the kitchen pantry.

I decide to move on from the topic of firsts and ask, "Do you get flashes of memory? Do you have my tastes?"

Henry looks over at me, his eyes unreadable, like he's still caught in the memory of his first time. Then his expression clears and he nods, scooting closer on the bed. "It startled me at first. I was in . . . I think it's your backyard. I was looking up at the night sky, it was cool, the scent of pine was strong, and I saw a comet and I felt . . ."

"Happy?"

He glances at me. "No. I felt . . ."

Don't say it.

"Like I was falling in love."

He said it.

My stomach drops, but I say, "Anything else?"

He lifts an eyebrow at my curt tone but doesn't comment. Instead he says, "Sometimes I'm lying on your bed at night, your parents are watching TV in the living room, and you're reading a quantum mechanics textbook and your vision is blurry, teary, because you're . . ." He pauses. "Alone, lonely—"

Denial rises fast and strong. "I wasn't." I shake my head. "I was never alone. I was never lonely. That's not true."

He just looks at me. Doesn't respond to my denial. He doesn't have to.

I fall quiet, feeling exposed. Suddenly I hate it that Henry is me, that he can see my past and experience my most private feelings. I hate that I can't hide or blur the truth because he sees it now too.

I can't bear to ask him if he's seen the night we were together. I don't know what he'd see, what he'd think, if he did.

So instead I move on to something that won't feel like poking myself in the heart with a red-hot iron.

"What's a stag do?"

Henry smiles then slips under the covers. "Americans call it a bachelor party. It's the goal to embarrass the groom. The greater the embarrassment, the more you show your brotherly love."

"Hmm." I think about how Henry supposedly sent John to the middle of a lake, drunk and naked in a rowboat without an oar. "I guess you love your brother."

He nods, looking across the room at the stars wavering in the window. "My family . . . I'm one of the lucky ones. My family is full of wonderful people who love each other very much." He pauses then glances over at me. "I have to admit, it terrifies me to think I might lose them. If we can't figure this out and . . . I don't get to see my niece and nephews growing up or send Niall out in a rowboat before *his* wedding or be there for my parents when they grow old . . . If forevermore I'm not their son or their brother or their uncle, I'm just . . . cut off. Lost to them. I'm . . . It terrifies me."

He looks over at me then, and the lamplight is so dim that the shadows catch him and I think he's in danger of being pulled under from the fear of it all. So I slip under the satin duvet, inch across the cool sheets, and don't stop until I'm resting against him. Arm to arm. Thigh to thigh.

He's quiet as the sensation of skin to skin, the breath caught and then let free, the heat of me brushing over the cool of him, flows achingly between us. Then, slowly, he reaches over and rests his hand in mine.

It feels as if an electric current connects, crackles, and then settles into a steady, fluxing rhythm.

"Do you feel that?" I ask.

He nods, looking down at our hands.

"Don't worry," I tell him, "we'll, figure it out. I won't let you down. I promise."

He smiles up at me, but it's not a happy smile. "You can't promise that."

"I can. I just did. I won't let you lose your family."

He deserves his family because he appreciates them, and he loves them unabashedly. I won't let him lose them.

He squeezes my hand then traces his thumb along mine. "Lorna was my first girlfriend."

Ah. Lorna.

She must be the first time I keep remembering. I suppose it's good to put a face to a boob.

"Did you propose to her?" I ask. "Youthful enthusiasm and all that?"

Henry shakes his head and his long hair brushes the naked skin of my chest. I reach up and brush his hair back, tucking it behind his ear.

"I'm only doing this because it's tickling me," I tell him.

He takes his free hand and twists his hair, brushing it behind his shoulder. A puff of mint rises— the shampoo I use.

"I did not propose," he says, "although we did discuss marriage in a vague distant-future sort of way. We dated through uni, then when I turned twenty-two I mentioned marriage in a more concrete way, and then she mentioned having sex with my best friend over my birthday weekend while I was in Switzerland touring CERN with my dad. My dad had surprised me with the birthday tour. Lorna surprised me with the . . ." He shrugs.

"Best friend birthday bonk-fest?"

"Precisely."

"So why the striptease tonight?"

His thumb stops tracing over my hand. He studies our joined fingers. "My best friend, Harry, they took up together after my birthday. Last year Harry ran off to Barbados with his life coach. Lorna wrote me, told me she was sorry, now she understood how painful it was. I told her it was fine. All in the past. She said she was sorry how we'd left things, that marriage was more appealing now. I thought she was referring to John and Olivia's wedding. She asked if we could talk at the wedding, and I said yes."

I shake my head.

Henry peers at me. "What?"

"There was so much subtext to what she was saying it was like quicksand. You were sucked under, and you didn't even know it."

He huffs. "I'll have to talk to her tomorrow—"

"As Serena?"

He raises an eyebrow. "Ah. Right."

"Yeah." I think for a moment. "It'll be okay. We'll handle it."

He squeezes my hand again and presses closer, seeking the warmth of me. His toes press against my calves, and they feel like tiny little balls of ice.

That's one thing I don't miss. My hands and feet were always cold.

I shift my legs and sandwich Henry's toes between my calves.

"You're like a brick warmed by the fire," Henry says, sighing happily as he wiggles his toes.

"And you're like an ice cube in a subzero freezer."

"Funny, isn't it?" he asks, and I assume he's talking about how we're now the opposite of ourselves.

I nod then ask, "Do you think maybe this is just a twenty-four-hour thing, like *Freaky Friday*? Maybe we'll wake up in the morning and we'll have switched back. Magic done. Poof!"

"Maybe," Henry says, looking up at the line of my jaw and the whiskers there. "I suppose it depends on whether this is magic or science."

"But isn't magic just science that we haven't yet explained?"

He smiles at me, a wry, joking light in his eyes. "You know, I always wanted to be a California girl. There are all these songs written about them and I wondered, what's it really like?" He shrugs. "Now I know."

I nudge him with my shoulder. "Likewise. I always said in my next life I want to be a stuffy British man, drink buckets of tea, and have erections every time someone mentions the word 'boob.' It was my dream."

He snorts and then drops his head to my shoulder, resting his cheek against the heat of my hard-planed chest and the beating of my heart.

The bedroom is quiet now. The suit of armor stands at attention in the corner, dully gleaming in the moonlight streaming through the window in gentle waves. The rest of the house is asleep. Not a noise penetrates the thick stone. I'm warm and comfortable, and it feels natural and right to have Henry touching me, resting against me, in my arms.

Maybe it's because Henry is in my body and my spirit is drawn back to my body. Or maybe it's something else.

All I know is that with the quiet settled around us like a warm, feathery duvet and Henry's breath fluttering over my chest and his thumb stroking the back of my hand, I feel more right, more centered, more myself, than I ever have in my entire life.

That thought frightens me, though, so I ask, "Are you really leaving ATLAS?"

Henry stills. His breath cuts short, then after a moment he relaxes and says quietly, "The first of October."

"What! Why? That's a terrible decision. ATLAS is the center of our universe. It's everything. I don't want . . ." I wrinkle my brow. If Henry had told me two days ago that he was leaving ATLAS I would've felt relief. But now I don't want him to go. Ever. Even worse, if we haven't switched back in a few weeks' time, it'll be me that's leaving. ATLAS is my dream. My one love. It's what I've given up everything for.

"I'm taking a position at FermiLab."

"FermiLab! Why? No! Are you kidding me? I don't want to go to Chicago. It's windy there. I hate wind. There isn't enough tea in the world to put up with that amount of wind."

Henry looks up at me, his brow wrinkled in a quizzical expression. "It's not that windy."

I beg to differ.

"It's called the *Windy City*." Besides, that's not the point. "It's not CERN. It's not . . . Henry, why? You have an amazing job. You have an amazing life. Why would you go to Chicago? I don't want you—" I clear my throat. "I don't want to go to Chicago. My life is in Geneva."

Henry turns away, pulls his hand free of mine, then shifts his feet free of the warmth of my legs. He leans against the headboard again.

"You're right," he says, his voice low and almost regretful. "If we haven't switched back, you'll have to decline the job. You can't go to Chicago. We have to stay together."

I nod emphatically. Of course we have to stay together. That was the deal, wasn't it? We stay together until the end.

"Okay," I say. I look across the room at the suit of armor. "Does it have a name, that armor?"

Henry nods, glancing over at the suit. It's about the same height as me—Serena—maybe 5'3" or 5'4". It's polished silver with gold filigree and a spiked helmet with a visor. It's almost menacing in a comical way.

"Fitzy Butterbottom."

"What?" I look over at Henry.

Henry smiles at me, his eyes dancing in the soft light. "That's his name. Fitzy Butterbottom. I was frightened of him when I was small. Lizzy told me if I named him something silly he wouldn't be scary anymore."

"Did it work?"

"No," he says. "I hid under my covers every night until I was fourteen."

"Then what happened?" I ask, drawing close to him again.

He gives me a quirky smile. "I discovered breasts and I had something else to occupy me at night."

I laugh at the joking light in Henry's eyes.

Then I ask, worried suddenly about the moment when we turn out the light and curl up under the covers, Fitzy Butterbottom keeping watch, "Can we hold each other tonight? In case that's what we need to switch back. Contact like we had during the storm."

Henry considers me for a moment, and for some reason my heart drums in my chest, rising up to my throat.

Finally, he nods. "Yes. And then in the morning we'll wake up and everything will be right as rain."

"Exactly. *Freaky Friday*. Our twenty-four hours is almost over."

Henry clicks the lamp off then and the room floods with the darkness of a stone tower room deep in the English countryside. I slip lower into the bed, the warm sheets gliding over my skin. I'm tall—so tall my feet reach the end of the bed and poke out of the sheets. The bedding whispers and rumples as Henry burrows down under the covers.

Then there's a sigh. A questioning silence. A held breath.

I lie still and wait, staring up at the dark beams of the ceiling and breathing in the minty scent of shampoo and the woodsy-starlight scent of the night.

Then, with a soft exhale, Henry shifts over the mattress. His hand brushes over the bare skin of my chest —just a whisper, a careful touch. Then he curls into my side, his legs tangle over mine, his chest presses into me, and his head rests in the cradle of my shoulder. His hair is smooth and silky and his weight is a warm blanket.

My breath comes steady and even, and with each rise and fall of my chest Henry rises and falls over me. His lips rest above my heart. I can feel a warm puff of air across my skin with each of his exhales. The feel of him burns into me.

I drop my hands to the bed, bury my fingers in the sheets, and close my eyes, praying that when I wake up I'll be me again.

24

The morning dawns bright and hopeful. The blue sunshine licks over us and paints the inside of my closed eyes a flossy red. I'm a tangle of limbs, legs, and arms wrapped together, bodies pressed tight, bare skin whispering over bare skin, so I can't tell up from down or what belongs to who.

I'm floating, half-asleep, hopeful.

Perhaps . . . maybe . . . I draw in a shaky breath, but the moment I open my eyes, I know.

The bedroom is blurry. Across the room, Fitzy Butterbottom is a shiny, indistinct figure, the computer is a blob, and the window, with sunlight streaming through the shield, sends rainbow prisms across the rug, showing a clear, bright, wavy blue sky.

It's the perfect day for a wedding.

My stomach drops as I tilt my head and look down at Henry.

He's still asleep, his cheek nestled against my chest, his leg thrown over mine, his hand curled over my heart.

His hair is tangled—it always does, which is why I usually braid it before bed—and his mouth is parted, letting out little sleep sighs. I can see well enough up close without glasses or contacts. I've never seen what I look like sleeping before. I look younger than I am. Innocent. Soft. Vulnerable. I'm not any of those things though. So maybe it's Henry that makes me look that way. Maybe when I'm in my body and asleep I don't look like this at all.

I let out a sigh, and it's then that Henry wakes. He stretches, squeezes his eyes tight, and makes a sleep noise. Then I think he remembers that we might have—maybe—could've— switched back, because he stiffens like a kid remembering it's Christmas morning and flings open his eyes. And then as quickly as the hope came, it dies. His body sags and he gives me a soft smile.

"I suppose it was too much to hope," he says, his voice sleep-thick and husky.

I nod, shifting under him. Henry untangles himself from me, sitting up and pulling the covers free. The cool air of the bedroom rushes over my skin, bringing up goose bumps.

"All right," he says, nodding like a man facing a duty he doesn't want but will do to the best of his ability anyway. "Onward."

I squeeze his hand. Then, before I can say anything, there's the sound of feet pounding down the hall, the excited voices of kids and the yipping of dogs, and then banging on the thick wooden door as a voice calls, "Uncle Henry! Uncle John says get up or he'll get you up because he's getting married today!" That's Michael, Maeve's five-year-old brother, and then Maeve yells through the door, "Grandma says Serena needs a fascinator! Does she have one? If not, I can help her pick one! It can be pink with sparkles!" There's a bark of excitement to emphasize the point.

And I'm left wondering what a fascinator is, which means I most definitely didn't pack one for Henry. Especially not a pink sparkly one. Since he balked at wearing my floral dress, I think he'll definitely balk at wearing something sparkly.

"Did you bring a hat?" he whispers.

Ah. That must be a fascinator. I shake my head. In the rush to get to the airport and the head-spinning disorientation of being Henry, I forgot that not wearing a hat to a wedding in England is worse manners than showing up wearing only gold nipple tassels and a G-string.

"I do not have one," Henry calls, then he kicks the covers off and gives his cheeks a quick wake-up slap. "We'll be out in a moment!"

"Coming!" I add.

Then Henry swings his legs off the side of the bed, gives me a bracing look, and says, "Ready?"

Am I?

Can I do this?

Can I stand as best man for his brother? Can I navigate a wedding as Henry and fool his entire extended family? Can I give his speech as best man?

Oh gosh, what's that saying? "Pride goeth before the fall"?

I nod confidently. "Yes. Absolutely. I'm ready."

∼

John and Olivia were hitched without a hitch.

They were married in a little stone church from the 1500s on top of a little green hill in the center of a little stone village with green grass and bright-blue skies and hedges and sheep fields in the distance. Olivia arrived in a Rolls Royce and her white dress snapped around her and her veil lifted like a cloud in the wind, and I couldn't help but think there really never has been a more beautiful, happy bride. When John saw her I heard his breath catch, and the light in his eyes made my chest ache.

Then the wedding began and Lizzy's kids tumbled down the aisle dressed in finery, with oohs and ahhs from both sides of the church. And then the corgis trotted down the aisle dressed in gray tails to match the ushers, and only one of the corgis stopped to chase not his actual tail, but the jacket tail. When he couldn't catch it he settled on chewing the white ribbon at the end of a wooden pew. Everyone laughed, and then Henry, sitting in the row behind his parents, scooped up the dog and held it in his lap.

After that the wedding went like weddings do. Henry's mom cried into a handkerchief that Charles handed her. The kids fidgeted and the dogs sniffed the guests. I stood behind John, and Niall stood behind me, all of us dressed in tails and gray trousers. I remembered the rings. There were lots of brightly colored hats and flowery, whimsical dresses. Olivia and John stared at each other and forgot everyone else in the entire church while they said their "I dos."

And Henry . . .

He sat in the pew behind his parents, the only sibling not standing up with his brother. The entire service he sat pin-straight wearing my pale-pink knee-length chiffon dress and the hot-pink fascinator with its lace folding like pink sea-foam and tall fuchsia feathers flowing like ocean spray. He didn't complain about the chiffon or the feathers, or when I put on makeup or twisted his hair into a chignon.

"I'm sorry you aren't standing up with him," I'd said while I pinned the chignon in place.

"Not to worry. I have a better view sitting down," he'd said, and we left it at that.

But the whole wedding I couldn't help but recognize the look on Henry's face. It's the one I wore so often when I was younger—the one I vehemently denied last night. Watching his family, watching his brother marry the love of his life, Henry looked . . . alone.

He was alone.

All that has passed though, and now we're gathered under the marquee in the garden outside the family home. The white tent was erected this morning as soon as the sun rose, as well as long tables and nearly a hundred chairs, and more bunting and flowers than I've ever seen drape from the tented ceiling and mound from gold vases on the tables.

It's a dreamy, flowery tented wonderland, and all the family and wedding guests are crowded under it, sitting at the tables, milling about, and congratulating the newlyweds.

There's a heady, bubbly feeling in the tent—one of celebration and excitement. The air smells of roses and lilies and champagne. There's a towering five-tier wedding cake spilling over with icing and tropical fondant flowers, and there's the joyous bubble of conversation and laughter.

I stand, take the microphone, and clear my throat, facing the sea of faces.

It's time for the best man's speech. Henry handed me a folded sheet of paper this morning with the warning to read it *exactly* as it was written.

I hate to say it, but in the hectic rush of preparations I didn't have time to read it.

Now he watches me, his finger nervously tapping on the white tablecloth, the drumming making the champagne in his glass ripple and bubble.

I give him a weak smile and he nods back, reassuring me. If I manage this, we're home free.

I lift the mic and say, "Hullo, I'm Henry, the best man."

There are a few chuckles as everyone turns toward me and someone shouts, "We know who you are!"

Oh gosh.

You don't. You actually don't.

At the long table next to me, the wedding party, Henry's family, Olivia and John, and of course Lorna, all turn their attention to me.

Well, it's showtime. I lift the paper up and squint. Henry's glasses work, but one eye is still kind of swollen, so I'm working with half-vision. Not to mention Henry's writing is *terrible*. It's like a toddler took a crayon and wrote this speech with the crayon between his toes. It's chicken scratch. It's cursive gobbledygook nonsense. What is this?

My word. My word.

Someone coughs.

The silence grows thick.

The back of my neck burns and Maeve whispers

loudly, "What's the matter with him?" and then Lizzy shushes her.

I throw a quick pleading glance at Henry, and he lifts his eyebrows and gestures for me to *read*. "Go on," he mouths.

I glance back at John. He grimaces at me.

I look back at the marquee full of Henry's family. His sisters, his parents, his niece and nephews and brother and new sister-in-law, at the aunts and uncles and cousins I only just met today, and his neighbors and even his primary school headmistress, the infamous Ms. Treacletee, whose teacup he glued to its saucer. They're all here, staring at me —Henry—with either pity, concern, or embarrassment.

I've been silent for a good sixty seconds. They think I'm tongue-tied with stage fright.

So.

I can't let Henry down. I can't let his family down.

I can give speeches. I give poster presentations at academic conferences all the time. I defended my thesis —that was nerve-wracking, let me tell you—and I gave my valedictorian speech at my high-school graduation. So. Okay. I can give a wedding speech.

I'll . . . wing it.

Another cough sounds.

A mutter.

Another whispered "Is he all right?"

And so I read what I can, and as soon as I start talking I see Henry's shoulders relax, and everyone nearby gives a communal sigh of relief.

"Olivia," I say clearly, chanting in my head, *British accent, British accent, do a British accent*, "is kind, charming, intelligent, warm-hearted,"—I narrow my eyes and try to decipher what comes next—"lovely as a . . ." I shake my head and then look at Henry. "Sorry, I can't read your writing."

Every head turns to Henry—who to them looks like Serena—and then his mouth falls open and everyone—Henry's dad, John and Niall, his sisters—they all start laughing.

I give them Henry's cheeky grin and shove the paper in my pocket. "You know how it is." I nod to John. "You do what the lady says."

"I do!" John shouts, clearly happy with his lot in life.

"Right. Well, John. Congratulations. Today you married the most wonderful woman. You'll get boundless love, undying support, kindness, a woman who will stick with you in hard times and in good times. You get the woman of your dreams."

Henry gives me a small smile—one that says he doesn't know where I'm going with this, but he trusts me. Lizzy clasps her hands to her chest and gives an "aww," and John and Olivia gaze lovey-dovey at each other.

"It's true," John says, and everyone sighs.

I smile. "And Olivia."

She nods and clasps John to her side, hugging him tight. Her dress is a white fall of lace around them and her bouquet of white roses rests on the table nearby.

Olivia waits for the list of John's virtues.

"You get," I say, pausing, looking around. "Well. I think you can keep the flowers. If you treat them right, they might last a week or two."

There's a stunned silence, and then everyone starts laughing.

"No," Kate shouts, "the flowers are consignment! They have to go to another wedding this afternoon!"

I grin at her and say, "Sorry then. I suppose just the dress will have to do."

"Henry," Olivia laughs. "I love John, thank you very much." Then she tilts her head and says, "But I love this dress too."

I wait a moment for the laughter to die down. Then I lift my champagne glass, the bubbles rising in a rainbow of gold, and say, "I was wrong. I forgot to mention, you get a man who loves you more than himself, who can't wait to spend every day of his life with you, and who told me last night that he couldn't wait to be married and endlessly happy . . ." I pause, wait for the awws to stop, and then say, "I wish you all the happiness. I'm so glad you get to join this family who loves you, and I know we are endlessly happy to have you as a part of it." I turn to John. "I'm proud of you for recognizing 'the one' when you saw her." I look back at Olivia. "And I'm grateful to you for making my brother happy." I lift my glass. "To the bride and groom."

"To the bride and groom!"

I tip back the glass and let the golden apple bubbles of the champagne slide down my throat.

When I look back at Henry, he smiles at me—a bright, clear, grateful smile—and it seems like the champagne bubbles are floating around inside me, because an odd buoyant feeling rises in my chest and bounces like shining effervescence through my veins.

And I'm not quite sure how to make it stop.

25

"THAT WAS AN INTERESTING SPEECH," LORNA SAYS, EDGING
next to me at the dessert table.

I keep my attention on the confections—raspberry
gelee, tropical trifle, sticky toffee pudding, and something
with strawberries called Eton mess that Lizzy complained
she can't eat—and avoid looking at Lorna. She inches
closer, snags a cup of trifle.

Back at the table, Henry is on his second glass of
champagne and having a jovial argument with Niall over
whether he should study law or move to a surfer colony
for a year in Australia. You'd think Henry would tell Niall
to go to school, but he's actually advocating for hemp
shoes, avocado smoothies, and surfing. I think he's having
fun playing California girl.

He's turned down offers to dance from at least half a
dozen cousins and three uncles, and each time, he gives
me a wide-eyed "can you believe this is happening to
me?" look. I can. His Great-Aunt Tilda asked me to dance,
and of course, I said yes.

Finally, I choose the sticky toffee pudding, which actually looks like it might be better than the one they serve at The Cock and Bull in Geneva. I grab a fork and say a terse thank-you to Lorna.

I turn to go, but she puts her hand on my arm. "Henry?"

I pause.

Lorna glances up at me with doe eyes. She's in the gold satin bridesmaid dress and the V at her neck plunges low. I purposely do not look down because I don't want a flashback to last night, and I don't want a hard-on (there aren't any pillows handy).

She squeezes my arm. "You said you'd forgiven me. I was under the impression when you said we would talk at the wedding that you wanted as much as I do to get back together."

Oh.

Oof.

Carefully I pull my arm from her grip. Then I put it out there as nicely as possible, one woman to another.

"I forgive you, but I don't have feelings for you. That's done."

She blinks at me, her lashes fluttering quickly. She takes a deep, trembling breath. "But you wanted to get married."

"Years ago," I say. "Many years ago. I changed. You've changed. Lorna, you shouldn't look to the past to fill a hole you have today. You should respect yourself more. I can't make you happy. I'd just distract you for a bit. Then, soon, you'd realize you still aren't happy, except you'd have the mistake of me to deal with. Fix your stuff, Lorna." I point to my heart. "Fix it in here. A man can't make you complete. Only you can do that."

I wait then, thinking I did a pretty good job of letting Lorna down easy and giving her some sister-to-sister advice. But the look on her face isn't one of gratitude. In fact, her lip curls and her nose looks narrow and pinched.

"You sound just like her. You don't sound like yourself. You don't even sound English anymore. You sound like a California hippy peddling self-help rubbish." She sniffs then turns her glare on Henry. "You weren't there, but I heard her last night cozying up to Eugenia. Bragging about her California roots and her career and her brilliant physics awards. Who cares if she has a double doctorate? Who cares if she's been published? She's a braggart. You can't see it because she's gorgeous in a pushy, showy way, but mark my words, Henry, she won't make you happy. She's awful."

I stare at Henry across the marquee. His cheeks are almost as pink as the fascinator he's wearing and he's laughing at something Niall said. Some strands of hair have slipped from his chignon and his eyes sparkle with mirth.

"You don't like her?" I ask, glancing back at Lorna.

She weighs my expression, then her hard gaze softens and she says, "I don't. And I don't think you should either. She's awful, and she's changing you. I don't like her."

I smile at her and nod. "Then you don't like Henry."

"What?" Lorna's brow wrinkles in confusion, and I realize I sound as if I'm speaking in the third person.

"Then you don't like me."

"I do—"

I shake my head. "You don't. Good luck, Lorna."

I grab another sticky toffee pudding—one for Henry too, because the smell of cinnamon and caramel has been teasing me for the past five minutes and I'm certain he'll like it—then I walk away, back to Henry.

"You should dance," Niall says when I get back to the table.

I set the desserts down on the white tablecloth, one for me, one for Henry. "I should eat this pudding."

Niall shakes his head. "No. You should dance."

The band—oddly, a group of rowdy octogenarian accordionists—is playing a rousing waltz that has people galloping across the dance floor.

Niall nods his head toward the long table. It's practically empty because nearly all the couples are dancing. The only people who aren't are Henry's parents. Eugenia waves her hands at me in a "dance with her, you fool" sort of gesture.

Henry gazes at me, a resigned, humor-filled light in his eyes.

"Would you like to dance?" I ask.

Niall scowls at me. "If you can't do better, I'll dance with her."

Henry stands faster than I've ever seen anyone stand in my entire life. "I'd be honored to dance with you, Henry. Thank you."

I give one last longing look at the sticky toffee pudding and then hold out my arm. Henry weaves his arm through mine and rests his hand on my forearm.

As we walk toward the open dance floor, the fabric ceiling floating above us with hanging ivy, flowers, and twinkle lights, the accordion waltz wheezes to an end and the band bridges into a beautiful, haunting slow song. It's the one you hear on the corner of a bridge in Paris as you gaze over the rippling Seine, or at sunset in London when the golden light glints off the fountains in Trafalgar

Square. It's the song that makes people either fall in love or weep because they're not in love.

I stand in the center of the dance floor and Henry stands in my arms. John and Olivia twirl past us, and Lizzy and James sway by. Even Maeve is dancing with a corgi, and Kate is dancing with Michael.

"We should dance," Henry says, tilting his chin up to look at me. This close, with him not wearing heels, the top of his head only comes to my shoulder. It's hard to remember how tall I am now—how much larger. It's hard to remember that Henry isn't Henry, because when I look at him and see me, it still feels like it's him. I mean, it is him, but sometimes I don't see me—my face, my eyes, my smile—I see only him.

He lifts his arms and hesitantly wraps them around my neck, his fingers brushing the collar of my shirt and the ends of my hair. I rest my hands at the base of his spine, feeling his warmth through the thin fabric of the dress. He turns his head and one of the feathers on his fascinator tickles my chin.

I smile, and his cheeks flush.

"Sorry."

"I'm surprised you wore it." I sway to the music, trying to ignore the shifting of him against me, the whisper of space between us.

He smiles, his eyes crinkling happily. "Maeve chose it."

I think he's a bit giddy on the champagne. I'm a lightweight, and two glasses usually has me feeling like my head is floating with the stars and my feet are dancing on clouds.

"You're a good uncle."

"Thank you." He smiles at me and my heart does a cartwheel in my chest.

Between us the air is thick. My hands rest on the curve of Henry's spine. Our chests brush, coming together then parting, and our hips sway, matching the longing romance in the song. It reminds me of bed and tangled limbs and whispered words. And sex. This dance reminds me of sex.

I can taste champagne and wonder if Henry can too. My breath is heavy, my lungs aching. The memory of the night Henry made love to me is tangible, and the magnetic pull between us keeps our bodies tight and our hands on each other.

I stare into Henry's eyes, not seeing my brown eyes and my wry expression. I see Henry's eyes and Henry's earnest, thoughtful expression. I tilt my head down, moving close so we're in our own world—one that's contained in the limits of our arms.

"I think," I begin, "that this has been one of the most magical days of my life, and it's not even mine. Isn't that strange?"

He blinks up at me, his deep forest-pool eyes rippling with hidden emotion. "I thought you didn't like commitment. Or love."

I say defensively, "Why would you think that?"

But then I realize how ironic that sounds. He'd think it because he feels it. He'd think it because of how I blew off our one night together.

He doesn't answer my question. Instead he says, "Lorna talked to me."

My swaying stills, but he keeps dancing, so I start again. "You too?"

He smiles—a little sad, a lot understanding. "She doesn't like me."

"No," I agree.

"She's watching us now."

I nod. "If you want, I give you permission to put your hands on your butt."

"Excuse me?"

I nod, putting on a stoic face. "For the cause. If she isn't convinced that you're with me and I'm with you, well . . . that'll convince everyone. Sometimes people need physical evidence. You can just put your hands on my butt for the rest of the dance. It's your butt anyway. I'm sure you've grabbed it plenty."

He chokes on a laugh and buries his face in the lapels of my coat. "That's indecent."

"Oh, please. I saw your Granny Myrtle pinching the butt cheeks of your Grandpa John, and don't tell me he didn't like it."

Henry snorts, then his hands tighten on my shoulders and he grins up at me. "You truly want me to grab your butt?"

"It's your butt. Besides, I'll grab mine if you can't handle it. That is if you're too squeamish to hold your own bum."

"I can handle it," he says cockily. "I'm action. You're all talk."

I laugh, a smoked whiskey challenge of a laugh, and Henry's eyes widen.

"It isn't a big deal," he says, glancing at me disapprovingly. "I've felt my own arse plenty."

"Sure. That's a completely normal thing to do, feeling your own bum. I'm sure you do it every day, just for kicks."

His mouth tightens. "Do you?"

I nod smoothly. "Oh yeah. You've seen my drawer."

His lips quirk. "What drawer?"

Yeah. Right.

"She's still watching," I remind him.

Henry's hands drift down. He stares into my eyes as his hands graze my shoulders. The muscles of my back tense under his fingers. He slides down, down, tracing my spine, until his hands rest gently on my bum.

Annnnnnd . . . insta-hard.

For. Crying. Out. Loud!

I cannot handle it.

I let out a shaky breath and try to breathe through the honeyed, viscous feeling flowing over my skin and settling deep inside. There's a ball of heat glowing in my belly, sending tingles up and down my spine.

Oh jeez.

I'm dizzy.

The marquee is shifting around me, spinning like a carousel.

My breath is tight and my mouth is dry, and I'm craving . . . The memory flashes again, the taste of mint and apples strong as I send my mouth over her breast, my hands questing over her satin skin, and there's a sharp cry and she grips my butt, pulling me close—

Frickin' Lorna. I do not need to be fantasizing about Henry's first time with Lorna right now.

I don't need to be fantasizing about anything.

"Is this all right?" Henry asks, and his voice is low and husky.

So I say what I'm thinking—what's chanting through my mind. "No sex. Under any circumstances. None."

Henry frowns at me. "What? Who said anything

about sex? Besides, I'm related to practically everyone here. That's disgusting. And I'm not exactly interested in going for a test drive. It's your body." He peers up at me. "Why are you so stiff and uptight?"

I choke on a laugh. One of disbelief and irritation and confusion. Me, uptight? Me, stiff? Well, okay, yes on that one.

But clearly Henry isn't feeling what I'm feeling. Not at all. I'm the fifteen-year-old horndog. I'm the one who still has feelings after nearly two years. I'm the one who, in my own words, needs to fix myself right (pointing at my heart) here.

"She's gone," I say to Henry, noting Lorna has left the marquee. "You can let go of my butt now."

He steps back then, drops his hands, and whatever intimacy I felt while we were dancing, it pops like a helium balloon suddenly burst.

Then I notice Henry's cheeks are flushed and his eyes are unfocused as if he's been in another world and he's slowly pulling himself back into this one. He looks . . . dazed.

When he glances up at me, he blushes.

And with that crimson blush I'm certain, one hundred percent certain, he just relived a memory of mine. And from the dreamy, unfocused look in his eyes, I know it was the night we made love.

26

THE SCENT OF AUTUMN ROSES TWIRLS BY, TEMPTING AND
teasing, and the accordions play on while the wedding
celebration swirls around us. Everyone is high on cake
and champagne and love, so the swirling of floral dresses
and feathered hats and the happy barking of corgis and
the laughter of family mixes into a potent bouquet of
wedding-day bliss.

Henry stares up at me, his cheeks flushed crimson,
and his dazed expression slowly shifts from unfocused
post-orgasm bliss to stunned surprise.

I stiffen, standing stock-still, looking (I'm sure) uptight
as John and Olivia waltz past and Grandma Myrtle and
Michael spin by. Henry and I stand to the side of the
dance floor, just outside the whirl of accordion-filled glee.

I brace myself, dreading his outburst, which will
probably sound something like this: "You lying liar, you
dastardly deceiver, you panhandler of pretense, you
fabricator of falsehoods! You lied!" Because, honestly, if
he just experienced what I think he did, then he just

remembered our night together. And if that's the case, then he knows.

He *knows*.

At the other end of the wedding tent, under an arch of white roses and trailing clematis, Olivia gathers all the women around her. A ripple of excitement buzzes across the tent. It's time for the bouquet toss.

"Henry, Serena, over here!" Kate calls, her pea-green feathers nodding as she waves us over.

I nod and wave, feeling like a man just granted a stay on his execution. I gesture toward the arch and the gathering crowd. "We should—"

"You lied," Henry says, his voice stunned, his eyes traveling over me as if I'm a new particle he just discovered and my properties break all the laws of physics. "You lied to me."

Oh gosh.

He did see it.

When he experienced me looking up at the stars in my back yard he swore it felt like love. He experienced all my emotions and he knew exactly what they were.

So if he had a memory of us making love, or really anything from the night we met, then he'll know. That night with him . . . it felt like falling in love.

Henry steps closer—so close that if I move an inch our bodies will be pressed together. He looks up and says, "You told me it was just a bit of fun."

His cheeks burn red, deep crimson against pale skin. I get the feeling he's reliving whatever he saw all over again. A sting of electricity zaps between us, and a painful, needy ache rides over me.

"Well, it was—"

"No," Henry says, shoving his hand against my heart.

His fingers scorch my chest through the fabric of my shirt. "You lied to me. All this time. Serena, what the hell? Why?"

"I ... I ..."

The look on Henry's face. He's angry, he's confused, he's upset. And I don't know what to say. How to explain it. *Well, Henry, I love my career. I love it more than love. I'm willing to give up anything for my career, including you. There isn't anything more important to me than discovering the fundamental laws of nature. There isn't anything more important than physics. Not love and not you.*

That's what I've told myself for years. That love obliterates common sense, ambition and achievement. That love is the antithesis of everything I want. That love would kill me and my dreams.

But now, after being Henry, I'm not so sure. I don't know what I think anymore.

My heart feels like a taffy being pulled in two directions, and soon it's going to break from the strain. I want my career, I want to be myself, and on the other hand, I want Henry. I've always wanted Henry. But the ripping, tugging—that struggle between what I want and what I shouldn't want? It stings and burns and tears. It hurts.

"Henry!" Kate yanks on my jacket, pulling my focus off Henry and onto her. "The bouquet toss. We're all waiting on Serena."

Henry blinks up at his sister, wiping away the tangled memories he was wrapped in and the heat of our discussion. "Sorry, what did you say?"

Kate grins, grabs Henry's arm, and says, "The bouquet toss! Archaic wedding tradition, all in good fun. All the ladies are there. If you catch it, you'll be the next married.

And Mum's praying it's you because she's wanted Henry married forever now and she likes you. We all do, even Lizzy, who is quite picky and typically prefers my corgis over Henry's girlfriends."

Kate drags Henry across the marquee toward the rose archway, where Olivia stands in the middle of hundreds of white roses holding her bouquet out like a prize. I trail after Kate and Henry, weaving past tables covered in crumb-filled plates and lipstick-stained wineglasses. Henry shoots a warning look over his shoulder—one that tells me he may have been detoured, but our conversation is not over.

"There she is!" Eugenia calls, and then Kate tugs Henry into a crowd of unmarried women. Lorna's in the crowd, elbowing Henry's cousin Fliss aside, and then Henry flashes me another look—one of "this is insane, are you seeing this?"—because the jostling and scuttling for position looks a bit like a rugby match played in pastel dresses and feathers. And then Olivia tosses the bouquet in the air and it arches and spins and tumbles and turns, and the women are jumping and reaching and elbowing and lunging, and Henry turns to me again, an appalled look on his face, when the bouquet smacks him on the side of the head and drops into his arms.

"Serena caught it!" Eugenia shouts gleefully. "I knew it!"

Kate laughingly shoves me toward Henry, women parting around me.

I stumble to a stop in front of him and he stares up at me, his feathered hat askew and his eyes wide as he grips the silk-bound bouquet. He looks a bit shell-shocked from getting whacked in the head by it, but maybe he's still stunned from the memory of us making love.

"Well done," I say, smiling down at him, trying to ignore everyone clapping and laughing and snapping pictures.

"Does this mean Miss Serena's getting married?" Maeve asks in a voice that carries across the tent.

"You bet!" Kate calls back jokingly.

"Kiss her," Olivia calls, because like I've always said, when people fall in love and get married, they want everyone else to fall in love and get married too. "Kiss her!"

And then the chant is taken up—*Kiss her, kiss her*—and even Maeve, the little traitor, and Grandma Myrtle join in.

"That's not necessary," I say, holding up my hands, trying to disarm the chant.

I don't want to kiss Henry. I can't kiss Henry. Besides, it would be weird, strange, unnatural to kiss Henry when Henry is me. That's like kissing yourself. Or . . . hmm. No. It's weird.

"No," I say.

Henry frowns at me, and I think everyone misinterprets it as embarrassment or annoyance, because Niall swaggers to the center of the group and proclaims, "Then I'll kiss her!"

He has a goofy, joking smile on his face and his reddish-gold hair glints under the twinkle lights. He leans forward, lips puckered. Henry lets out a squeak that sounds like Purrk when he's outraged at the lack of sausage in his food dish. Niall's eyes are closed, his lips extended. Henry swings the bouquet over his head like a claymore and wallops Niall, punching him with a mouthful of rose petals.

I shove a stunned Niall aside as everyone bursts into laughter.

"That'll show you, Niall!" Kate calls. "Serena only wants Henry! You're the wrong brother!"

Oh jeez.

"Kiss her, Henry!" Eugenia shouts, and then little Maeve joins in and the chant begins again.

I look down at Henry and he scowls up at me.

"It's just a kiss," I say, quietly enough that it can't be heard over the chanting.

"It's not just a kiss, and you know it," he says through smiling teeth, beaming at the crowd around us.

"Ready?" I ask.

"Fine."

He tilts his chin, leveling me with a gaze that lets me know he sees me, that he *knows*.

And so I take him in my arms, tug him close, amid cheers and whistles, and lean down, determined to give Henry a quick, passionless, closed-mouth peck on the lips. Enough of a kiss not to raise eyebrows, but also not enough to—well, be anything.

But then my mouth meets Henry's, my lips brush over his, and before I can pull away there's a jolt, a bolt of electricity, that punches me in the chest and stops my heart. My vision dims, the rose petal and champagne scent vanishes, and I'm left in a dark cavern, a black, empty space, where there isn't any sound or any light or anything at all.

There's just . . . us.

His hands grip my shoulders. He makes a small, need-filled noise. His lips whisper across mine, tasting of champagne and starlight, and then my heart kicks to life again and I rocket out of the dark space where it's just him and me, back into the dazzling bright light of the wedding.

"Now that was a kiss," Kate says.

"Well-snogged," Niall laughs.

"I hear wedding bells!" Grandma Myrtle crows.

A corgi yips in agreement.

And that's when I gaze down at Henry, disoriented and still spinning. He's still me. I'm still him. But for a second there, for just a moment, I thought we'd switched back.

His hands tighten on my shoulders, then he stands on his tiptoes and whispers, "I've figured it out. I know how we switch."

27

I SIT CROSS-LEGGED ON THE TIME-WORN RUG IN HENRY'S tower bedroom, Fitzy Butterbottom the only witness to our kiss. A waltz fraying at the edges drifts muffled through the lead pane window, and the gold-tinged light of the setting sun sprays across us, dappling us with champagne-colored warmth.

Henry's mouth is warm, apple-colored, and soft. He tastes of cake crumb and wedding toasts, and his lips are fleshy and yielding while mine are firm, slanting over his.

Henry sits on the floor across from me, cross-legged too, leaning forward, his hands in mine, his lips . . . pressed, waiting, waiting . . . waiting.

His sigh feathers across my lips and then he glances up at me, his mouth still against mine.

"It isn't working," he says, his words tickling my lips, vibrating over me.

He's right. There's no tumbling, no spinning, no falling into darkness, no switching.

However, there is that liquid warmth spilling over me

and filling me with a bright, luscious tingling that makes me dizzy and breathless and so out of my mind that all I want to do is tumble back on the floor, roll into a bed of rose petals, and lay Henry on top of me.

Which is when I pull back, because clearly I'm losing myself in this kiss.

A splash of cold air rushes between us, and I drop Henry's hands.

"Sorry," I say at the look of disappointment on his face.

A line appears between his eyebrows. "I thought it would work."

I nod.

"Do you remember how you always lecture anyone who will listen on the human mind being like the control panel on the Starship Enterprise?"

I scoff. "I don't lecture."

He lifts an eyebrow, so I shrug and let him continue. I'd rather talk about *Star Trek* than the memory of mine he experienced earlier.

"We humans," he says, "can only experience reality through our control panel. We have our five senses and that's how we interpret the world. I'd say we also have a sixth sense—our intuition. What we feel here." He points to his heart.

"Right."

"Our senses and our brain are the control panel of our ship. And just like a captain can navigate the ship from the control panel without ever looking through a window, so can we. But the captain would never mistake the readings on the control panel for the entirety of the universe. They wouldn't be so foolish to think the readings on their panel *are* the universe."

"Exactly. They wouldn't think it's the entirety of reality. And neither should we," I say.

"Just because we can't perceive it doesn't mean it's not out there. There is an infinity of things we can't perceive, that as humans we will never perceive—"

"And if we can't perceive them—"

"We can't conceive them," he says, having heard my "lecture" more than once.

I smile at him then ask, "You think what happened to us is something we can't conceive?"

"I think there's a good chance of it. If it was a side effect of the particle accelerator, then we wouldn't have felt what we did when we kissed earlier. I think the atom smashing was a red herring. You said yourself that the scam-artist psychic told you she's seen this before. I doubt they were smashing atoms when it happened."

"The ones who died," I say, and the golden light loses its rosy hue, turning stone-gray and evening-weak.

"We aren't going to die," Henry says. It's more a command than a statement. "We're going to figure it out."

He stares at me for a moment, not really seeing me, lost in thought. He drums his fingers against his knee, rustling the fabric of his dress. "It's as if we're walking along a rope, confined to the surface, when all of sudden ants walk along from the bottom-side and we think, 'What? There's another side!' But of course there's another side, another dimension to the rope. We can't walk on it, but ants can. I think it's the same thing. We only need to figure out how to flip the rope."

"But if we can't conceive it . . ."

Henry reaches over and grips my hand. "I've always believed one of the best things about humans is that we always strive, always hope, even when there isn't any reason to. Isn't that why we built the LHC? Isn't that why we keep searching for the answers to the universe? It's all right, Ducky. We'll find the answer."

I draw in a sharp breath. He hasn't called me Ducky since we first met. When I believed . . .

Well, when I believed things were only impossible until they weren't.

But then I met Henry and he became my impossible.

"I didn't think you remembered that name."

"I liked Ducky. She was . . ." He sighs, shifts on the carpet.

Outside the accordions wheeze to a festive finale and there's cheering and whistles. We've been gone ten minutes. Soon we'll be missed and will have to head back down. Henry peers at me from under his eyelashes, and between us a stream of sunlight carries dust motes on its current.

"You liked her. But . . ." I leave the question in the air, letting it drift like the specks of dust floating between us.

Henry could easily brush it aside and ignore it. Instead he says, "You fell in love. That night. It wasn't just me. You fell in love too."

I hold very still, barely breathing, as the quiet of the stone-walled room sinks over us. I wait for noise from outside, laughter or another song, but I'm captured in stillness.

Henry's hand curls in mine, his warmth whispering over me. "Serena, you felt what I felt, and then you . . . you . . ."

"Told you it was only fun."

"When it wasn't," he says. "And you knew it. What I saw, your memory, it was . . ." He looks at me, his cheeks flushed, his eyes burning with a flame I recognize.

"Perhaps you misunderstood the memory."

"No. There's nothing to misunderstand."

My stomach drops and I tug my hand free. I turn away and look at the comically menacing stance of Fitzy, the ancient suit of armor. Behind me the white bed sheets are still rumpled and the soft scent of mint and apples teases me.

Mint.

And apple.

My stomach rolls again and I'm short of breath, like I'm plunging down a raging waterfall in a barrel about to sink into the frothing rapids, because I've just realized. I've finally put it together.

"I was your first time!"

Henry looks as if I just surprise-kicked him in the head and he's trying to shake out of the shock. "What?"

"You and me!" I thrust my finger between us. "That memory of boobs that makes me rock-hard like a horny fifteen-year-old every single time I get a flash of it. That was your first time. With me!"

Oh gosh.

I got aroused at a memory of my own boobies. Whhhhhhy?

Henry stands then, quick as flash, and scowls down at me defensively. "And?"

Oh no.

I'm right. That explicit, erotic, incredible memory that keeps flashing in my mind is Henry's recollection of making love *with me*.

I flush hot. Flames lick over my skin. I tug at my collar. "I can't believe this."

"What? Why? Are women the only ones allowed to be virgins? They're the only ones who can have a first time?"

Henry glares at me, arms cross over his chest, pink dress flaring around him. The fuchsia hat tilts precariously, the feathers bobbing.

I stand too, feeling ridiculous for sitting cross-legged on the rug while he scowls down at me, a petite pink-dress-wearing woman angry at the injustice of virginity politics.

Well, I'm upset too. "You should've told me!"

"I did," he says. "I said, I don't ever do this."

"'I don't ever do this' is a million miles away from 'I've *never* done this.'"

He lifts up his hands. "Fine. Yes. Thank you, Ducky. You took my virginity and then you broke my heart. How's that? Now I've told you!"

Henry's chest heaves, his cheeks pinken, and he looks like the epitome of a spurned innocent, deflowered and unjustly tossed aside by the philandering rake, a.k.a. tall, handsome, manly me.

For crying out loud.

And . . . oh no. Are those tears? Is he crying?

"Don't cry," I say, holding out my hand. "Henry, don't cry."

Henry sniffs. "I'm not. I never cry."

A tear slips from the corner of his eye, falling down his cheek and leaving a trail of mascara. Another tear falls and Henry sniffs, his lips wobbling.

"I don't ever cry," he says, shaking his head. He wipes at his wet cheeks, smearing the mascara, and gives a little hiccup-sob. He looks at me, pure mortification in his expression. "I don't cry."

And that's when I remember the date, and I know exactly why Henry is crying. "I'm really sorry, but you do now."

Henry is about to experience all the wonderful joys of my menstrual cycle. It should hit tomorrow or the next day, right after he's had a crying jag, a load of cramps, bloating, and extreme cravings for peanut butter and chocolate.

"Serena?"

I walk to the desk, grab a tissue, then decide on the entire box. Knowing my cycle, he'll probably need it. I once went through two boxes of tissues the night before my period while watching *The Wrath of Khan*.[1]

I hand him the box and he mumbles a thank-you, then he noisily blows his nose. I look away, frowning at that leering suit of armor. What a Peeping Tom. He's privy to all sorts of drama, isn't he?

"Are you all right?" I ask after Henry's had a moment to dab his eyes and blow his nose.

He nods. "I don't know what happened. Sorry."

Should I tell him?

Yes? No?

Maybe we'll switch back by the morning.

"My period is due," I blurt out.

Henry's hand drops and the tissue flutters to the floor.

"That's why you're crying." I shrug. "Sorry."

His hand curls, fingers closing around the tissue box. But then his grip relaxes. He takes a deep breath and says, "You never told me why you lied about that night. I want to understand. Let me understand."

It clicks then. Maybe if I tell him, if we understand each other, we'll switch back and we can put all this behind us. I can go back to my life. Henry can go to Chicago. Maybe it wasn't the kiss that made us almost switch back. Maybe it was the growing understanding between us.

I nod. "All right. I asked my friends at the pub to help . . . dissuade you, because . . ."

Henry waits, his chin tilted, cheeks covered in smeared mascara and tear stains. I don't want to hurt him, at least not more than I already have, but if he has to understand . . .

"I don't want love. I've never wanted love. Feeling anything for you was a complication I didn't want. You saw one flash of one moment. You didn't get the aftermath when all I wanted was to leave. I realized you were going to be working with me and I didn't want anything to go further, so I . . . put a stop to it. I'm sorry it was so, well, badly done. I can't go back. I would if I could. I'd tell you thank you, but no thank you. I think love ruins people, it kills them and their individuality, it takes away their dreams and robs them of their careers. I think love is a mistake. So . . . that's about all you need to know to understand me."

I nod, feeling sick to my stomach, as if I've just swallowed spoiled milk and it's burning my throat and curdling on its way down. I want to throw up, especially with the way Henry's looking at me.

It's the way he looked at me that night at The Cock and Bull when I turned him away. It's how he looked at me the first day he saw me at ATLAS. It's not at all like the warm, laughing expression he's had since we switched. The expression that's been there to comfort me and reassure me and make sure I keep hope.

"I'm sorry," I say, my voice—no, Henry's voice— breaking. "It's not pretty, but it's me."

Henry shakes his head, the fuchsia feathers drooping listlessly. "Do you know why I'm leaving ATLAS?"

I don't. And I'm not sure I want to know either.

"It's because I can't keep coming to work every day seeing you. I thought I could. I thought I'd get over you. But I didn't. Seeing you every day, watching you work in your messy, chaotic office, arguing with you over theories, listening to your convoluted stories about *Star Trek*, hearing your laughter in the hallways, smelling your mint-and-apple perfume in the break room and knowing you'd just been there—it didn't make me get over you. It made me fall even more in love. Every damn day. I can't keep on. I couldn't keep on. That's why I wanted to go to windy, cold, not-enough-tea-to-warm-you Chicago. Because it hurt falling in love. At first it felt like flying, then it just felt like falling and crashing over and over and over again. But now . . ." He holds out his hand. "Now I'm here. You're here. And it's still the same. I love you, and you . . ."

He waits for me to say something. Anything.

To say, I love you too.

I fell in love that night and I haven't stopped.

But I can't. It wouldn't be true.

"I'm sorry," I whisper, my voice a desert, barren and dry.

We stand in shrouded silence, the gray light of dusk folding around us. If I could cry, I would, but like Henry says, he never cries.

Instead I reach out, take a tissue, and wipe the mascara and tear tracks from Henry's face. "I never meant to hurt you. I like you, very much, but I can't love you. I made a mistake, but since then I've only tried to do the right thing."

Henry reaches up and closes his fingers around my wrist. My pulse throbs beneath his hand. I pause, leave the tissue pressed to his cheek.

"It's funny," he says. "Sometimes we can do everything right, not make a single mistake, and we still fail. We can do everything right and still lose everything."

"Maybe. But not this time. You said we'll figure it out, and I promised you that you wouldn't lose your family or yourself."

He drops my wrist then. Breaks our connection. "Right."

I sigh, stepping back.

A ringing chime sounds from my luggage. I turn toward the noise.

It's my phone—the ringtone for my parents.

They call twice a month: the second and fourth Sundays at 4 p.m. Geneva time. We talk for exactly thirty minutes. My parents update me on the shows they're watching, my dad's projects around the house, and what my mom will cook for Sunday dinner.

This isn't the second or the fourth Sunday of the month, and it's not 4 p.m. Geneva time.

I hand Henry the phone, a niggling fear sprouting in my chest.

"It's my parents. Can you please answer it?"

His brow wrinkles at the tension in my voice, but then he nods. "Hello?"

His face freezes, becoming as smooth as ice, his stance like a statue. He stands still, makes a noise, then another, and then he says, "Yes. I'm coming. I'll be there."

When he turns to me I take a step back, frightened of what he's about to say.

It reminds me of when I was a kid, four years old. I had a pet hamster. I named her Sally and I carried her in my coat pocket, stroking her soft fur and wrapping my hand around her warmth. I fed her pellets and sang her made-up songs and told her she was my best friend. Then one morning when I woke up she was lying in her wood shavings, and she was stiff and cold. My dad came in while I was standing there poking and prodding her, trying to get her to wake up. There was something that I knew but didn't want to acknowledge. But when I looked up at my dad and saw the lines around his mouth and the grave expression in his eyes, I knew. I knew, but I thought if I could keep him from saying it, it wouldn't be true. That it was the words that made it happen. It took me a long time to forgive my dad for saying, "She's dead."

It's like that now. My heart pounds, my skin is clammy, and sweat beads and slides in cold fingers down my neck. Henry looks at me with knowledge in his eyes—knowledge I don't want spoken. But I'm older now, and I know saying it out loud or not saying it out loud doesn't change the reality.

"What?" I say, my lips numb.

"It was your dad," he says. "Your mom had a heart attack. She's in surgery. He asked that you come. They don't know if she'll make it."

28

I'M ONE OF THE LUCKY ONES. THOSE PEOPLE WHO MAKE IT far in life and never set foot in a hospital.

Hospitals are a foreign country I've never needed a passport for. There isn't a single stamp in my book. Not a broken arm, not a blood draw, not a grandparent lost or a parent sick.

I've only seen hospitals portrayed in movies or shows, which means I've always thought of them as places where:

1. Stunningly attractive doctors rush down halls to the blaring of "Code Blue!" "Code Green!" "Code Chartreuse!" while intense music crescendos and a fragile woman with a gushing wound but a pretty face desperately needs help (a.k.a. dramatic doctor edition).

—OR—

2. Doctors and nurses jab at each other, pranking and joking in jovial conviviality, sometimes treating patients but mostly gossiping about their lives to the sound of a laugh track (a.k.a. comedy clinic edition).

—OR—

3. Heartthrob overworked doctors seek out supply closets, abandoned stairwells, and empty patient rooms where they are *constantly* having quickies, longies, and other hot-and-heavy sexathons (a.k.a. horny hospital edition).

That's my knowledge of hospitals: drama, comedy, or horndog. What can I say? This is the media's portrayal of hospital life. And who am I to argue?

But now here I am, jet-lagged, weary-boned, and scratchy-eyed, striding down a painfully bright fluorescent-lit hallway, Henry barely able to keep up with my ground-eating strides.

There aren't any dramatic scenes or "Code Chartreuse!" blaring over the sound system. Instead there is the droning buzz of air vents, the gasping squeak of wheeled beds pushed by slope-shouldered attendants, the high-pitched, plaintive beep of monitors emitting from open rooms, a weak, phlegmy cough, a moan, a hushed voice, and a sharp laugh. The hospital noises scrape over my skin like a knife over an open wound.

There isn't comedy either. Most of the people here, the visitors, walk timidly and unsure, reminding me of that old chant, *Step on a crack, break your momma's back.*

They are quiet, careful, as if stepping on the seam of one of the ugly linoleum tiles will break the spell keeping their loved one alive. Even the staff, dressed in teal scrubs or white coats, lanyards jostling, are perfunctory and purposeful, like keys clicking steadily on a keyboard.

And the sex? Well, I haven't peeked into supply closets or poked my head in empty rooms, but the sterile air, dry atmosphere, and tension tinged with exhaustion? It isn't exactly a fertile field for fornication if that's what you're wondering.

So all the shows were wrong, and now the reality drags across me, a curtain scraping over its metal rod, closing out all the false stories.

The lights wash over the long hallway, giving it a harsh antiseptic tint that matches the sting of sanitizer and alcohol in the air. The taste rides bitter on my tongue, and the dry hospital air bites at my bloodshot, tired eyes.

The halls of the hospital are almost as long as some of ours at CERN, but they don't have the same feel—that of magic and wonder and exploration. No. The halls here remind me of tunnels carved in an ant hill, deep underground and hidden from the light. There is no sun, and if a thunderstorm comes and the anthill floods, the only way out is by dying.

Henry takes a half-jog, half-step to keep up with me. His eyes are blue-rimmed, dark from lack of sleep. He looks worse than I did after pulling two all-nighters in a row during a particularly hellacious exam week during grad school.

We've been traveling for nearly thirty hours, having left Henry's family shortly after my dad called. When we left Henry hugged his mom for seconds longer than necessary, his arms tight as if he thought he might not see her again. Eugenia gave him a surprised pat, and said, "There, there, your mom will get sorted. The doctors will fix her right up." And then we sped to London, Henry driving like his rally navigator dad, cutting through traffic, speeding past roadblocks, swerving around diversions, shifting skillfully, gunning the engine. Two flights later, another rental car, and a long, speedy drive northward up the winding, fog-shrouded coastal road, and here we are. Exhausted, hungry, and in need of a shower, a change of clothes, and a bed, but here.

I glance down at Henry, giving him the flickering of a grateful smile. He nods, giving a quick tilt of his chin. I told him everything he might need to know to be me. To be me for my mom.

I stop at a tall gray laminate desk, where the attendant downstairs directed us. Behind the desk a young woman stares at a computer screen, clicking the mouse, ignoring Henry and me. I put my hand on the cold laminate, ignoring the hand sanitizer and the poster for handwashing and hygiene, and clear my throat.

"I'm looking for Caroline Otaki. Room 3047."

"Are you family?" she asks, giving me a quick cursory glance lacking interest or warmth. "Visits are restricted to family only on this floor."

I nod. "Yes, I'm . . ."

I stop. I'm not. I'm not family. I'm Henry Joule, British, male, 6'1", thirteen stone. My mother's Eugenia Joule, my father Charles Joule.

In no way am I related to my actual mom.

The woman takes her hand from the keyboard and waits for me to continue.

Down the long hall of rooms, somewhere on this

floor, is my mom. She was thousands of miles away, and now she's only dozens of feet. Yet she may as well be across an ocean if I can't see her.

I know my mom won't know me. She'll think I'm Henry. I won't be able to tell her I love her. I won't be able to tell her I'm sorry for not visiting in two years or for running off into the world and leaving her and dad behind. I won't be able to tell her to get better because if she doesn't I'll be angry with her, so angry, even if she's gone and you aren't supposed to be angry with the departed.

But still. I didn't think I'd be blocked from even seeing her face.

"Yes," Henry says, stepping beside me, leaning into me. "I'm Caroline's daughter, Serena Otaki. This is my husband. We're family." Henry stops and brushes his fingers over mine, a steadying, reassuring touch. "Where's her room?"

His voice is soft, gentle, with that California accent firmly in place.

I hold my breath, my mind a tangle of yes and no and yes.

And then we're on our way down the hall with twenty minutes left during visiting hours.

Before we step into my mom's room, I tug on Henry's hand, pull him back to me, and trap him in a circle as if we're still slow-dancing back in England. A nurse hurries past, her shoes thudding on the floor. She barely gives us a passing glance.

"What?" Henry whispers.

My mom's door is only five feet away. It's open, and the sounds of a TV show on low-volume filter into the hall.

I study him. The purple smudges under his brown eyes, the wrinkled, travel-worn buttercup-yellow wrap dress I packed for the post-wedding celebration, the mess of his hair tucked in a low bun. What will my parents think when they see him? That he's tired, yes. That he's rumpled, yes. That he loves them?

I reach out and tuck the flyaways and loose strands of hair behind Henry's ears, then I straighten the wrinkled dress over his shoulders.

He stands still, watching me with a solemn gaze.

"Please." I clear my throat, dropping my hands. "Will you please tell my mom I love her? Please say . . . please say, 'I love you.' I know you don't know her. I know you won't mean it. But if you could—"

"Yes. Of course."

I take a breath, ignoring the tinge of antiseptic. "Thank you."

He nods, giving me a small smile.

And suddenly I know exactly how Henry felt when he faced his family as me. When I saw him standing outside the circle of their love looking like a boat adrift at sea without the stars to guide him.

I'm about to see my mom. She might die. She might live. But I'll be outside of it all. Unknown. Unseen.

Henry studies the expression on my face. A light of compassion flickers in his eyes, then he reaches out and folds his hand around mine. His fingers thread through my own, sewing us together. Once I would've been terrified of the feeling—the feeling that our hearts are being stitched together one moment at a time—but now, here in this moment, I can only be grateful that he's here.

Then we walk into my mom's room together.

29

THE MURMUR OF THE TELEVISION, THE *PING PING* OF AN electronic monitor, and the rustle of starched hospital sheets greets us. The room is small, claustrophobic. There's a narrow plastic-framed bed, a blue plastic chair, a laminate counter with cupboards, and a wall-mounted TV with a whiteboard under it that says in green marker, "Hello, my name is Althea. I'm your nurse today."

The ever-present hospital antiseptic smell is clouded by the strong aroma of my dad's favorite coffee—a habit I picked up from him—mellow and soothing and sweet.

The scent of it mixed with chemical antiseptic makes my throat clench and the back of my eyes burn.

I hover at the doorway, a specter outside my family's circle.

Henry kneels at my mom's bedside, his hand gripping hers, while she brushes his hair back from his face just like she did when I was a kid, trembling from nightmares and unable to sleep.

"It's okay," she says, her voice as thin and crackly as a

dried-out leaf crumbling in winter. "It's okay. I'm fine. I'm fine."

I watch her hand shake as she smooths his hair back. There's a needle, a tube, tape on the back of that hand. It pulls her skin tight as she soothes him, thinking that he's me.

I grip the cold doorframe and stay still and quiet, giving her this moment without the intrusion of a stranger.

My dad stands next to Henry, his hand on Henry's shoulder gripping him tightly. When we stepped into the room Henry went to my parents. The reception wasn't a joyful, chaotic tumble like I had in England. Instead it was like the painful, jagged inhale of a person after they've held their breath underwater too long. I don't think my parents saw me—they were too consumed by hugging Henry and reassuring him everything was well, even though to me nothing looked well.

My mom never looked like me. Or, I should say, I never looked like my mom. She has wispy blonde hair, pale blue eyes, and fragile pinkish skin that bruises and cuts at the smallest provocation. She is the reflection of the moon wavering in a shallow mountain stream. And me, I've always looked like the night sky. Brown-black eyes, black hair, luminescent skin. Now, watching Henry murmur a response to my dad's question—"Out of London. Two stops,"—I see what I always missed before.

I look like my mom in subtle ways. The line of my jaw. The tilt of my nose. How my fingers taper and my lips curl at the corners. And something else. It's an unspoken thing, maybe an unseen thing, but it's there nonetheless, a whisper that says "mother and daughter."

It's so subtle I'm not surprised it took me viewing it through another pair of eyes to notice it.

My mom looks to me then, in response to something Henry said. She blinks in surprise—so she hadn't noticed me—and then she takes me in. I push away from the doorframe, step into the confines of the hospital room, and offer a tentative smile.

My mom has a maze of clear plastic tubes running from her—from her arms, her nose, her chest—so that my own skin feels punctured and tight in response, and I want to rub my chest to take away the ache I imagine in hers.

"This is Henry Joule," Henry says, glancing between me and my mom and dad. "Henry, this is my mom, Caroline, and my dad, Matt."

My mom's brow puckers, and she lifts a hand worriedly to her tangled, wispy hair and then to the taped, bandaged incision on her chest. Color infuses her pale grayish cheeks and she sends Henry a reproachful look.

I don't want my mom to feel awkward or shamed by her appearance, so I bend down, give Henry's disarming smile, and say in my best British accent, "I'm sorry I look a shambles. I promise, Mrs. Otaki, I clean up well. Perhaps when you're better you'll let me prove it."

And with that, my mom's gaze softens. She skims her eyes over my thick, unshaven stubble, my bruised, now yellow-green black eye, my finger-raked hair, and my rumpled clothes. I'm a mess, and now she's at ease.

My dad, on the other hand, is not.

"Excuse me. Who are you?" he asks, stepping between Henry and me and eyeing me up and down.

I bite back the sudden urge to grin at my dad. Even in

the hospital, with my mom post-coronary bypass surgery, he still has to play protective dad for his only daughter. But seeing the tension around his mouth, the worry in his eyes, and the tightness in his shoulders, I think maybe he needs this as a distraction.

"Henry Joule," I say, holding out my hand.

My dad grips it in his, and then he pumps my hand and proceeds to try to crush my bones into dust. Actual dust. *Ow. Ouch. Ow ow owowowow.*

"Matt Otaki," my dad says, watching my reaction to his pulverizing palm shake.

My dad is giving me the manshake, the alpha grip, the jeez-it-hurts. I smile at him, hiding a wince, and continue to shake his hand.

Henry looks between us, comprehension in his eyes. I suppose he knows a hand-crusher when he sees one.

"He's Henry, my boyfriend," Henry says. "He's a colleague at CERN and—"

My dad finally lets go of my hand. He slaps me on the arm, a bit harder than friendly. "Let's get a coffee, Henry," he interrupts. "Leave Serena and her mom to talk."

I resist the urge to shake out my tingling hand.

I glance at Henry and he gives a subtle nod. He's okay if I go.

"Coffee," my dad repeats.

"All right, sounds good," I say, even though it doesn't and what I'd really like is to sit by my mom, hold her hand, and drink a steaming-hot cup of tea.

As my dad leads me out of the cramped room, my mom murmurs, "I'm so glad you're here. I love you, Ducky."

And Henry whispers back, "I love you too, Mom."

I leave them then, letting my mom's words fall around

me, knowing I can pick them up and remember them whenever I like.

I stride down the hall, my dad next to me. Once we're out of the room his shoulders fall and he seems to diminish. He looks worn, exhausted. But that only lasts for a moment. As we turn the corner, following the signs for the waiting area and vending machines, my dad straightens and levels a piercing gaze on me.

"So, Henry. Why did you come here with my daughter? That's a serious step, international travel, visiting her mother in the hospital. It's not something a man does lightly."

Oh gosh.

You're telling me.

My dad, Matt Otaki, has always seemed tall, stocky, powerful. Now, with me as Henry, he's about four inches shorter than me and less bulky than I remember. He has silver in his black hair, sun-browned wrinkles on his forehead, and the air of a man just past his physical prime but still in charge of everything he surveys. And now he's leveling a cool gaze on me, waiting for my response.

All I want to do is give him a tight hug and have him tell me everything is going to be okay. But that isn't an option.

"Well," I say, wondering what exactly my dad wants to know, "I care about Serena. Very much. I want to support her . . . and you and M—" I stutter, almost say Mom, and then finish, "Mrs. Otaki."

My dad gives me a sardonic look—one I've never received from him before.

"I don't doubt that, Henry." Although, honestly, it sounds like he does.

We round the corner and spill into a small square waiting area. There are two gray vinyl couches, a smattering of fake potted trees, and a few ugly paintings of lighthouses and sailboats to liven up the gray wallpaper. On the wall next to the TVs are two vending machines. One has snacks, all unhealthy food that shouldn't be in a hospital, and the other has coffee, hot cocoa, and tea.

Thank goodness. Tea.

My dad jangles the change in the pocket of his khakis and scowls at the machine. "The coffee is bad, but I finished what I brought from home. What do you like?"

I glance at the machine then back at my dad. "Tea with milk and sugar."

That would fix things. It'd be heavenly. It could cure the jet lag. It could sooth the raw, scraping feeling lodged in my throat. It'd make everything better.

"You want tea?" My dad looks at me like I'm a stray dog that just peed on his shoe.

Okay. Maybe tea wouldn't make everything better.

"Coffee?" I ask.

My dad nods. "Good choice, Henry."

He drops a dollar in quarters into the machine and jabs the button for black coffee. A foam cup drops from the machine, is grabbed by metals claws, and then an anemic whirring noise sputters as a thin black trail leaks into it.

The smell is chemical-bitter and *not tea*.

"How long have you and my daughter been dating?"

I watch the liquid stream patter into the cup. We're the only people in the waiting room, probably because it's depressing and smells like dirty socks and spoiled creamer.

"Um, we had our first date two years ago."

Technically true. Although it was our first and last date.

"That's interesting. Serena never mentioned you. Why do you think that is?"

Ha.

"I couldn't say. We only became serious recently. She came with me to my brother's wedding, and I suppose we felt it was time to . . . commit."

My dad lets out a stiff huff—the kind he would give me when I hadn't cleaned my room well or when I didn't finish my broccoli. "What do you mean, commit?"

"Date."

"You're already dating."

"Um, exclusively."

My dad shakes his head. He grabs the foam cup out of the machine and thrusts it into my hand. "No milk. No sugar. What do you do for a living?"

I take the cup and the hot coffee burns my fingers through the thin foam. "I work at CERN with Serena, we're on the same team," I smile. I can talk about work.

"Uh-huh," my dad interrupts. "Are you planning on marrying my daughter?"

I choke on the bit of lava-hot coffee I managed to sip. I wheeze and cough while my dad watches me with one raised eyebrow.

Oh jeez, that's where I got that annoying habit from.

"I see," he says, then he jams more quarters into the machine and punches the coffee button. Then he levels me with a wrathful dad gaze. "So you aren't planning on marrying my daughter. That leaves one thing, and being men, we both know what it is."

Oh no.

No, no, no.

I am not having the "don't poke my daughter before marriage or I'll castrate you" conversation with my dad.

"I didn't say that. Marriage is nice. It's good. Great. I mean, who wouldn't want to marry Serena? Every man who meets her wants to marry her. She's . . ." I hold up a hand, motioning in the air, trying to come up with a suitable word, and then I realize it looks as if I'm doing that boob-grab, great titties motion.

My dad's face turns a furious shade of purply red.

I choke on another cough and drop my hand, hiding it behind my back.

"Why, you little—" My dad looks at me as if I've lost my mind, calling me on my apparent pervy player vibes.

"No, I mean . . . I don't believe in intimacy before marriage," I say quickly. "I'm . . . like a monk. Abstinent. Serena and I have a pure love. Soulful . . . and pure. I'm abstinent."

Sorry, Henry.

My dad perks up and his wrathful expression shifts to one more good-natured. He considers my expression then nods. "That so? You have good intentions?"

I nod. Uh-huh.

Gosh, I have a renewed appreciation for Bernie Berger and all my other high-school and college boyfriends who met my dad. I never quite understand why they looked shell-shocked if I ever left them alone with him. Now I do.

He watches his coffee slowly sputtering from the vending machine, then he says, "How much debt do you have?"

"What?"

"Debt. Credit card. Student loans. Mortgage. Car

payment. Personal loans. Bills. If you're serious about my daughter, I don't want her involved with someone in debt up to his eyeballs."

I shake my head. I have no idea. "Not much."

"Define not much."

I make up a reasonable number. "A monthly car payment. Credit cards paid off each month. I'm British. I believe in optimistic pessimism, not debt."

He scowls at that. "Do you own your own home, or rent?"

"I own," I say, remembering Henry's orderly apartment, soothing and organized beautifully.

And then the rapid-fire interrogation begins.

"Are your parents still married?"

"Yes."

"Siblings?"

"Two brothers, two sisters."

"Oldest, youngest, middle?"

"I'm the oldest."

"Career ambitions?"

"Many."

"Doctorate?"

"Yes."

My dad's questions rain down on me like a barrage of bullets, and I answer as quickly as I can, dodging from one question to the next.

"Speeding tickets?"

"Rare."

"Criminal record?"

"Yes."

Oops. I didn't mean to admit that. Henry told me the story on the plane, trying to cheer me up.

My dad does a double take. "For what?"

"I was stripped and wrapped with cling wrap to a parking meter while drunk in university and, well, many people decided to drop coins into the cling wrap instead of the parking meter, and—"

My dad waves his hand, dismissing Henry's criminal past. "Prison time?"

"None."

"Where'd you get the shiner?"

"My best friend."

He doesn't even blink at that.

"Gambler?"

"Only at work, when it comes to science."

"Drugs?"

"No."

"Alcohol?"

"Occasionally."

"Smoke?"

"Never."

"Have you been married? Engaged? Divorced?"

"None of the above."

"Will you treat my daughter right? Always put her first? Make her happiness your priority?"

Awww. Dad.

"Yes to all of the above."

"Good."

"Good?" Does this mean the interrogation is over?

My dad nods and claps me on the shoulder, this time a friendly cuff. "Good. Thanks for coming. Serena will need a shoulder to lean on. She loves her mom a lot even if she doesn't always show it. Don't let her down."

"Thank you. I won't," I say, feeling a rush of affection for my dad. He loves me. He wants to make sure Henry isn't a douche.

My dad grabs his foam cup from the vending machine, takes a long swig of the steaming liquid, grimaces at the terrible flavor, and then, cool as you please, says, "By the way, Henry, it goes without saying. Hurt my daughter and I'll break both your legs, your arms, your fingers, and both thumbs so that abstinence becomes a permanent state for you." My mouth falls open as my dad cheerfully adds, "Enjoy the coffee."

30

"I THINK IT'S NICE," HENRY SAYS, GLANCING OVER AT ME AS I wend our rental car down the old country road leading to my childhood home. "Your dad concerned about you breaking my heart. Using me as a plaything. If only he'd talked to you two years ago, before you popped my cherry and tossed me aside."

The corner of Henry's lip lifts in a teasing smile. I know what he's doing—he's trying to distract me, loosen the tight rope around my throat and make me laugh. But since we left the hospital, when my mom kissed Henry goodbye and smiled at me absently, I've had a heavy weight in my stomach that feels like a lead ball leaking doubt and worry into my bloodstream.

We've been driving for an hour and the ball hasn't dissipated. Instead it feels as if it's settled inside me and burrowed in for a nice long stay.

"Serena?" Henry asks, tentatively touching the back of my hand.

I nod and smile. "Yeah. He's a good dad."

I look at Henry out of the corner of my eye. In thirty minutes we'll be at the cedar cabin in the woods that I grew up in. A tiny two-bedroom home built in the 1920s when "luxury" and "cabin" weren't two words that belonged together. My dad added indoor plumbing and a bathroom when they bought the cabin back in the nineties for exactly eight thousand dollars. Which probably tells you exactly as much as you need to know. It's a "project" house and always has been.

We've long made our way from the coast, driving away from the cobalt-blue ocean waves capped with white froth and the noise of the ocean's steady crash and roar relentlessly beating against the meadow-topped bluffs. We've left the rocky shorelines dressed in sheets of pearly-gray fog. We've left behind the howling winds, the salted sea-spray, the tide pools that hold an entire ecosystem of crabs, sea urchins, and anemones dependent on the ebb and flow of their sanctuary waters. Gone is the keening silence of the brown pelicans and the piercing, plaintive keer of the murrelet. And gone is the hospital.

Now we're in the deep woods where cedar and fir live, where the redwood have stood as silent sentinels for centuries. I've always wondered what the redwood who have lived for two thousand years think of humans. They watch us flash in and out, bright like fireflies, lighting for a second and then disappearing in the dark. Do they know we're here? Sometimes when I turn my gaze skyward, unable to see to their treetops, I feel just as small as I do when I stare up at the stars. A lone human in the vastness of the universe. Some might think this is a depressing feeling, but for me, it's only ever left me filled with awe and wonder.

Outside the car window the road is a flat gray, with cracks, potholes, and gravel, giving way to the roots and rends of the encroaching forest. The cracks are familiar, the *thum-thum-thump* of the tires over the uneven road soothing in its jarring familiarity. Every day for years I took this road to school, to swim team, to the grocery store with my mom.

The sky, a pale pearl-white tinged with the faintest smudge of blue, peeks through the towering redwoods. The cabin is only a few miles away now, but suddenly the thought of going inside without my mom being there makes the ball in my stomach twist in revolt.

I pull to the side of the road, gravel crunching under the tires. There's a small trailhead just off the road, unmarked and unused, except by locals.

"Do you mind?" I ask Henry. "I know we should sleep, but I need a minute."

"Of course," he says, following me out of the car and onto the dry, caramel-colored needles that litter the ground.

I step onto the trail. The needles crackle underfoot and the scent of home hits me. Except it doesn't smell like home, because I'm not me right now. I suppose when scent retrieves memory you have to be in your body for it to work its magic. Because now the smell of the forest is new. It's redwood, a teasing scent that floats in and out, mysterious and spiced with a hint of sweetness. It's not heavy like cedar or loud like fir. Instead, smelling it for the first time as Henry, it reminds me of the faint hint of a woman's perfume after she's left a room, there and then not.

I walk along the trail, Henry silent, following close behind. This section of forest is filled with interspersed redwoods. One redwood alone is enough to take your breath away, but a forest of them can soothe your soul. I've always known this, I've just forgotten.

Leaving home, living in another country, settling into adulthood—all of that can make you forget the wisdom of your childhood.

So I step over the matted-needle forest floor, catching sight of a banana slug trudging along and spying the tail of a deer as it flashes past, darting behind a wide trunk. I listen for the gurgle of the forest stream, the water flowing over slippery rocks along fern-lined banks. The stream has always sounded like softly murmured conversation, and when I hear the chatter I smile.

The air is cool. A wet mist always hangs in the forest, and goose bumps rise on my arms at the wet chill. The redwoods grow thicker, reaching toward the sky, hundreds of feet into the air. Their bark is deep, grooved canyons that I once loved to run my hands over, exploring the rough textures. They block nearly all the light, settling a dim hush over the forest, broken only by our feet crunching over the dry needles and the call of the stream.

Then the trees open, the sky shines through, and a trail of sunshine breaks the mist and shines through the redwoods, lighting their bark in reds and golds. I pause in a spray of sunshine just at the stream's edge and bend down to dip my hand in the water. The cold shocks my skin like burying your hand in a pile of snow. I let the water run over my fingers and watch a red-bellied newt slip by.

Henry kneels down next to me, a deep green fern brushing against his arm. "I . . ." He looks around and takes a breath. "I know . . . I remember . . . this . . ." He can't seem to put into words what he's feeling, but I know. I felt the same thing at his home.

"I know," I say, pulling my hand from the cold water.

"You loved it here," he says, "in this place."

I nod. Sit back on my haunches. Then, when the fatigue of being awake for nearly two days straight threatens to crush me, I lie back on the soft ground.

Towering above, taller than church spires and skyscrapers, the redwoods extend to the sky.

Henry studies me for a moment and then settles down on the ground next to me, his side tucked next to mine. I stare at the sky—at the glimpse of an eagle wheeling overhead, barely visible through the spiring trees.

"Henry?" I ask, my deep voice rumbling over the tumbling gurgle of the stream.

"Hmm?"

"Will my mom be okay?"

He stills at my question, then very slowly he reaches over and takes my hand. His grip is reassuring, steady, a quiet show of support.

The ball of doubt in my stomach eases, and when he moves closer and drops his head into the crook of my arm, it completely dissipates. All the worry and doubt lifts away like a leaf swept down the forest stream.

"I'd like to switch back now," I tell him, staring up at the flickering shadow and light. "Before I didn't want it enough. Now I very badly would like to switch back. I want to be there for my mom."

Henry squeezes my hand. "I know."

My eyes are dry when I ask, "Was it this hard for you at the wedding?"

Instead of answering, he says, "How about we make each other a promise?"

"What?"

"We take care of each other. When we're happy, like at the wedding, or when we're hurt, like now. We take of each other as best we can."

"I already promised that," I say, looking down at him.

He rubs his thumb over the knuckles of my hand, tracing the furrows and the grooves, setting a soothing rhythm. "I wish we could switch back too," he says quietly. "Your mom told me she's proud of you. And she's grateful you came. And she loves you. You deserve to hear that. Not me."

I wrap my arm around Henry's back and pull him closer against me. The warm, reddish-golden glow of the sun blankets us, and overhead a forest butterfly flits past, darting between shadow and light.

It's magic. This place feels like magic.

"Do you mind if we rest here for a while? Maybe the forest will work some magic."

Henry lifts up on his forearms, gazing at me with dark, solemn eyes. Pulled to him, drawn into the warmth of him, I reach up and brush my lips across his.

It's not a kiss. It's sunlight stroking over skin. It's butterfly wings stirring the air. It's the murmured caress of a forest stream. It's over before it's begun.

Henry sighs, his lips soft, gentle against mine.

Then we drop back to the forest floor, the scent of earthy spice rising. Henry settles into the groove of my shoulder, wraps his arms around my middle, tangles his legs with mine, and presses his cheek to my heart. His hand is warm in mine.

"A few minutes," he says sleepily. "We'll sleep for a few minutes and then go."

His eyelids flutter closed, and in seconds his chest is rising and falling in the steady rhythm of sleep.

I stare at the cathedral of redwoods for long minutes wishing, *Switch back, switch back, switch back* . . . If the particle accelerator can't do it, if blood and tea can't do it, if kissing can't do it, then maybe the magic of an ancient forest can.

I close my heavy eyes with the thought. *Switch back* . . .

And then another . . .

If Henry and I switch back, does that mean he'll leave and I'll never see him again?

31

I WAKE TO A MOANING, PAIN-FILLED GASP THAT SOUNDS JUST like the abject caterwauls of a dying baby llama. It's pathetic, miserable, and wretched.

I yank open my heavy eyelids and squint into the late-morning light streaming through my bedroom window. The small room is as cluttered as it has been for years, full of rustic wood furniture, swim team trophies and science fair medals, constellation posters, *Star Trek* posters, piles of textbooks, sci-fi novels, random stacks of driftwood, weathered ocean pebbles, and laminated passes to the Trekker conventions I attended as a teen with Jillian. There's even an unopened bottle of gas-station coffee on my computer desk that I think I bought two years ago—the last time I was here.

The moan sounds again.

I rub my eyes and reach for Henry's glasses. My mouth is dry, my eyes gritty, and there's a crick in my neck from pretzeling in my twin bed with Henry. It's not made for anyone over six feet tall, and it's definitely not made for two sleep-deprived adults.

And then there's that noise.

"Serena . . ."

It's Henry. His fingers dig into my abdomen and he says my name with a plaintive mewling.

"What? What's wrong?" I shake my head and sit up, trying to wipe away the cobwebs of sleep.

We came back to the cabin after an hour's nap in the woods, collapsing into bed without food, a shower, or changing into pajamas. By the green-tinged forest light filtering into the room, I'd say it's at least ten o'clock in the morning.

"I think I'm dying," Henry gasps.

That gets my attention.

I scramble fully upright and grip Henry's shoulder. His hair is matted, his is face pale, there's the sheen of perspiration lining his forehead, and his eyes are clouded with pain. His mouth is tight, and then he winces and his fingers dig harder into my skin.

"It hurts."

"Where? What?" I ask, glancing over him expecting to find a broken limb or gushing wound.

His knees draw up to his abdomen. "My stomach. I'm being ripped apart. This must be what spaghettification feels like. My insides are being rammed through a pasta maker and shredded. This isn't right. Something's wrong. We need to go to hospital."

I would take a moment to appreciate Henry's use of spaghettification to describe pain, but I'm too busy scrambling off the bed, ready to throw on a change of clothes. But then what he said sinks in.

"Your stomach?"

He nods. Presses a hand to his lower abdomen. "Here. It's a piercing, knifelike pain with a dull, raging ache underneath—"

"And your back hurts?"

"Yes," he says. "Perhaps it's appendicitis? I might need surgery. I'm sorry—"

"Do you have a headache?"

He pauses and touches his head. "Yes."

"And you want to cry?"

His lower lip wobbles. "No."

That's a yes.

"Stay there. I'll be right back."

I hurry from my bedroom and into the living room, ignoring the hunter-green La-Z-boys, the plush couch, and the half-finished golden retriever puzzle on the coffee table. Instead I head for the cedar-paneled kitchen. I grab a spoon and then a jar of peanut butter from the pantry. Then I find one of my mom's hidden chocolate bars in the back of the Tupperware cupboard. You'd think after twenty-plus years she'd find a new hiding spot, but no. On the counter my dad left a fresh pot of coffee and a note: "Gone back to hospital. Mom discharged today. See you soon. Love, Dad."

I pour Henry a cup of coffee, add two spoonfuls of sugar, then rush back to my bedroom. Henry's curled in a tight ball, his eyes shut tight.

"Peanut butter, spoon, chocolate, coffee." I drop the items one by one onto the wooden nightstand next to my bed.

Henry opens his eyes then blinks in confusion. "I thought you were calling an ambulance. Instead you brought peanut butter? Serena, I don't think you understand how much pain I'm in."

I crack open the jar of peanut butter, let the roasted peanut scent drift up, then stick the spoon in. Then I unwrap the dark chocolate bar, the metallic paper crackling, and crumble a bit of the chocolate on top.

"Eat this," I say.

"What?"

"Eat it. You're not dying, you're on your period."

Henry jerks upright.

"My period?"

"Well, my period. But—"

"*This* is what a period feels like?" Henry is aghast. He sounds like I just told him Little Bo Peep was actually a man who habitually stole lady's underwear. "This hell is a period?"

"Hold that thought," I say, then I hurry to the bathroom to find a painkiller, a heating pad, and a tampon. On second thought, I drop the tampon and grab a pad instead. Henry might not be ready to graduate to tampons on his first go around.

Back in the bedroom Henry has already finished half the coffee and is hugging the peanut butter jar like it's a teddy bear. The chocolate bar is nowhere in sight. His eyes are a bit glazed and he's licking peanut butter from the spoon.

"Here," I say, handing him the bottle of painkillers and the heating pad.

He gives a grateful smile and swallows the pills with his coffee.

"You can put this on," I say, holding out the pad. "Do you need me to describe how to—?"

"I'll figure it out," he says, his pale cheeks filling with red.

"Do you need more chocolate?"

"How do you do this?" Henry asks, eyeing the empty chocolate wrapper. "How do you do this every single month? How do you go to work? How do you sit in a meeting and listen to me natter on about maintenance while you feel like this?"

I shake my head then point at the nightstand. "Peanut butter, chocolate, coffee, and painkillers."

"But..." he stops. "It's awful. And I feel quite honestly like it might be a grand idea to go on a murderous rampage if I don't get another chocolate bar."

I hold back a smile. "I'll be right back then."

There's one more dark chocolate bar in the back of the cupboard, which I hand to Henry. "You'll feel better in about an hour," I promise. "It hurts the most first thing. It gets better."

I can tell the painkiller and heating pad are already at work. His color is better, and his face isn't tight with pain anymore.

"You can take a shower," I tell him. "Fresh towels are in the bathroom cupboard."

Then, at the vulnerable, pained expression on his face, I sit next to him on my bed. When the mattress dips he slides toward me. I rub my hand over his lower back, knowing I've always wished I had someone to rub my back when my cramps are raging.

"Thanks for taking one for the team," I tell him, giving him a small smile as I draw slow circles over his back.

"Serena?"

"Yeah?"

"I'd like it very much if we could switch back before next month."

I hide a smile. "Me too."

"I think if men truly knew what a woman goes through every month, they'd never envy them."

"Do you envy me?"

"Not anymore."

I laugh. "Well, I mean, men have to get their prostates checked."

"Doesn't compare."

"Morning wood?"

"Please."

"Getting kicked in the balls?"

"That's nothing on this."

"You know," I say, thinking about when Jillian nailed me in the testicles, "I might just have to disagree."

Henry sends me a quizzical glance and I grin at him. "Theoretically speaking."

"Your theories are terrible," he says grumpily.

I laugh. "That's not true. You love testing my theories. It's why we work so well together."

He drops his head to my shoulder. "I suppose so."

Ha. He knows so. I can hear it in the smile in his voice.

Which reminds me. "When we switch back, don't go to Chicago. Stay in Geneva."

He stills, his breath held, waiting for me to say more. When I don't, he pushes away from me and gives me a small smile. "Why?"

"Because . . ." I pause, search for the reason why, and then, lighting on the answer, say, "We're good together. I know how you think. You know me. We work well together. We could be a powerhouse. Think about everything we could do together. The theories we could prove. The papers we could write—"

Henry stands suddenly. His arms wrap around his middle as if he's holding himself together. "No."

"What?"

"That's not a future I want."

I shake my head. "But—"

"No," he says. Then, "If you want me to stay, at least be honest with yourself and admit the reason why."

He waits to see if I will, if I'll say the words, but I don't. So he turns and walks away.

32

I TRY VERY HARD NOT TO HOVER OVER MY MOM. I RESIST the urge to hug her, fluff her pillows, help her to the bathroom, or ask her every thirty-nine seconds how she's feeling.

When my dad pulled into the pine-shadowed drive I hurried outside, opening the truck door and offering my arm for her to lean on. I realized at Henry's startled glance that I was being a bit too helpful for a man who had supposedly only met my mom once.

After we shuffled inside, my dad asked, "Where do you want to stay, Caroline? Couch or bedroom?" To which my mom said, "Wherever you want to put me." Then my dad asked, "What would you like to drink?" To which my mom said, "Whatever you'd like to make." Then my dad asked, "What should we have for dinner?" To which my mom said, "What are you in the mood for?" Then my dad asked, "What should we do now?" To which my mom said, "What would you like to do?" My dad said, "Watch the news?" And my mom said, "You do like the news."

This wasn't unusual. This, in fact, was the soundtrack of my childhood. My dad asks what my mom wants, and my mom says, "Whatever you want." My dad asks, "What do you like?" and my mom says, "Whatever you like." It's a familiar refrain. As familiar as an afternoon rain showering over the coastal forests. But with every question and every subsequent answer, the wrinkle between Henry's eyebrows becomes more and more pronounced.

At the last question Henry stared at me, his forehead wrinkled, gaze searching. I could feel the unspoken questions moving between us, back and forth. *Is this why you think you'll lose yourself?* his gaze asked. *Is this why you're afraid? Is this what you think will happen if you let yourself love?*

The unspoken questions weighed heavy in the air, as present as the rich scent of coffee percolating in the kitchen.

"How about we play Scrabble?" I said then, turning from the knowledge in Henry's searching gaze. And then, realizing my statement was unexpected and I was Henry, not my parents' daughter, I said with an offhanded smile, "I know Serena likes Scrabble."

So now I'm sitting cross-legged on the smooth cedar-plank floor next to Henry while we play a game of Scrabble with my parents. My mom is propped on our old plaid couch, the cushions sinking under her, threatening to swallow her. She's tucked under a fleece blanket, sleepy-eyed and wispy-pale.

"Ducky," my mom says, motioning for my dad to place the letters for her.

He sets each wooden tile down with a distinct *click,*
click, click against the board. "D—U—C—K, and there's
the Y, connecting to your Yttrium, Henry."

My mom beams down at the word then says, "Did
Ducky ever tell you how she got her name?"

"Ye—" I begin.

But then Henry shakes his head firmly and says, "No.
Never."

"I did—"

"Didn't," Henry says.

I glance over at him, all pink-cheeked and rosy. He
widens his gaze and flutters his eyelashes at me, the
picture of innocence, then he says sheepishly to my
parents, "I told him my name was Ducky when we met,
but I never told him why."

Ha. I could've told Henry I've never been sheepish a
day in my life, but my mom doesn't seem to notice.

Instead she's smiling at Henry with a soft, dreamy
expression that reminds me of the look someone has
right before they nod off tucked securely under a fuzzy
blanket.

"It's all right if you're too tired," I say, thinking the
Scrabble game was too much and my mom should be
resting.

"I'm not too tired," my mom says, smothering a
yawn.

Henry folds the floral dress he's wearing around his
crossed legs and leans forward, resting his elbows on the
coffee table like he's a kid preparing for storytime.
Clearly, the painkillers and chocolate worked and he's
feeling better.

"How did you two meet?" my dad asks.

It's clear he still isn't one hundred percent sure about

me, especially since I laid the word "Yttrium" and edged ahead of him in the game.

Henry's face lights with laughter, his eyes dancing with humor. "I was stuck to a bench in a pub. An adhesive glued me in place. Henry rescued me, and after that I decided I liked him more than any other man I've ever met. I imagine the adhesive was fate."

"Really!" my mom says, incredibly, joyously happy with Henry's pronouncement.

He has no idea what he just stepped into.

I nudge his leg with my foot, casting him a quelling glance, but he's too busy agreeing with my parents about the fortuitous foundations of fate to pay me any mind.

"Adhesive, huh?" My dad studies me, chewing this new information over, and then, coming to the exact mental destination I knew he would, he gives his grunt that means "good" and leans forward to clap me on the arm.

I nod and give him (I hope) a happy smile.

"So . . ." Henry says, scooting closer to me, "do you want to tell the story about my name, Mom?"

"I'll tell it," my dad says. He sets his letter tiles on the table and then settles down into the couch cushions, adjusting my mom's legs on his lap. He rubs his hand over her calves absently as he ponders where to begin.

"My background is biochemistry," he finally says, a weathered smile on his face. He looks at me expectantly, and I realize he's waiting for my—Henry's—reaction.

"Ah-ha. Excellent. Biochemistry is a wonderful field."

My dad agrees. He points to the wood paneling lining the living room walls. "I specialize in adhesives. You see that paneling? I created the adhesive that holds it to the wall, sixteen times stronger than the current products on the market. Granted, it stinks like a skunk ate rotten cabbage and sprayed it on your walls, which is why I can't sell it, but the odor dissipates after eighteen months. Unfortunately, most people don't have vision. They don't see that the benefits outweigh the detriments."

My dad waits for me to agree, and because I lived with the rotten-skunk-cabbage stink and his lecture on benefits outweighing detriments, I nod.

"Absolutely."

My dad gives his "good" grunt. "In college I was working on pressure-sensitive adhesives. Those are PSAs if you know the jargon."

I nod. I know the jargon.

"Good. Ducky's told you some then."

I nod again.

"I was experimenting with van der Waals forces, which is—"

"Electrostatic forces that attract atoms to one another." Henry smiles and his California accent slips a bit—I think because he's talking about physics, his other native tongue besides British English. I nudge him, but he doesn't notice. Instead he continues. "There can be an attraction or a repulsion between the atoms because of the transient shift in electron density. " He's warming to the conversation and forgetting, I think, that he's supposed to be me. "You have to use quantum mechanics to understand it. It's a weak force, distance-dependent, caused by the fluctuating polarization of particles. It vanishes at greater distances between interacting molecules. In fact—"

Henry's gaze flies to mine, his expression tinged with surprise.

I shake my head. *What?* Is he thinking he and I

swapped, are held together, by a force as weak as van der Waals?

I frown and Henry shrugs.

"Duct tape," my dad interrupts, not able to hold in his glee.

"Pardon?" Henry asks, looking back at my dad. Clearly, he's completely forgotten he's supposed to be a California girl, not a proper British man.

I elbow him.

Luckily, my dad doesn't notice. He's busy reliving the glory of duct tape, and my mom is too happy with the way Henry keeps smiling at me to notice his sudden change in accent.

"Duct tape uses the principle of van der Waals forces. It's a PSA, the greatest human achievement after the pyramids. I was working on my thesis, improving on the idea, when I met Caroline." He pats my mom's leg, and she sends him a sleepy smile. "She was driving in her old Mazda, wheeling by campus, when her muffler fell off."

"Matt taped it back on with duct tape," she says.

"Which you should never do, so they say."

"But he did, because duct tape can fix anything."

My dad pierces me with his "do not question this" glare, and I nod. There's no way I'm about to argue that point with my parents.

But apparently, Henry doesn't know any better. "Well, I do think there are some things it can't fix. For instance—"

"Broken leg," my dad says.

"Duct tape cast," my mom replies.

"Wart?"

"Duct tape cure."

"Wrinkles?"

"Duct tape Botox."

"Broken window?"

"Duct tape glass."

"Cat hair on couch?"

"Duct tape," I say, and my dad gives me an approving nod.

He's not done though. He wants to make sure I get it.

"Blisters?"

"Duct tape," my mom says.

"Splinter removal?"

"Duct tape."

"Bug trap?"

"Duct tape."

"DIY hammock, bleacher seat, snow shoes, fix-any-broken-thing, first aid, and Ducky, may I ask, what saved Apollo 13 and the Apollo 17 Lunar Rover when nothing else could?"

Henry stares wide-eyed at my dad. "Duct tape?"

My dad nods then turns and gives me a wide, face-splitting smile. "You see? Duct tape."

Henry shakes his head, still not comprehending my dad's abiding love of all things adhesive, and more specifically, duct tape.

"But tell Henry what duct tape has to do with my name," Henry says. Luckily, his California accent is back in place.

"Well. There's the story. I fixed Caroline's muffler. I invited her out for ice cream. Two weeks later . . ." My dad clears his throat, scowling at me as if *I'm* the first-date fornicator (I'm supposedly abstinent, remember?), and then says, "Caroline told me we were expecting."

"So Matt proposed," my mom says, settling deeper into the couch and smiling at my dad.

"When Caroline's muffler broke off, she'd been on her way to LA. She'd been cast in a big role. Her first. She was set to play Ophelia in that Hamlet remake—you know the one? The one with the modern pop music?"

I nod. I know the one.

"The actress that went on to replace her became one of the biggest stars in Hollywood. Isn't that something?"

Henry reaches over and takes my hand. I let him thread his fingers through mine. His hands are cool and soft.

"It didn't matter," my mom says. "I wanted to be an actress for twenty years. Acting lessons, community theatre, studying, practicing, but as soon as I met Matt, it didn't matter. Nothing else mattered. That's the way it is in my family though. It happened to my mom. She was a teacher, but when she met my dad, all she wanted was to settle down with him, so she quit her job. It happened to her sisters, every one of them. They met their man and then nothing else mattered. My grandma, my great-grandma too. As soon as we find our partner, nothing else is important."

There's a twisting in my stomach. A queasy nausea.

When I was a teenager, self-righteous and disgusted with my mom for giving up her dreams, I asked her, "What do you want out of life?"

And she smiled at me, elbows-deep in dishwater, and said, "For you and your dad to be happy."

And I said, "No Mom, what do *you* want?"

"That is what I want," she'd said.

She didn't get it, and I couldn't make her understand.

"Matt proposed," my mom says. "We didn't have much money, so we moved north, to this cabin. It was quite the sight."

That's an understatement. For the first five years of their marriage, this place was held together with duct tape and a prayer. That's part of the reason my parents swear duct tape will fix anything. Leaky roof? Broken window? Leaky pipe? Broken cabinet? All fixed with duct tape.

"And when I proposed," my dad interrupts, "I said, 'We don't know each other well, Caroline, but this baby is going to be the duct tape that holds us together.'"

"Duck Tape is a brand," my mom tells me, thinking as a British man I might not know about it. "So I said the baby's name should be Ducky."

"And that is how our daughter got her name," my dad says, leveling me with the satisfied gaze of a story well-told.

"Well, Serena first, since we didn't want other kids to tease her, but Ducky to us." My mom smothers a yawn after saying this.

"That's a good story," Henry says, brushing his thumb over the back of my hand.

"Well, you've heard it plenty!" my mom says.

Henry nods. "Thank you for telling it."

I sit still, Henry's hand in mine, the green-gold light of sunset falling across the cedar floor. My back hurts from the hard wood and my legs are cramping from remaining crossed for so long. The Scrabble game remains unfinished on the coffee table in front of us.

As the shadows fall and the tiny cabin living room grows small and closed, my mom beams at me—Henry— and says, "Now you know. You meeting Ducky because of adhesive was fate. And if you're lucky enough for our Ducky to love you? Well, then nothing else will matter anymore. You'll be the most important thing in her life. Isn't that just the best thing you could hope for?"

I stare at my mom's earnest smile. Her belief that I'll be ecstatic that her daughter will give up her dreams, her career, her *everything,* for love. Her desire for me to subsume myself for another person is laid out like letter tiles on the game board.

I'm unable to answer. The nausea has risen to a hard lump in my throat so that it's impossible to respond.

Henry isn't looking at me, but I can feel all his attention on me. On the way I'm sitting rigidly, on the tightness of my hand in his, on the way I can't respond.

He loosens his grip, brushes his fingers over the back of my hand—gentle like an angel's kiss—and then says, "Henry told me just last week, if I had to choose between my dreams or him, I should choose my dreams. He's never wanted me to lose them."

He never said that. He didn't. But he's saying it now. He's telling me here and now.

"Dreams change, Serena," my mom says. "You get married, have a baby, dreams change. Sometimes we don't know how much a dream can change until we experience it for ourselves."

Henry nods. He doesn't look at me to see how I've reacted to his declaration or to my mom's response.

"I know," he says softly. "I understand."

Knowing Henry, I'm sure he does. I'm sure he understands it all.

33

THE PERFUMED NIGHT AIR DRIFTS EARTHY AND SWEET through the back yard, sifting through the grass and rattling the dried needles of the nearby forest. The sky is indigo-black, the deep purple of ripe cabernet grapes, fleshed with streaks of moonlight and stars.

I lean back on my forearms, letting the grass tickle my skin while I dig my bare feet into the loamy soil. I tilt my head up to the sky and drink in the stars.

"The sky is just like I saw," Henry says, rubbing the goose bumps on his arms, "from when you were younger. You loved this. Have you missed it?"

"I have. I just didn't realize it."

Henry nods. His legs are tucked under him and the grass bows around him. The night temperatures have dropped, lending the forest's edge a damp coolness.

I'm warm—the benefit of being Henry—but I know he's feeling the chill. I strip off my button-down shirt, leaving only a T-shirt, and drape it over his shoulders.

"Thanks." He flashes me a quick smile and pulls the shirt tight around his arms, shivering.

"Come here," I say, pulling him against me, tucking him into the warmth of my chest. His cheek brushes my heart and his hair tickles the bare skin at my throat. I wrap my arms around him, and after a moment he settles close, soaking up my heat. "Better?"

He nods. "I have to admit, I miss being warm."

I smile. "I miss being cold."

He laughs. "I miss liking tea."

"I miss *you* liking tea."

He twists in my arms and grins at me.

"I miss Purrk," I say.

"I miss craving a dog at my feet instead of a cat in my lap."

"I miss spicy food."

"I miss meat."

"I miss being messy."

"Do you?"

I shrug. "Maybe not."

He grins, and I add as an afterthought, "Is it wrong to say I miss my breasts?"

His eyes light up, reflecting the moonlight, and he gives me a laughing smile. "Only if it's wrong to say I miss my—"

I elbow him and he lets out a huff of laughter. I grin at the stars.

"Well?"

"Fine," I say. "Of course you miss it. I imagine you miss your daily . . ."

He lifts an eyebrow.

"Weekly?"

His expression goes flat. Aha.

"Daily exercises," I say.

His mouth twitches with suppressed laughter.

"And I miss my drawer," I admit.

"Still don't know what drawer you're talking about," he says even though I know he does.

I smile and rub his arms, trying to keep him warm. A white moth flits by, landing on a fern at the edge of the woods, and then it flutters past.

"I've kept my end of the bargain. No test drives," I tell him. I wait for him to confirm that he hasn't done anything, but the only sound is the *who who whoooo* of a northern spotted owl echoing through the woods.

"Henry?" I tilt my head, looking down at him, but he keeps his face averted.

"Henry!"

"What?" He finally glances up, and I see his cheeks are suffused with a bright red flush.

"Did you . . .?" I gasp. He did. "Unbelievable!"

He shakes his head. "I didn't. I . . ." He chews on his lip. "It was a dream. Before your period, I was . . . you know . . ." He drums his fingers on his leg in nervousness and I watch him, appalled and fascinated at the same time.

"And?"

"I was . . . needy. Your body was very . . . needy." His fingers drum faster, and the red in his cheeks deepens as if this is the most uncomfortable conversation he's ever had in his entire life.

"You have got to be kidding me," I say.

"No. Look, I didn't violate our agreement. I didn't touch anything. But I was so sensitive. And I had this dream and I woke up and . . ." His eyes widen meaningfully.

"And you were coming your brains out?" I ask.

"Maybe."

Ha.

It's my body. I know exactly how I feel before my period. As horny as a fifteen-year-old boy ogling mammary clouds—that's how horny. And I've had sex dreams that I've woken up from in the middle of an orgasm. So yes. I know exactly what Henry's describing.

"Did it feel good?"

"It was fine."

Uh-huh.

"Was I still asleep?"

"I don't know. You were . . . spooning me."

Ha.

"What was the dream about?"

He flushes.

"Was it about my boobs?"

No answer.

"Henry. Were you dreaming about my boobs?"

"I plead the fifth," he says.

"You can't plead the fifth. You're British. You don't have the fifth."

"Not true. I'm a Californian now. I can plead the fifth all I want. Regardless, I didn't break our agreement. Not intentionally."

"It's not really fair, though, is it? I think maybe I'll try to have a nocturnal emission. Do you have those? Can I count on one?"

Henry gives me an appalled look. "Not in at least fifteen years."

"Too bad."

He levels a gaze on me—one censuring and disapproving—and then my mouth twitches, his eyelashes flutter, and we both start laughing. He drops his head against my chest, his shoulders vibrating with laughter. I tug him close, wrapping my arms around him.

"Feel better?" he asks after our laughter has faded into the night.

I nod. The ridiculousness of our conversation, the buoyancy of laughter, has lightened me and set me free from the worry and the fear that lingered most of the day.

"Did you do that on purpose?" I ask. "Try to make me forget everything?"

"Did it work?"

"For a bit."

"Good," he says, leaning into me. Then, gazing up at the sky, watching the shadow of an owl soar above us, blotting out the stars for a millisecond, he says, "I meant what I said earlier. I never want you to lose yourself for me. That's not a love I'd want."

I still. The chill of the air tugs at me, brushing over the skin of my bare arms.

I take a deep breath and sense the faint perfume of starlight. I don't know if it's from the sky above or from Henry held in the shelter of my arms.

"Isn't that what's happening though?" I ask him. "I'm losing myself in you. I like tea now. I eat meat. I like dogs and organizing things, and the thought of marriage gives me a cozy, happy feeling. Isn't that losing myself?"

Henry shakes his head, pulls back from me. "Even when you look like me, even when you like the things I like, you're still you."

I disagree, but he continues.

"Don't you think I'm still me? When you look at me, don't you see me?"

I stare into his deep brown eyes—my eyes—but he's right: I stopped seeing him as me, the petite, dark haired, big-eyed woman, and have only seen him as himself since—

Well, since we switched.

He's always been him, even if he does crave coffee and clutter and cats now.

"I see you," I admit. "I only see you."

He twists in my arms to face me, sets his hands on my cheeks, and cups my face, his fingers stroking the stubble on my cheeks. "Your soul burns so bright it doesn't matter what you look like or what body you're in—it's you. Nothing can change that. And if being me can't make you lose yourself, then how could loving?"

I lean into his touch. His thumb brushes over my lip. I look at the question in his eyes.

"I love too much," I tell him. "I'm my mother's daughter. I love too much. I only have room for one great love in my life. I've already chosen it. I don't want to lose my dreams. I don't want to lose everything for love."

"I wouldn't let you."

"It wouldn't be for you to let me or not. It would just be. That's what love does."

He shakes his head, dragging his fingers over my skin. "No."

"It is. You see it everywhere. I see it every day. I grew up with it. I lived it."

Henry drops his hands, leaving only cold air behind. He looks up at me, the moonlight playing over his skin. "Every expression of love is different. No two people love the same. Our way of loving would be infinitely different from anyone else's. Don't you see?"

I don't. I don't see that, and Henry recognizes it.

He nods then settles back, leaning against me. We stay outside in the chill long into the night, staring up at the stars.

34

A WEEK PASSES IN A BLUR OF MORNING MIST BURNED INTO afternoon sun, dipping to star-filled nights where I sleep tangled with Henry in my tiny twin bed. We sink into a rhythm of morning walks through the forest, the matted earth crackling beneath our feet and sending up boughs of spice and mossy wood.

Sometimes Henry reaches for my hand, sometimes I reach for his, but most of the time I can't remember who reached first. It's for comfort or friendship or because often I feel adrift and he's the one I reach for to settle me.

Under two-hundred-foot-tall redwoods, in sunlight streaming in lacy stretches, we debate the fundamentals of nature, question why gravity is so much weaker than the other forces, and discuss whether chaos or order rules our universe. I point out red-bellied newts along the creek bed, the slow trudge of a banana slug over dried redwood needles, and the flickering tail of a deer as it springs into the shadows. Neither of us mentions love.

Instead, after our walks, Henry makes healthy breakfasts of oatmeal with blueberries and strawberries for my family. He sits with my mom while she rests on the couch, tucked under the same blanket while he reads to her from my favorite *Star Trek* novels, making her laugh with his ridiculous impressions and alien accents. While my mom naps, he works with my dad in his toolshed/workshop in my dad's latest attempt to make a tape that is twenty times stronger than duct tape but costs half in production.

All the while, I do what Henry would do when under stress. I clean. I vacuum, I do the dishes, I dust all the bookshelves, and I ask my mom if she'd like me to deep-clean the kitchen. I never appreciated before how meditative cleaning is and how much Henry must've used it to have a bit of control in a chaotic world.

His family texted, his mom and sisters asking if my mom was okay. I sent back Henry's love. Niall texted to ask about law school, and Henry texted back get a surfboard already. His brother John asked if we were all right, and I told him to get back to his honeymoon.

Slowly our lives are weaving together. When Henry and I are close, I feel something like van der Waals. It's a shifting of electrons, an awareness, an elemental attraction I can't resist. But it's stronger than that. When our limbs are tangled together at night, when we're pressed close, it feels as if we have an unbreakable connection. As if that night years ago, when we came together, our molecules broke apart and then coalesced again with a new property where we only resonate one for the other. It was there before, but I ignored it. Now I can't ignore it.

At the kitchen table my mom slowly flips through a photo album crammed with photos of me as a kid, and full of abstracts of all my publications. I didn't know she had those. As I wipe down the cabinets she points out photos of me at swim meets and a picture of me at my college graduation.

"Thank you for doing all this," she says again, and I wave it off. "I'm not tall enough to dust the tops of the cabinets. It's a big help."

"Don't worry about it. I like cleaning."

She smiles. "You're a good fit for Ducky then. She's allergic to brooms and dusters."

I am not.

I just have a different relationship to cleaning than Henry. It's more like casual dating rather than marriage.

I set the dusty rag down and smile. "I don't mind. She has her own way of organizing. It works."

"This is why she loves you, I'm sure. You understand her." My mom runs her hand over a photo of me dressed in my *Star Trek* science officer uniform.

My mom's skin has shifted from gray to pink over the past week, and she's able to sit up longer and move about. She's dressed in loose cotton pants and a button-up-shirt, and her soft, wispy hair is loose. She looks so hopeful that I almost hate to deny what she said, but—

"I see the denial in your eyes, but you can't hide things from a mother. I know my daughter and the way she looks at you . . . That's love."

She means the way Henry looks at me.

My mom smiles down at the photo album then says absently, "My dad died when he was fifty-one. A heart attack. The same age as me."

"You aren't going to die," I say. My gut churns at the way she's looking down at the photograph. Me at my graduation, her and my dad on either side of me.

"I think I hurt Ducky more than I realized. Moms do that."

I shake my head, but she doesn't look up.

"I think I frightened her. I realized that the other night. Do you mind me telling you this? I'm feeling a little . . . wobbly," my mom says, looking up at me with pale cheeks and searching eyes.

"I don't mind," I say, then I walk to the Tupperware cupboard, reach into the back, and pull out the chocolate tin. When my mom lifts her eyebrows, I shrug and say, "I found it while cleaning."

She gives a short laugh then pats my hand as I pull out a chair and sit down next to her at the old wooden table.

"We'll share," she says, sorting through the milk chocolate, the chocolate-covered almonds, the white chocolate, and the distinct lack of dark chocolate. The sugary chocolate scent wafts from the tin. My mom sighs. "No dark chocolate. Ducky must've raided my stash."

I hide a smile.

She picks out a handful of chocolate-covered almonds—"good for the heart"—and pushes the tin toward me.

I don't know what Henry usually eats, but I reach for the white chocolate (gross), which I guess is what he likes. When I taste it, I smile. I was right. I hate white chocolate (what's the point of it? It's like the appendix—totally useless), but here and now, the creamy flavor is delicious.

My mom nibbles at her almonds then says, "I've been thinking the past week about my life."

As you do when you almost die.

"Understandable."

"I've spent almost thirty years being a wife and a mom. Just a wife. Just a mom. And as I was strapped in that ambulance racing to the hospital, I kept thinking, 'If I die now, will that be enough? If I die, will I regret my life?'"

My mouth goes dry and it's impossible to swallow the chocolate. Instead it lodges at the back of my throat, a tight lump.

My mom shakes her head. "Ducky would think that I'd regret it," she says. "I know my daughter. She's always been a bit disappointed in me. A bit ashamed. I never quite lived up to her expectations. I remember when she was eleven and she won first prize in the county science fair. All the parents came for the awards ceremony. The other kids, their parents were doctors or professors or engineers. One of them, this mom, a chemist, asked me what I did. I said, 'I'm a stay-at-home mom.' 'Yes,' the woman said, 'but what do you *do*?' I joked, 'Well, I bake cookies all day and fold laundry—what else?' Then I happened to look at Ducky, and she . . . Her cheeks were red and she wouldn't look at me." My mom flips through the album, the pages turning quickly, until she stops on a page near the front. She points to a picture of me holding a trophy nearly as big as I am. My dad has his hand on my shoulder and my mom stands a bit off to the side, her hair neat, her eyes worried. "Here it is. She never looked at me the same after that night."

I stare at the picture. I don't remember that being the night I stopped wanting to be like my mom. For me it was a more gradual fade rather than a red line slashed through a specific date.

"I'm sorry," my mom says. "I don't know why I'm telling you this." She closes the album and then pushes away the tin of chocolates.

Outside a pop like a muffler backfiring sounds, then I hear my dad's shout. I'm not concerned. The noise of small chemical explosions was a common sound during my childhood. I'm sure both my dad and Henry are wearing safety gear.

"Don't worry," my mom says, glancing out the window toward the toolshed, "it happens all the time."

I nod. "You don't have to be embarrassed," I tell her. "People say I'm easy to talk to."

"That must be it," she says, giving me a grateful smile.

Outside, my dad throws open a window on the workshop and a thin stream of smoke slips out.

"I think," my mom says, "having a heart attack made all the emotions I've been keeping in . . . well, it made them all seep out. Sort of like cracking an egg. It's a mess."

"Don't worry." I reach into the tin and pull out a handful of chocolate-covered almonds, setting them in front of her.

She smiles in thanks and picks at one, peeling away the soft chocolate shell with her nail. "I suppose all I wanted to say was, I don't regret my choices. I'd do it all the same. I was born to love Matt, and I was made to be Ducky's mom. That's what I meant about loving and having no choice. It's like my daughter. I've always been so proud of her. She knows what she wants. She was born to be a scientist. Just like her dad."

My mom smiles as another muffler-backfire-popping noise sounds.

"I worry about her though. So I'm glad you're here. I

realized earlier this week that I might have frightened her off commitment. Going on about giving up acting for marriage and motherhood."

"You don't regret it?"

"No. Never. But I misspoke the other day. I had a choice. We all have a choice. It felt inevitable, but that's because I wanted it so much. I was always proud to be Matt's wife and Ducky's mom. That made me more proud, more happy, than acting ever could. But everyone has a choice. It's just, when you're in love, the choice is easy. You choose love."

"But you didn't have to give up your dreams."

She pats my hand. "You sound like Ducky. I made new dreams."

I follow the line of my mom's jaw, the smile that looks so much like mine, and the tired wrinkles at the edges of her eyes. There isn't anything in her expression that looks like regret or sorrow, just happiness at a life well-lived.

"You have at least forty more years ahead of you," I tell her, urging her silently to be healthy, to stay alive. "Maybe you can have more dreams in the coming decades."

She nods. "What I'd like is to see Ducky as happy as I've been. She loves her job. But . . . you know . . . when you're waking up in the hospital, maybe dying, maybe not, your job isn't there holding your hand. That award you won or that article you published or those colleagues you impressed, they aren't there holding your hand. If I'm gone, if Matt's gone, and all Ducky has is her job? Who will hold her? That's what I worry about. I don't want her to change or to give up her career or become like me. I just want to know that she'll have someone to hold her when she needs it. When I'm gone."

My mom looks at me, tsks at the look on my face, and pats my hand. "Moms think about things like this. I'm sure your mom is the same."

I nod. Finally manage to swallow the lump in my throat. "She is. She's just the same."

"Good." My mom stands then, her chair scraping on the wood. "I'm glad you and Ducky found each other. When she was little, she always asked if people paired up like electrons and protons, and I told her yes, that she'd find her match someday. I'm glad it's you."

I stand then too, and before my mom can leave the room, I wrap her in a quick hug. "Thank you."

She pats my back in surprise and peers up at me, nearly a foot taller than her. "Well. I'm going to take a nap. You might want to check on Matt and Ducky. There's been a few too many booms this afternoon."

I smile and step back. As my mom leaves the kitchen, I say, "Wait. Ducky . . . she . . ."

My mom pauses in the kitchen doorway, her hand resting on the wood molding.

I close my eyes, my throat thick. I need to tell my mom this, even if it's coming from Henry. "When Ducky told me about you, she said you were the best mom she could have ever hoped for. She's sorry she doesn't visit more or call more. She misses you and thinks about you. And even though you are as different as a mother and daughter can be, she said she's grateful you're her mom. She loves you. Very much."

My mom doesn't turn, she just stands still in the doorway, the afternoon light from the kitchen window falling over her. After a quiet moment with only the hum of the refrigerator and the creaking of the wind over the shingle roof, she lowers her hand from the doorway, nods, and walks away.

Her bedroom door creaks shut. I collapse back into the chair, drop my head into my hands, and then, after a moment, I get up and search the cupboards.

For tea.

35

WE LEAVE IN THE MORNING AFTER OATMEAL AND ORANGE juice and tight-wrapped hugs in the driveway. I promise my mom I'll look after her daughter, and I promise my dad I'll study up on adhesives so I can help him and Ducky in the workshop on my next visit.

I watch their figures in the rearview mirror until the road curves and they disappear, replaced by the shifting greens and browns and grays of the forest.

The windows are down, and a soft, warm breeze filters the scents of old wood and moss, mixing with the cups of coffee my dad foisted on us for the long drive to the airport. The tall redwoods filter out most of the light, leaving the narrow country road in subdued quiet, the only sound the wheels of the car flicking over the gravel-strewn road.

The steering wheel vibrates under my hands as I slow for a deer and her fawn crossing ahead.

"It's beautiful here," Henry says. "Not at all like England. Or Geneva."

"They're beautiful too though." I glance over at him. He's holding the travel mug of coffee in his hands, cradling it as he takes a long, heavy-lidded sip. I smile. "In England you have thousand-year-old buildings. Here we have thousand-year-old trees."

Outside the car window the shrill *ke-eee-eeer* of a hawk sounds, muffled by the thick canopy and then swallowed by the ferns and the understory. The soft light filters across the car window like the flickering of an old black-and-white movie.

In a few hours we'll make it to the coast with its salt-scented air and meadow-topped bluffs and craggy hills. But until then we're in the solitude of the forest.

I glance over at Henry. His eyes are closed as he savors my dad's coffee. He's tired. I think being me, caring for my mom and helping my dad cope, really took it out of him.

"Thank you," I say. "Thank you for everything. In case I didn't mention it."

Henry blinks at me owlishly. "Only a hundred and twenty-two times since we arrived." He smiles. "It's nothing."

It's not nothing. We both know it.

"Do you think I'll see my parents again?"

"Yes," he says, barely giving me enough time to finish.

"As me?"

"Yes."

"Why? What makes you so sure?"

"I'm an optimist. And tomorrow we'll be back in Geneva and I'm certain we'll figure this out."

I study him for a moment and then turn back to the road. "We go back to work in two days. If we haven't switched, I'll—"

I'll be him at work, and he'll be me.

Henry tilts his head back against the car seat and stares out the window at the Douglas fir, the cedar, and the occasional redwood. I turn onto a larger country road. The blue sky and sunlight spreads out overhead as we leave the forest's canopy.

The breeze blowing through the car tugs at Henry's hair, pulling the strands from his braid and tugging at the sleeves of his wrap dress. He takes another sip of coffee and then absently drums his fingers on the lid of the mug.

I smile. He has my habits, but he's still Henry through and through. He was right. Switching hasn't changed us. It's only given us a new perspective and a new understanding.

"I've been thinking," I say, rolling up the windows so we don't have to compete with the rushing air to talk.

"Hmm?" he asks, then he frowns at the empty mug.

"You can have mine." I nod at the still full cup my dad offered me.

"Thank you. What about?"

"Did you ever think about how when you grow up in a family, or in a culture or a place, you have a specific outlook on life?"

"I suppose."

"Well, I mean, a girl who grows up in rural Northern California as an only child is going to have a different outlook on life than a boy who grew up in a castle in England with four siblings."

"It's a latrine," Henry says, smiling over at me.

Right. I smile at his grin.

"It has a castle ruin and a World War II airplane."

Henry settles back into his seat, happily holding my full

cup of coffee. "You asked about that plane. I forgot. My great-grandmother lived in Shanghai during the late thirties and forties with her parents. They didn't evacuate. Her parents died in a train accident and she was sent to a Japanese internment camp, Weihsein. She was held there with other British expats for two years until the Americans liberated them. They flew over with a B24 Bomber. A year later, when she married my great-grandfather, she asked if someday he could find her a plane. I was told that seeing the paratroopers was one of the happiest moments of her life."

I glance over at him, surprised at the story. "I didn't know your great-grandma was in an internment camp."

"Her and more than a hundred thousand other British, Americans and Canadians . . . mostly missionaries and businessmen and their families living in northern China and Japan. They were considered enemy nationals."

I shake my head. "It's odd because half a world away, in the US, my grandparents were in an internment camp too."

Henry reaches over and touches my hand. "Do you think it's strange, what people do to each other?"

I shake my head. "No. I think people do all sorts of things that they're later ashamed of when they're afraid. Fear robs us of reason."

"It reminds me of something my family says. There is no fear in love." Henry runs his fingers over my knuckles, tracing them lightly over my skin. His hands are delicate, his nails slightly rounded.

"You're right. My grandparents met in that camp as young teenagers. A little girl there told them they were soul mates. They died before I was born. My dad was a late-in-life baby. But he says their love was something special. No place for fear."

Henry studies me, an understanding in his eyes. "Sorry, you were saying ... about outlook on life?"

"Oh, only that I didn't realize how much growing up like I did colored my world. It's like ... " I take a moment to think, staring out at the gray of the road rolling past the green fluorescence of the ferns and mossy rocks and the tall roadside grasses shifting in the breeze. "It's like when I was little I put on a pair of colored glasses. They came from my family and my experiences, and everything I looked at was tinged by those glasses. Say they're yellow—well, then blue looked green to me, and red looked orange. So if someone was kind, I'd wonder, what do they want from me? Or if someone wanted to date, I'd think, they want to change me. While your glasses, maybe they're blue, so red is purple and yellow is green. You have a completely different outlook."

"But you can take the glasses off," Henry says.

"Right. I thought I did. When we leave home, we think we take the glasses off. But what I didn't realize is that when I smashed the lenses and broke the glass, the shards caught in my eyes and slithered all the way down my bloodstream and lodged in my heart. So even if I wasn't wearing the glasses anymore it didn't matter, because the tint was coming from inside me, and I didn't even know it. I didn't see it. Not until—"

"Until we switched."

I nod and pull to stop at an intersection. To the left there's a hand-painted sign for fresh eggs two miles away, and to the right is the highway.

No one is behind us. The intersection is quiet. The only movement is the shadow of the fir trees dancing on the road and the clouds skittering across the sky like sea-foam cresting over azure waves.

Henry turns to me then, the air between us electric and heady.

"I understand." He reaches over and places his hand on mine. I look down at our fingers laced together on the steering wheel. I keep my foot on the brake, suspending us in this moment.

"I don't want to change you." His hand whispers over mine, stroking me. "The more I know about you, the more I feel. I'm wrapped so tight in you that I can never be free. I don't want to be. I love the way your mind works. I love your humor. I love how much you care. I love how you leave a trail of paper and dishes and dirty clothes behind you. I love how you sip coffee nonstop and doodle theorems on cereal boxes and napkins. I love how loyal you are, and how stubborn. I love your optimism and your hope. I love how you find magic in the stars and believe in the goodness of humanity. I love that you care about others, even people you've never met and those who are vastly different from you. I love how you don't want to wake up in the mornings and how you wrap around me in your sleep, and how you reach for me without realizing it."

Before, even two weeks ago, if Henry had said these things to me, my mouth would've gone dry, my stomach would've clenched, and I would've broken out in a cold sweat.

But now . . . I understand.

I understand him.

He's not trying to control me or change me or anglerfish me. He's just . . . telling me he knows me. He understands me.

"You understand me," I say.

He nods, his dark gaze as solemn as a starry night. "I understand you."

I lean across the car, my seat belt tugging at my chest, and rest my forehead against his. My breath shudders from my lungs as I cup my hand over his cheek.

"I thought I wouldn't, or that I couldn't. But I understand you too. Sometimes I think I understand you better than I understand myself."

At my words, the thick electric tingle in the air stings and buzzes as it moves across us, raising the hairs on my arms. The air smells of static electricity, and my insides quiver at the energy roiling around us.

Henry's eyes widen and he stares at me, a question in his gaze. *Do you feel that?*

I do.

I press closer to him, bringing my other hand up to cup his face. He reaches up and rests his hands on the bunched muscles of my shoulders. Crackling heat arches between us.

"Serena," he breathes—a question, a prayer.

Keeping my eyes on him, I lay my lips over his, tasting the buttery-sweet coffee and feeling the soft, giving heat of his mouth.

I hold my breath for the space of a heartbeat, two. Henry's fingers grip my shoulders, his lips slide over mine, a low sound pulls from his throat, and the car seems to vibrate with the thrumming energy pooling between us.

I bite his lip, pull his mouth to mine, swim in the feel of him, keep my gaze locked with his. He feels it just as much as me.

The electricity.

The spinning.

The tearing apart.

Is this what we had to do? Understand each other?

His tongue slides across my mouth. A violent spark lights inside me, thrumming at the base of my spine, building in an ache that urges me to take, to kiss, to make love.

And then—

And then—

A car horn blares behind us, loud and insistent. I jerk back, yanking my hands from Henry's face. My foot leaves the brake and the car lurches forward before I can jolt us to a stop. Henry's hands tear free from my shoulders and he thuds back in his seat, his seat belt yanking him back.

A red pickup truck swerves around us, the driver laying on his horn as he passes, turning toward the highway.

I draw in a shuddering, painful breath. Spots dance in my vision and the road tilts. My body feels as if a thousand stars are lighting me from the inside out.

I grip the smooth surface of the steering wheel and look over at Henry.

He's still me. Still Serena.

He's watching me, one hand pressed to his rosy, kiss-swollen mouth.

And then—

The electric fades, the stars wink out, and I turn right to fly home.

36

Geneva welcomes us with cloud-strewn skies, dove-gray afternoon light, and a cool, rain-damp mountain breeze that tickles my nose with the promise of cobblestone streets, alpine forests, and romantic stone buildings perched on icy blue waters.

The city is cradled below us. Church spires and old hotels, gardens and museums congregate around the deep azure lake, nestled under the benevolent gaze of Mount Blanc.

As soon as the plane skipped, skidded, and jerked to a stop I felt the warm happiness of returning home. I ate a croissant with strawberry jam from an airport kiosk and sipped a delicious, piping-hot tea. Henry drank a double espresso and smiled at me over the rim of the cup as we waited for our bags to arrive on the luggage carousel.

We slept on the transatlantic flight, my seat back, Henry curled against me, his head on my chest, my arms around him. All the way to London, then London to Geneva. And now.

Home.

Well, almost home.

I knock on Jillian's front door, Henry standing back and to the side.

From the front, Jillian's place looks like an unassuming modern chateau set on a forested mountainside, seamlessly blending in with the blue-green pine, the rustling meadow grass, and the moss-covered rocks. However, once you're inside it's a sprawling haven with walls and walls of windows overlooking the city. Henry doesn't know Jillian or her husband Daniel, but he does know my cat.

That's who we're here for.

Purrk.

And then Henry and I will head back to my apartment, where we'll stay until . . .

Well, until.

The front door is flung open. Jillian's there with a fuzzily annoyed Purrk in her arms. He's using Jillian's rounded belly as a perch, squirming and batting at one of her dark curls. Daniel, her husband, stands behind her.

Daniel is . . . well, you might describe him as combustibly hot. His face is regularly plastered in magazines and newspapers, and I know for a fact that he was once on a hundred-foot billboard in Times Square, shirtless. He's not the kind of guy I would ever have imagined my best friend ending up with, but after seeing the way he looks at her, like they have their own secret language and their own secret world, I can't imagine her with anyone else. Plus, Jillian actually talks with him. Which is a big deal.

Now she narrows her eyes on me, then she looks at Henry, then she looks back at me.

"Serena?" she whispers, not quite sure if I'm still Henry.

"Yeah." I hold out my hands like, "What you see is what you get." "Does he know?" I nod at Daniel.

Jillian nods, biting her bottom lip. Then, still holding Purrk, she holds her hand out to Henry. "Hi, I'm Jillian. Serena's best friend. You must be Henry."

He grips her hand. "Nice to meet you. Henry Joule." He says this in his crisp accent, and when he does Jillian's hand falls limp and she gives him a stunned look.

"Unbelievable," Daniel breathes, which pretty much sums up the look on Jillian's face.

Henry pulls his hand back and smiles uncomfortably at my two friends eyeing him as if he's a bizarre species.

"I thought you would've figured it out by now," Jillian says. Purrk squirms again and gives a cranky meow. He's never liked being held. He prefers to sit on your lap with the freedom to move whenever he pleases.

"You remember what Zelda said," Jillian says, glancing worriedly at Henry. "She knows what she's talking about."

Daniel steps close to Jillian, resting his hand on her lower back and rubbing her spine. She smiles up at him, and for a moment something passes between them. An intimate, private moment that ends with Daniel reaching out and tucking a loose curl behind Jillian's ear. She turns back to me, a flush on her cheeks. I guarantee, as soon as we close the door, those two are going at it.

"Thanks again for watching Purrk." I reach out to take him, but when I do, Purrk's ears flatten and he hisses, swiping at me, his claws extended.

"Purrk," I say, "it's me! The distributor of sausages. The purveyor of cat treats. The sprinkler of catnip crack."

I try again, but Purrk swipes at me a second time, letting out a long hiss.

"Maybe . . ." Henry steps forward and holds out his arms. Without missing a blink, Purrk jumps from Jillian's arms to land in Henry's. He settles in like a swaddled baby and begins a loud, rumbly purr.

"You've got to be kidding me." I glare at Purrk. "Aren't cats supposed to have a sixth sense? Shouldn't you know who I am?"

Henry's smiling down at Purrk, rubbing his fingers through Purrk's long, glossy black fur. Purrk rubs his face along Henry's chest, nuzzling him.

"I quite like this cat," Henry says, sounding surprised. "I've never liked a cat before."

Jillian rubs a hand over her rounded belly and gives me a smile. "Don't worry, Serena. I still like you, even if you do look like a tall, rough-hewed Captain Kirk with too much facial hair."

My hand goes to my chin, rubbing the thick two-day growth. "I've been traveling."

"Captain Kirk?" Daniel asks doubtfully, pulling Jillian closer.

She grins up at him, and at her smile his eyes practically burn off her maternity dress.

"So," I say, gathering up the cat carrier, Purrk's food, and his bag full of treats, toys, and dishes. "Thank you again. We'll be . . . we'll see you—"

"When you're back to yourself again," Jillian says. Then she hurries forward, stands on her tiptoes, and gives me a hug that's so tight the air rushes out of my lungs. "I'm glad your mom's okay. I'm glad you're okay. Now hurry up and switch back." Then she whispers, "I called Zelda again. She told me to remind you that you don't have much time."

I nod and Jillian steps back. Daniel lifts his hand in goodbye, and then Henry and I take Purrk and head to Geneva.

The clouds gather thick and threatening, pressing a gray, heavy weight on top of us.

37

I UNLOCK THE DOOR TO MY APARTMENT AND SWING THE old, creaky wooden door wide. A splash of light shines over us, a cool afternoon gray. My apartment has the quiet feel of a home that's been empty for a long time. The air is still and silent and tinged with the scent of old stone walls and overripe apples left on the counter.

Nothing has changed. There's still unopened mail piled on the kitchen counter, laundry mounded on a living-room chair waiting to be folded, and dishes stacked in the drying rack waiting to be put away. It's a cluttered, messy, lived-in home.

Purrk jumps down from Henry's arms, landing on soft feet, and then skitters, tail up, into the dark gray light, I'm sure to reacquaint himself with his domain and his food dish.

Even though it's been less than two weeks it feels as if I've been gone much longer. I almost don't recognize my own home. Or maybe my home hasn't changed, but I have.

I look over at Henry, about to ask if he wants to prepare for work tomorrow, but then I see the expression on his face.

Confusion giving way to surprise.

He wrinkles his forehead and a line appears between his eyebrows, then his eyes widen and he turns to me.

Behind him, the wooden door to my coat closet is half-open. There are piles of tennis shoes, boots, and heels on the floor, and coats crowded inside—trench coats, raincoats, winter coats, and then, right at the front of the line, Henry's coat.

It's the one he gave me the first night we met. The one he wrapped around me so I could leave the pub with him. The one I dropped to the hotel-room floor so we could make love.

The edge of his mouth lifts in a small half-smile. "You kept it."

He reaches out and runs a hand over the fabric. It's been nearly six months since it stopped smelling like Henry, that cedar and starlight scent. For the first year, every time I opened my closet I caught the ghost of him.

"You told me to keep it," I say, closing the apartment door with a soft click. We're shut into the silence and the stillness.

He pulls his hand from the coat and turns to me, a soft, questioning light in his eyes. The luggage is between us, so I step around it and take Henry's hand.

"I distinctly remember. I said, 'I have your coat,' and you said, 'Keep it.'"

"I said that because I was angry and hurt."

"And I kept it because . . ."

"Because?"

"Because I wanted something to remember the best

night of my life. Especially if I wasn't going to experience anything like it ever again."

We watch each other, the stillness of the apartment closing around us, the only noise the soft pad of Purrk prowling from one room to another and the humming wind mounting toward a storm. Outside the air is electric, and inside a buzzing energy rides over my skin, filling me with a tingling, painful need.

I want to hold, to kiss, to be as close to Henry as possible. I want to run my hands over him. I want to touch, to feel. I want to pull him close and spin in the dizzying circle of us until I can't tell where I begin and he ends. But it's more than that. I don't just want another night where we make love. I don't want a moment that ends. I want to be close to him for the rest of the time we have. I want to keep discovering more about him. I want to keep understanding him. I want to wake up tangled with him in twisted sheets. I want to share breakfast with tea and coffee. I want to have discussions that span the universe. I want to be with him for the rest of my life, not because I'm losing myself, but because I'm finding myself. And while I'm doing that, I want him to be doing it with me.

And no matter what I look like or who I have to be, it doesn't matter, as long as we can do it and be it together.

"Serena?" Henry steps forward, his shoes whispering over the wood floor. He clasps my hand and then enfolds me in the circle of his arms.

The warmth of him wraps around me, and the electric buzzing grows until I feel like I'm standing inside a tuning fork that's been struck and is vibrating across every inch of my skin.

"It doesn't have to be only one night," Henry

whispers, his cheek pressed against my chest, our bodies fitted to each other. I lean into him, molding to him. "I'd stay with you every night. Every day. If we never switch back I'll stay with you. If we do switch back I'll stay with you. It doesn't matter, as long as it's you."

I hold him, dropping my lips to the top of his head and spanning my hands along the base of his spine. For a moment, in the dim light of the entry, it feels as if we've merged, as if our hearts are beating as one.

"If we switch back, you'll still want—"

"I'll always want you. We're like binary stars—we're bound tight. Gravity keeps us orbiting each other. When people look at the night sky, they think binary stars are one star. It's only with a telescope they can tell there's actually two stars there. That's how I feel about you. Switching back isn't going to change that."

I think about binary stars, about how they're as close to soul mates as you can get. And how even if they wanted to, they couldn't separate. It's like the anglerfish, but instead of one sucking the life from the other, the stars make each other shine brighter.

[Here we have a diagram of Binary Stars, labeled me and Henry.]

And isn't that the way a relationship should be? One person shouldn't subsume the other. Instead they should both help the other shine bright.

"You're right," I say, staring down at Henry, my eyes wide, skin tingling. "You're right."

He reaches up. Rests his hand against my heart. A bolt of electricity flows through me, like his palm has the nuclear fusion of a thousand stars pulsing through it. I jolt, and outside the window a streak of lightning cracks through the sky. The apartment fills with a sharp blue light and a deafening boom rattles the windowpane.

Purrk yowls and streaks across the living room. He launches himself under the couch, and from the dark his green, glowing eyes peer out at us.

"Wow. That was . . ."

Rain bursts from the clouded sky, driving against the windowpane and drumming against the roof, drowning out my words. Another bolt of lightning cracks the sky, spearing Geneva. The gray light is swallowed by the storm and the apartment descends into an unnatural darkness. The drumming rain is almost deafening, and outside the old, narrow streets are already swelling with roiling streams of rainwater.

An electric current tinges the air and a strange, expectant buzzing vibrates through me. I've not felt this way since the last thunderstorm. Since Henry and I—

"We have to go," I say, grabbing Henry's arms. My hands vibrate on his skin.

"What? Where?"

"To switch! Can't you feel it? We have to go!"

With that I grab his coat from the closet and thrust my arms into the sleeves. I grab a raincoat for him, clasp his hand, and then we fly down the stairs and out of the apartment building, into the driving rain, the violent lightning, and the heart of the storm.

38

ONE HUNDRED METERS DOWN, DEEP IN THE COOL DEPTHS of the earth, Henry and I stand in the center of ATLAS.

Outside it's unnaturally dark, sheets of rain and ominous clouds blot out the sky, and wind rips through stands of mountain pine and flips streetlights horizontal. The rain slashes sideways and beats the ground so violently that it springs upward and defies gravity by falling up. The howling wind, the driving rain, and the crash of thunder have created a storm of Big Bang proportions. Every streak of lightning thrust across the sky is like a particle beam racing from one end of the LHC to the other.

The air crackles with otherworldly energy, infusing my blood and making me feel as if I've closed my hands around an electric fence and I can't let go.

Deep in the underground cavern, well below the bellowing storm, I still feel the pulse of every bolt of lightning.

The particle detector is quiet, shut down and put to

rest. It feels as if I'm standing at the feet of a sleeping giant. The hum of cooling fans and electronics is the gentle snore of a mammoth. The air is cool and tinged with the scent of metal, oil, and cool underground circulated air.

Henry and I stand on a metal catwalk suspended twenty feet above the ground. The glint of metal—gold and silver, bright and flashing—surrounds us. The space is cavernous, twenty-five meters high, and right now the sleeping/dreaming air is filled with thrumming energy.

Henry faces me. Under his hardhat his hair is wet and dripping. Water drops glisten on his face and lips. His cheeks are pink from the chill and his eyes glow with a sparking electricity.

I'm just as wet, my skin just as chilled. But inside I'm glowing with a current that's growing with every second.

"You feel it, right? This is it."

He grips the handrail, his knuckles bleeding to white. "Yes. I feel it. It's just like the night we switched."

I nod, moving closer to him. When I do, an electromagnetic pulse of energy rockets around us. Henry's eyes widen and he reaches out to steady himself. He's shaking. His whole body is shaking. I reach out. Grab his hand.

And then I realize I'm shaking too.

But it's not us.

It's the catwalk. Or —no, it's ATLAS. The entire space is vibrating as if we've been gripped in a giant's fist and he's shaking us. All the metal machinery flashes. The catwalk groans. We're caught in the grips of an energetic anomaly.

I twist my hand in Henry's as the tug of the energy

increases, as the catwalk sways, groans, and shrieks, and the molecules inside me start to twist and rend.

This is it.

This feels like it.

I cling to Henry's hand. Keep my eyes on his. Last time, when the world started to spin, I didn't want to be held by Henry. This time I don't want to ever let go.

"Ducky," he says, and I smile at his use of my name as a glowing sensation builds inside. "If this doesn't work," he says, his words dying under the growing roar and the swaying of the catwalk, "I don't feel . . . hurts . . . if this doesn't work . . . I—"

"What?"

The wind—How is there wind underground?—tears away his words. The vibration exponentially increases until everything inside me is breaking apart.

"Henry?" I grip his hand, the whirling inside me a maelstrom.

"Ducky . . . I don't think this . . ." His face pales, his mouth tightens, and he flinches. In pain?

"I can't hear you!" I shout, feeling as if I'm losing him, as if a whirlpool is gripping me and he's slipping away, his hand about to be ripped from mine.

He steps forward and the harsh light glints over his pale skin, casting him in gray.

He flings himself against my chest and grips my still damp coat as if he's feeling it too, that force tearing and ripping, desperate to yank us apart.

And then the howling wind, the feeling that we're in the center of a lightning bolt, thunder booming around us, it stops.

It all stops.

And there's only silence.

Dead silence.

Henry looks up at me, his eyes unfocused, his face wreathed in pain.

Suddenly I'm scared. I'm terrified. Something's wrong. The energy is gone, the electricity is gone, everything is gone.

"Henry?"

"I love you," he gasps as if he's run a thousand miles across the universe just to say those three words.

They hit me with the force of a supernova. It's not love at first sight. It's not friendship-to-love. It's not hate-to-love. It's not blind love. It's love built from understanding. A love that knows all my flaws, everything I'm afraid of or that I've done wrong, all my idiosyncrasies and all my blind spots—a love that knows I'm human and often bullheaded and stubborn and mistaken. A love that knows me and still loves—loves every hidden corner of me, every dark depth, and every idiotic thing I've done in the past and may do in the future, and still, still loves me. It isn't a passing love or a superficial love. It's a deep, abiding, accepting love. A burning, undying love.

With that knowledge my entire universe explodes in a sheer, brilliant white light. A booming flash blinds me with its heat and its force.

The light fades slowly, white seeping back to color—silver, gold, blue, orange. The yellow of the catwalk. Sound returns—humming electronics, beeping, the whir of air vents. Smell—oil, metal, rain.

And then feeling—cold skin, goose bumps, and—

Where's Henry?

He's not in my arms.

He's not holding my hand.

I spin around. My heart booms in my ears like thunder.

I look down. I'm still Henry. Strong hands, biceps, long legs—

There.

Lying on the ground. Face pale, black hair fanned out, mouth parted, eyes unseeing.

Henry lies dead at my feet.

39

FOR ALL OF HUMAN EXISTENCE WE'VE SEARCHED FOR answers. One of humanity's enduring traits is the undying quest to understand our place in the universe. To understand ... why.

At the height of particle physics, where the language of science no longer adequately describes what's happening, the only thing left is poetry of the soul. It's this place where many scientists meet God. Every day I see how the universe hangs on a particle's edge, how one alteration to the laws of nature, a billionth of a billionth of a change, would result in the annihilation of *everything*. In physics, we understand either we are very, very alone—the result of chaos and coincidence—and we will die alone, or someone out there cares very, very, very much to have created a universe that would collapse with the slightest of changes to the fundamental laws that build our existence—but won't, because we aren't alone and never will be.

When I was younger, I fell in love. I thought the only

thing that mattered was my love of science, my passion for physics, my quest to understand the fundamental laws of nature. I believed I only had room for one love. I believed if I fell in love with a man then I would no longer love my career or pursue my passions. I was scared that the all-consuming love I'd experience would make me leave my job for marriage and family.

I promised myself I would never, ever, ever give up my life for a man.

I grip Henry's cold, limp hand.

He has no pulse.

No breath.

I kneel on the cold metal next to him, the hard floor digging into my knees, the scent of fear clogging my nostrils and constricting my throat. The harsh lights cast him waxen and still.

"Henry?" I grip his shoulders, shake him. "Henry."

He's gone.

How do I know?

Because that constant magnetic pull that thrums between us like a clear stream flowing in a lush forest—it's gone. That electric buzz that dances over my skin whenever we touch—it's not there. The resonance I feel, the sense of rightness—it's vanished.

In its place is an icy finger trickling down my spine, dragging away Henry and leaving cold emptiness.

"Please," I whisper.

And then I look down at my body lying still, unmoving, dead, and I know exactly what I have to do.

I'm at that fork in the road again. Not many people get to stand at the same fork twice in their lives. Once the choice is made, it's made. Before, I chose to lose Henry, to deny love.

This time around, I can choose to let Henry go. I can go on living my life as him, pursuing all my goals. Serena Otaki will be gone, but I'll still be here. I'll visit Henry's family. I'll take care of his parents like he'd want me to. I'll write articles under his name and attribute all my achievements to him as well. I'll visit my family in California as Henry, and after a while, I'll forget I was ever Serena. I won't have Henry, but I will have science.

Right now, Serena Otaki is lying on the ground without breath or a heartbeat. I can choose to let Henry go. For the second time I can choose myself, not give up my life for a man.

It's funny. I never meant that phrase literally.

But now I do.

I think about how much Henry loves his family. How he held his mom in a tight hug as if he was afraid he'd never see her again. I think about how he teased his brothers and laughed with his sisters and how he so clearly loved his niece and nephews. I think about how he wasn't ever afraid to tell me how he felt. How he made my mom healthy meals and read her books and made her laugh when she was tired or afraid. I think about how my mom asked me to take care of him—of me—by being there for him and giving him someone's hand to hold.

Henry has so many people who love him. He has so many people he loves. He's never been afraid to receive love, and he's never been afraid to give it.

Me? I've only ever been afraid.

I'm not anymore.

I can't let Henry die. I can't let him stay me and lose his life. I'd do anything to keep him here, even switch back. Right here and right now. So that I'm the one who's gone and he can keep on living and see his mom and dad again, laugh with his brothers and sisters, and have a nice cup of tea next to the kitchen fire on a rainy day in the country.

And with that cup of tea, or twenty, or two hundred, he'll start to feel better. And eventually he'll fall in love again and he'll have that cozy feeling he gets when he thinks of smiling over at the woman he loves, holding her hand on the couch, and reading her a line from the book he's enjoying.

I understand him. I know his capacity for love is endless. That's why I know it isn't me that should go on, it's him.

This is his body. This is his life. This is his future.

And that future spreads out before me like a ribbon unfurling from its spool. It spins out, and I can see all the years in front of him.

Love. Marriage. Kids. Happiness.

That's all I want for him.

And if my time is here? If I have to give up everything for him?

My life? My future? My passions?

So be it. I wouldn't want any of it without him anyway.

"Henry," I whisper, leaning over him, gripping both of his limp hands in mine.

Across the cavernous space, beneath the bright lights, the elevator doors slash open and a team of paramedics carrying a stretcher rushes out.

Someone must've seen Henry collapse on the video feed. They must've called for help.

But if they take him away? I know deep inside that I won't ever see him again.

So I lean down before they can reach us, and I press my mouth close to his.

Above, the lights flicker and the cavernous space pitches into darkness. I grip Henry's hand, hold myself against him, and press my mouth to his unmoving lips.

Then I'm whirling, flying, tearing through space and time, spinning, spinning, spinning in a dizzying rush that's faster than light and more violent than a cataclysm. Everything inside me tears, rips apart, and I collide with —Henry? Is he there?—and everything in me wrenches and rends, splitting into a thousand shards of being. And I know this time, there isn't any going back. This time Henry and I are switching—we're switching back—and he'll be alive, and I'll be gone.

And I'm not sorry to die. I'm only sorry to leave him.

As the electric storm raging around us slows and all the particles inside me start to coalesce, I'm pulled, hurtling back into myself.

But before I go, before I die, I have to tell Henry something. I pray, I hope, that as he slams back into his own body he hears me and understands.

I never told him. I never said the words that have always been in my heart.

So I say with my last remaining breath, "Henry, I lo—"

40

HENRY

I jolt upright, my heart pounding ferociously, practically banging free of my chest. A cold sweat beads on my forehead and an oceanic roaring fills the void between unconsciousness and wakefulness.

There's a metallic, acid taste in my mouth and the grip of antiseptic riding in the air. I fight down the violent hammering of my heart and blink away the darkness.

But the dark remains.

It's night.

The purple-gray light of Geneva, the half-night of the city bleeding light into the sky, creeps through the window. The storm died, and now the city sleeps in the dampened, lulled state of watchful quiet that always comes after the rain.

It's the perfect time for a cup of tea.

I suck in a sharp breath. Sleep has fallen away, and I remember.

I quickly reach up, splaying my fingers over my face. Feel the thick two-day stubble. Reach for the glasses tilted on my nose. Just to be certain, I pat my chest, feeling the pounding under my fingers. No breasts. I blink. Look down. My hands. My legs. My everything.

I'm at home in my body again. I feel like myself. Solid, steady, with dodgy eyesight and a love of football, physics, and tea and biscuits.

I'm me.

Dammit.

"Dammit, Ducky."

I run my hands through my hair and shove it back from my eyes. I remember now.

I was dying.

I squint into the dark, catching the glow of the vitals monitor hidden by the shadow cast from the room door. It's a small, sterile room, not dissimilar to the one Serena's mom stayed in when in hospital. Four close walls, dour and claustrophobic. A square window. A plastic wardrobe. A narrow cot.

And a hard, plastic chair, grossly uncomfortable so you aren't tempted to stay too long.

Except I'll stay all night, won't I? I'll stay as long as Ducky does.

"You've a nice cot," I say, my voice a low murmur in the silent room. "Perhaps we should trade."

Ducky doesn't answer.

Not that I expect her to.

She lies still and silent under the white cotton sheets, her black hair loose around her shoulders, her normally pink cheeks pale, her mouth drawn. When I was young I had an illustrated copy of *Grimms' Fairy Tales*. Right now, she looks just like Snow White in her glass coffin.

Ducky would hate that.

I hate it.

From the first moment I saw her she's been filled with life. She moves lightning-quick between one thought and another, her expression so animated you can catch a hundred emotions in one second. She's always reminded me of the English weather, where bursts of rain and bouts of sunshine leap back and forth as quickly as sun and shadow flickering beneath the swaying branches of a leafy sycamore tree.

She's always been like that. She sprints from one idea to the next, her enthusiasm contagious. When she walks she moves quickly, with a short skip to keep up with her racing thoughts. Her gaze continuously roves. Her eyes are expressive. She's . . .

She worried that being with me would change her, or that being me would change her, but she's always been herself. Filled with life.

When I was in primary school my parents celebrated their fifteenth anniversary. They hosted a garden party and invited the entire village. I asked my mum, "How do I find someone like you and dad did?" My mum said, "You don't have to find them—they'll come to you. The minute you look across a room and you don't see anyone but them, that's when you know you've found each other."

The day I first saw Ducky, when I looked around the pub and there she was, stuck . . . I knew.

I reach over to the bed and take her hand—too cold, too limp—in mine. I run my fingers over the back of it, draw a soothing circle, then weave our fingers together.

"You shouldn't have switched back," I tell her. "If one of us had to suffer, I'd rather it be me."

I was there, hovering on the edge of the storm. I felt myself slipping away. Then in the spinning darkness I felt Ducky reach out, grab my hand, and yank me back.

I was thrown into my body, alive and well. And Ducky?

I swear my heart stopped. My breathing too. The pain was excruciating. I know she chose to switch so that if one of us died it would be her.

That's what it felt like. It felt as if I was dying.

Yet when the paramedics arrived, Ducky was fine. Only . . . not waking up.

I think perhaps that psychic was right. If we'd stayed in the wrong body for much longer, we wouldn't have survived.

I'm not sure Ducky will survive now. Except she has to.

I called her parents. Her mom asked me to keep my promise, to stay by Ducky's side and hold her hand until they could arrive. I know I didn't make that promise, but I have no intention of breaking it.

Jillian raced here, her husband Daniel right behind her. When she first saw me, she said, "Serena?"

I shook my head. "No, sorry." And I was.

They left after two hours of pacing and questions and stress, and only because Daniel insisted Jillian had to rest.

Now I lean forward in the hard plastic chair and brush a strand of hair off Serena's cheek. I know she hates it when it falls over her face.

"You're all right," I tell her, keeping my voice low, blending with the echoing footsteps in the hallway, the low nighttime murmurs of the staff, and the gray light of the room. The cold air from the overhead vent drags over us, catching her hair and sending the metallic whisper of antiseptic through the air.

I grip her hand tightly, trying to infuse her with my warmth. Her features are more familiar than my own. I've spent nearly two years memorizing the way her lips curve into a smile, the way her hair falls from its braid, and the way her eyes spark and then glow like the milky way whenever I enter a room.

Switching places with her didn't make me want her less. It made me love her more.

"You're all right," I say again.

Her hand remains still beneath me, her breathing even and quiet. Her eyelashes don't flutter. Her heart rate doesn't increase.

"You should come back. You should wake up."

I wait to see if she will.

When she doesn't I pull the chair closer, scraping the legs over the floor, and then wrap close to her, cocooning her, just like we're dancing again.

"You should wake up because I love you. And I know you and I'm certain you'll have a lot to say about it. I wanted to tell you about everything I learned being you . . ."

I wait, smiling at the soft line of her cheeks and the high, questioning fling of her eyebrows. Even in sleep she raises her eyebrows at me.

A warmth settles in my chest, and I run my fingers over the back of her hand.

"At first I didn't like being you. I dislike coffee and cats and spicy food. Not to mention, you have a serious lack of respect for hoovering and tidying up. I tossed dirty laundry everywhere. It was disturbing. Not to mention, you fidget, you're too short to reach the top cabinet, and honestly, men stared at my breasts too much for my liking. And don't remind me about menstruation. Or chocolate. If I want chocolate, I want Cadbury white chocolate, not Ghirardelli Dark. It was strange being you, like I'd slipped on a pair of shoes that didn't quite fit and they were rubbing me raw and chafing my skin."

I wait to see how Ducky's taking my confession. She doesn't seem disturbed. Her eyes are still closed, her breathing still shallow, so I continue.

"Here's where it gets strange. It didn't take too long for me to get used to that shoe. I think it was your memories, the glimpses of your past and the emotions I felt that were clearly a fragment of you. The first memory I had was of your back yard, when I felt as if I'd swallowed starlight and a comet shot across the sky. It reminded me of the first time I saw you. I knew I'd experienced you falling in love."

I brush her hair back from her face and take a deep breath. Outside in the hallway two nurses walk past, debriefing on a patient. Their voices echo over the tile floors and the plaster walls and then fade.

Ducky and I stay wrapped in the intimate confines of her room.

"That wasn't all," I say, pulling the scratchy cotton sheets higher, trying to give her warmth. "I caught your loneliness and your dreams. I felt the awe and love you have for your home, but also your desire to leave and explore. I felt your longing in England for a large family that might love you. And I saw the night we first met."

I pause, waiting to see if Ducky will wake up to join in the conversation, but she doesn't.

"I know what you felt when we made love. Not because I saw the whole thing, but because I felt the same way. And then I felt your fear. I wish I could say I don't understand, but I do. I was scared too, but I thought we'd leap together. I was angry when I first saw that in your memories, you choosing to run away. But then . . ."

I take a deep breath, pull in the scent of mint and apple that clings to Ducky, and remember the scent of starlight that I always caught hints of when I lived as her. For her, starlight is love.

"Then I saw the night at the pub where you let me go, and I felt how much it hurt. And there was another memory. I don't know when it was. We were in the cafeteria at work. I was having a cup of tea by myself, and you were sitting at a table across the room drinking an espresso. I had the impression this was a common occurrence.

"You came and sat down far away but facing me and pretended for just a moment that we were at a table together. That we weren't separated by a room full of people and our own inability to connect, but instead we were enjoying a moment, just the two of us. The feeling of that moment, it was a yearning so intense it would have shocked me if I hadn't felt the same exact thing every single day I spent without you."

I squeeze Ducky's hand, feeling the thrumming electricity that's always there when we touch.

"So after that I didn't mind being you. I understood you, even though I thought I never would. I wanted to protect you and your family and be there for you in any way you needed me. Even if the only way you needed me was to help your family or be your friend. But Ducky, I'm not just your friend. I love you. I want to spend my life with you. I want to wake up next to you every morning, argue theories at work, bring you coffee and chocolate when you need it, and take you with me to visit my family and yours. You can make messes and I'll tidy them up. I can eat steak and you can have tofu. We'll let Purrk rule the flat, but we'll also ask Kate to find us a rescue corgi. You'll read sci-fi and I'll watch football. And sometimes we'll walk through Geneva and you'll take me and my coat on a magical tour to all your favorite places. And then, when we get home, I'll kiss you and you'll kiss me. And we'll live happily ever after. But we can't do that if you leave. We can't do that if you don't wake up.

"Please, Ducky, wake up. Wake up. You said you never wanted to give up your life for love. Don't. Don't give it up for love. Come back to me and *live* your life for love. Grab it. Take it. Live for love."

I clutch Ducky's hand. "Please."

I stare down at Ducky, at the shadows falling over her face, at the sweep of her eyelashes and the upturned corner of her lips. At first I thought what happened to us could be explained by science. I thought we would find the solution with our minds. But if it was science, it wasn't any science I can understand. Instead it feels as if it was another mystery we may never know the answer to. There are doors in the universe that we'll never hold the key to, nor unlock. So now I think what happened was beyond our comprehension. Yet when humans reach things beyond the understanding of our minds, we use our souls.

How did Chopin compose masterpieces? How did Galileo sail the stars? How did Tesla call down electricity? Through dreams. Perhaps through love.

How do you describe a feeling that can't be put into words?

Through a song? Through a handful of wild daisies? Through holding a hand in a darkened room when the only hope you have is each other?

Or do you take that feeling and package it in the most inadequate words to exist in the English language? Perhaps when we say them, we can only hope the other person understands—that they feel what we feel—that to them "I love you" means just what it means to you.

Starlight over redwoods, wind trailing over bare skin.

Sunshine peeking through the rain clouds, a cup of tea and a beloved book in your hands.

A cat purring in your lap, a corgi cuddled over your feet.

Your newborn niece curling her hand around your finger.

Your mom singing to you in the night, rocking you close when you wake from a nightmare.

A gentle kiss in the rain with the woman who will always stay in your heart.

There are a million expressions of love. They could fill the universe in all their infinite glory, and yet . . . we can only say—

"Henry."

Ducky drags in a sharp breath. Her eyes fly open as if she's still spinning, flying back into herself. She grips my hand, searching through the shadows and the gray light of the hospital room until she finds me.

I sink into the light in her eyes. It's all the stars, the entire universe, and my chest feels as if it breaks open and my heart tumbles to lie at her feet, hers for the taking.

"You're here," I breathe.

She came back.

And then I remember what she said. I remember what pulled me out of the deathlike darkness and yanked me back into myself. I remember.

And I decide that maybe those three words are enough after all.

Ducky squeezes my hand and says—

"I love you."

41

I'VE ALWAYS BELIEVED THAT THINGS ARE ONLY IMPOSSIBLE until they're not. For instance: me actually enjoying tea, people switching bodies, and true love.

Especially true love.

I always thought, "My gosh, true love is impossible! It can't possibly happen!"

But then it did.

It did.

And by "true love," I don't mean the kind where you're giving yourself up. I mean the kind where you're fully you.

My hand shakes as I take my apartment key and try to fit it into my lock. There's so much emotion inside me right now I can barely keep it all in. When I turn this key, when I open this door—well, let's just say, Henry and I aren't going to be messing around.

Outside the sky is a bright Tiffany-blue, the shade of jewelry boxes and future dreams. The rainstorm washed the old stone buildings clean, and now the spired churches, the stately hotels, and the French balconied apartment buildings glisten and shine in the sparkling sun.

The streets are full, as they usually are on a clear, calm day after a storm, full of couples at outdoor cafés, families in the park, and the stray office worker blinking up at the sun, wondering if they should take the afternoon off. There are snatches of laughter, the rumble of traffic, and animated conversations all bouncing like a child's ball around the narrow stone streets.

Outside my apartment the air smells like my nook of Geneva—wet leaves, stone, coffee, and croissants, with just a tinge of crisp lake air. Inside my apartment building the air is still and quiet, perfumed with floor polish and old plaster and stone. The tall windows in the stairwell let in the bright sky-blue light. The city sounds are muffled, especially beneath the loud thudding in my chest.

Finally, I manage to slide the key into the lock. I turn my bolt and the door opens to my apartment—all the clutter, my overstuffed couch, Purrk prancing to the door, tail up in greeting. He rubs against my legs (the traitor) and then, surprisingly, he rubs against Henry too.

At that, I finally look at Henry to see if he's feeling the same rush of emotions that I am.

When we caught the taxi from the hospital he said, "We have approximately six hours until my family and yours descend on us, to ascertain for themselves that you are in fact okay. Which means—"

"My place or yours?"

The smile he gave me . . . Let's just say, for the first time in my life, my knees went weak.

And here they are again, wobbly and weak, because

Henry's gray-blue eyes are just like the sky after a storm —full of hope and dreams and love.

There's a throbbing ache building inside me, brushing over my skin and electrifying the air between us. I sway toward Henry, the magnetic pull of him sweeping me up and drawing me close.

My breasts grow heavy, my nipples sensitive, and all I want is to feel Henry's fingers drawing over me, his mouth taking me in. I want to feel the quickening of his heart and the vibration of his moan as he tastes me.

Something in my expression must relay everything I'm visualizing, because his eyes shine cerulean like Lake Geneva under the sun. He takes one step forward, reaches around me, and shuts the door. He leaves his palm on the wood and then leans forward and places his other hand on the door, trapping me in the electricity of his gaze.

I reach behind me, grab the cold metal of the bolt, and click the lock.

I'm caged between his arms, the cool wood firm against my back. Henry leans close, the heat of him wrapping around me, the cool cedar-and-starlight scent of him streaming over me. He's taller than me again, broader, and so he dips his head, bringing his mouth close to mine.

He's so close his thighs press into mine. My pelvis scrapes against him and all my nerve endings thrum and glow incandescent.

"Ducky?"

I nod, swallowing down the hummingbird-fast beating of my pulse. My lips tingle as he swipes his gaze over them. He captures my eyes with his.

There's a question there. *Do you trust me? Is this*

forever? Can I do that thing with my tongue and my red tie again?

The answer is yes.

Yes, to all of them.

"Yes—"

I don't get out anymore, because the moment I say yes, Henry kisses me. And that—oh—we've kissed before. We kissed when we were each other. We kissed that first night together. But we've never kissed as ourselves—truly ourselves—and we've never kissed for the last first time.

Henry cups my face, digs his hand through my hair, and tilts my head so I'm at the perfect angle for him to make love to my mouth. He makes a small, deep noise against my lips, and when he does, I open for him. He takes what I give, sliding his mouth over mine and tasting me in long, languid strokes that build and build. I bite at his mouth, nibble and lick and taste.

With each nip and bite, with each stroke, the current between us grows until I can't help but lodge myself against him, clutching his shoulders and tugging him closer.

I press my breasts against his chest, the sensitive points tingling as he gasps. My hips rock against his and I feel him, hard and wanting. A spark lights and dances over my skin as I rock into him again. He bites my bottom lip and then drags his hand over my breast, down my hip, to hold me in place while he kisses me, devours me. I try to roll against him, but he keeps me pressed to the door, trapped, while he makes me glow from his kiss.

"Henry," I gasp, the heat of his mouth sending shockwaves through my veins all the way down to my core. "Now. I want—"

"A test drive?" he murmurs, his mouth trailing down my neck.

His hand splays over my hip, holding me tight. I rock toward him. He cups my face, his fingers curling over my cheek. I turn my head and press my mouth to the palm of his hand, opening my mouth and giving his palm an open-mouthed kiss.

"I don't need a test drive. You're already mine."

He smiles then, and with that smile I decide I'm done with clothes and I'm done with kissing. I want to feel him stretched over me, his heat sinking into me, the weight of him and the feel of him.

I grab the hem of my wrap dress and in a swift motion tug it over my head. Henry blinks as I unsnap my bra and let it fall to the floor. He devours my breasts with his eyes, and they grow heavy and voluptuous under his gaze. The memory of his touch, of his mouth, makes my nipples peak.

"I like them better on you," he says, and then I step out of my underwear and stand naked before him.

"I'm glad to have them back. I like my breasts."

My skin tingles under his gaze. He holds me there for a moment, a soft smile on his mouth. And then a sharp electric snap crackles through the air and the moment is gone, and Henry grabs my hips and lifts me so that I'm wrapping my legs around him, clinging to him as he strides past my cluttered living room, past Purrk lying in a stream of sunlight on the wooden floor, and to the dim light of my bedroom.

Henry drops me onto the bed and I sink into the cool white feather comforter, the scent of mint and apples rising around me.

He tears his T-shirt off, displaying his lean, flat

stomach dusted with hair and tanned skin. Then he flicks free his button and kicks off his jeans and boxers. And then he's with me, his thighs over mine, the dusting of hair on his chest scraping over my breasts, the pressure of his weight sinking me into the bed.

He reaches up, links his fingers with mine, and gazes into my eyes.

"I love you. It doesn't matter what you look like or what you do, or what your name is, or who everyone else thinks you are. I love you. The you in your heart."

I feel as if I'm falling, as if I'm spinning, whirling, trailing behind a falling star streaking through the sky, caught up in the stardust. This time, though, I know the spinning isn't foretelling a switch. It's foretelling a future.

"I love you too. I love you more than you can know."

Henry smiles down at me. "I think I know."

And yes, actually, I think he does.

Then he kisses me, his mouth taking mine. The hard length of him presses against me, his hands clutching mine. I roll my hips, starlight burning over me at every place we touch, at every place we connect.

He roves down my chest, tasting my breasts, kissing down, down, until he's tasting me and making me beg and clutch him close and cry his name as he breaks me apart and then pieces me back together.

And then I pull him back to me. He lies over me, presses his heart to mine, kisses me, clasps my hands, and then holds me in his gaze as he gently nudges my legs apart, and—

"Stop watching, you perverts."

"Who?" Henry looks around the room, his wheat-colored hair falling over his face, the dappled sunlight spreading over his flushed cheeks and the sweat glistening on his skin.

I smile, looking up. *You* know who I'm talking to.

"Never mind," I say.

And so Henry never minds by kissing me, nudging my legs apart, and slowly sliding into me. He makes a soft, male noise and the muscles in his shoulders and back bunch as he drives deeper. I clench around him, and he grips my bottom and tilts me so that when he's deep inside me he hits a spot that flashes electric-white.

And then he's moving, and I'm moving with him. His fingers brush over my clit, sparking a cascade of pleasure. And he strokes and thrusts, slow and languid like his kiss, until I'm burning and the current between us glows bright.

And then the room disappears and there's only Henry and me and a spinning, whirling, thrumming of shattering need where I break apart in his arms, and because he's holding me and breaking apart too, we come together and coalesce.

He falls over me, his weight pressing me into the soft mattress. The comforter rustles beneath me and the salty taste of him lingers on my lips. I brush my mouth against the curve of his shoulder and settle under the delicious weight of him.

His heart pounds against my chest and his legs tangle with mine.

Our hands are still clasped, and he's still inside me. He lifts his head and looks down at me, his eyes full of something I understand.

"Do you think we could do that again?" I curve my ankle around his calf and run my foot up and down his leg.

"I think . . . hmmm . . ." His eyes are sleepy, his lids heavy. "I think we have four hours, twenty-two minutes until family and friends arrive. That means we can do it . . . eight more times."

"Eight! A man can't—"

"There are tongues and lips and fingers and ties and . . ." He nods over at my nightstand.

I gasp. "I knew it! I knew you'd seen it."

He grins at me, unrepentant. Then he presses a kiss to my mouth.

"In my defense," I say, "I couldn't have sex after I was with you. We made love, and I couldn't bring myself to be with anyone else when the only person I wanted was you."

Henry's gaze softens, and he reaches up and brushes his fingers over my face. "Then it seems we have a lot of lost time to make up for."

"Are you going to marry me?" I ask, thinking about rain and books and corgis and cats, tea and coffee and kids and castles and holidays and normal days, and, oh . . . everything. Everything that being with Henry would mean.

"Are you asking me?" There's a small smile on his face, his eyes full of laughter.

"Of course I am."

His small smile turns to a grin. "Then yes. I'm going to marry you."

And then, because there are hands and fingers and ties and a nightstand nearby, Henry makes up for lost time—by loving me.

42

SPRING FALLS SOFTLY OVER GENEVA, WITH THE MURMURED
trickle of melting ice, the sigh of green shoots of grass
peeking through patches of snow, and the sweet song of
the nightingale finally returned from her travels.

August is gone, the vibrant leaves of autumn long
past. Christmas with Henry's family—wearing paper
crowns and drinking port in front of the fire while the
kids popped Christmas crackers—remains a fond
memory, as is our first New Year's kiss, and Valentine's
Day with a corgi rescue pup wearing a glossy red bow,
and now we've arrived at spring in our new home—a
quaint alpine cabin in the woods overlooking the city, not
far from Jillian and Daniel.

A lot has changed in the past nine months.

A lot.

I quit my job, I only eat red meat, I watch football
instead of *Star Trek*, my spice cabinet is alphabetically
organized, I drink tea with every meal, and I fondly call
Henry and me "Hecky."

Kidding.

I'm *kidding*.

Actually, I'm not kidding about the spice cabinet. Henry organized it, and I agree, it's really useful. But about everything else—I'm kidding.

I love my job. Henry stayed at CERN, and we recently published our first paper together. We presented it at a conference in Italy, where I gorged on fresh focaccia dipped in the local olive oil and avoided *all* noodles.

During the workday, at exactly 10:15 a.m., Henry and I meet for a quick break, and he drinks a tea and I have a double espresso, then we get back to smashing atoms and crunching data.

It may have been a surprise to some when we showed up at work engaged, and then a month later married, but then they shrug prosaically and put it down to another mystery of the universe.

On weekends we play with our corgi, Cupid, explore the hidden corners of the city, and take jaunts to the forests and wineries and medieval villages of the countryside. We go to the farmers' market and then cook together, and we cuddle on the couch, where I watch *Deep Space Nine* or *Voyager* and Henry reads a book (usually a biography of a British scientist), sometimes looking up with a smile and quoting a passage to me.

And then, of course, we do other things, many things, which you may think are impossible—things that make sex on a tree branch look tame. And I'm here to tell you, sex in a . . . um . . . while . . . er— Never mind. Needless to say, *nothing* is impossible.

But that isn't the point. The point is that tonight Henry's family, my parents, Jillian and Daniel, and their baby are all here. So is Fran, who is in heaven holding

Beau, the new baby, rocking and cooing and delighting in his baby sounds. And when Fran isn't cuddling Beau, she's in the kitchen stirring up vast quantities of food for everyone gathered.

We're having a delayed housewarming party and everyone is in the garden, twinkle lights overhead, soft music drifting over the daffodils and tulips, the scent of pine and fir mixing with curries and pizzas and fondues and fish and chips and tofu (spice level: make your grandchildren weep) and freshly baked bread and French cakes and apple pies and Swiss chocolate confections and practically every food ever invented except noodles.

I step off the back porch, a bucket of champagne and ice in my hands. The cool grass tickles my ankles and the night breeze tugs at my dress. The sky is a lush purple, velvety-soft and star-studded. The music—a slow love song—matches the swaying of the fir trees in the wind. The kids run across the lawn, Cupid yipping as he chases them. Fran holds Beau, patting his back as she laughs at something Daniel says. Jillian leans into Daniel's arms and beams up at him.

My dad pulls a roll of tape from his pocket, his latest adhesive success, and flourishes it for Henry and his brothers. Niall, who is back from his surfing holiday in Australia, holds out his hand in wonder. John, who paid Henry back a thousandfold at Henry's stag do, gives the tape a considering look, and I suddenly feel sorry for Future Niall.

My mom and Henry's mom chat in lawn chairs near a small patch of blooming yellow tulips. They hit it off at the wedding and have developed an abiding friendship.

Kate and Lizzy have their feet up, enjoying the local

Chardonnay they found at a nearby vineyard this afternoon.

Henry's dad offers Daniel a beer and then pulls him to the side, I'm sure trying to convince him—again—that he should develop a Swiss watch specifically for rally navigators. And perhaps, maybe, sponsor a team. I think if enough champagne is served, Daniel will happily agree. Or if it's suggested that they call the watch "The Beau," he'll most definitely agree.

The music and laughter drift over me like a warm spring breeze off the lake, perfumed with daffodil blooms and happiness. The lights twinkle overhead, and the stars, the ones that I've always wanted to reach—I feel as if I'm holding them in my hand.

Everyone here, all the love and friendship, it's as if we're making enough light to shine as bright and warm as an entire constellation.

Henry glances toward me then, and when he sees me standing at the back of the house, the sweet grass and daffodils around me, my dress rumpled and my hair blowing in the breeze, he smiles, the corner of his mouth turning up and his eyes crinkling. He says something to my dad and his brothers and then strides across the lawn, keeping his gaze on me.

I wait, feeling so happy that I can barely keep the emotions inside. I think I must be glowing with them.

Henry reaches me and tucks a strand of hair behind my ear, leaving a shivery glow at his touch, and then presses a kiss to the corner of my mouth.

"What?" I ask when I see the look in his eye—the one that, ever since the day we made love again, hasn't failed to make my knees weak.

"I saw you," he says, brushing his hand over my cheek, "and I couldn't resist coming to say hello."

"You said hello three minutes ago," I say, meaning the kiss he stole behind the trellis.

He makes a noise as if he's reliving a wonderful memory. "I did, didn't I?"

I grin at him, and he takes the bucket of champagne and ice from me. The ice shifts and crackles and the champagne clinks against the metal.

We're toasting our new home, our future, and then, I'm sure, we'll toast Beau, and my mom's health, and Olivia and John's announcement that they're expecting, and Niall getting into law school, and, well . . . it'll go on, until we have to open another bottle, and another, because there are so many things to be thankful for.

Henry takes my hand and I link my fingers with his, holding him tight as we step into the garden.

"I'm so happy," I say, even though happy can't begin to describe what I'm feeling.

But Henry understands what I mean. He always does.

He squeezes my hand, gifts me with his smile, and says, "Me too."

And we step together into the garden to the sound of laughter and cheers for champagne and the happy bark of Cupid and the delighted shrieks of the kids and the wild suggestions for first toasts, and then I think, "This must be what happily ever after feels like— something I thought was impossible but really isn't."

Some people think happily ever after is always going to be joyous and, well, happy and full of one wonderful moment after another. And then other people, they think it doesn't exist at all.

In reality, neither is correct. Life, love, and happily ever after looks more like this.

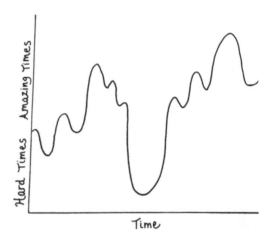

[Here we have a graph of hard times to amazing times on the Y axis and time passing on the X axis, with an up and down flow of experiences over time.]

Isn't that lovely? There are happy times, high moments and low moments, hard times and amazing times. The best moments—a first kiss, a baby's birth, discovering a new particle, moving into your new home—and the hard moments—your mom getting sick, you leaving home— and the everyday moments—walking hand in hand in the woods, reading together on the couch, standing in the garden holding hands as your family gathers around.

It's all there—all there in love and in happily ever after.

Why?

Because it's with the person you love most in the whole universe. In this universe, in another universe, in every single far-reaching corner of the entirety of existence.

"What are you thinking?" Henry asks as we step into the chaos of our family and friends.

I smile at him. "I'm thinking that I love you."

And so Henry drops the bucket of champagne to the grass, takes me in his arms, and kisses me. And when he does, I decide there is *one* impossible thing in the universe. One impossibility that will never be broken.

It's impossible that Henry and I will ever stop loving each other.

And that is exactly the way it should be.[1]

THE END

NOTES

Chapter 1

1. E.g. If a date asks me how many sexual partners I've had, I say 8. However, in the unspoken footnote they haven't read, I say sexual partners are like age—once you hit a certain number you stop counting. See, aren't footnotes fun?
2. Evidence of hearth fires in Wonderwerk Cave in South Africa from ONE MILLION years ago.

Chapter 2

1. Fish genitalia are varied and unique. Some have long appendages, others do not.
2. Pheromones.
3. Joule: a unit of energy equal to the work done by a force of one newton acting through one meter. (This is sexier than it sounds.)

Chapter 3

1. Five-sigma: probability of 3×10^{-7}, or about a 1 in 3.5 million chance. If it's five-sigma, it's the real deal.
2. Salubrious: promoting well-being. Used in a sentence? The salubrious effects of sex while paragliding are manifold.

Chapter 7

1. Or anyone else. My rule? One and done. Always. Dating is a distraction.

Chapter 10

1. I don't know if it's *the* red tie. It could be. It might be. I'll never know.

Chapter 12

1. The Worldwide LHC Computing Grid. It's the world's largest computing grid, with 170 computing facilities across 42 countries. Don't forget, CERN is the reason we have an internet.

Chapter 15

1. What the $*%@! is going on?
2. We are Klingons!
3. Happy Birthday.

Chapter 17

1. If a micro black hole were created by the LHC it would disintegrate in about 10^{-27} seconds and then decay into the standard model or supersymmetric particles. No need to worry. No need to fear micro spaghettification here.

Chapter 19

1. Twenty-three.

Chapter 27

1. In my defense, Spock dies. Tragically. I dare you to watch it and not cry.

Chapter 42

1. After all, physicists love a paradox.

Read the next book in the series: *Fated.*

When Fiona Abry is given a family heirloom that "makes your dreams come true" she meets the man of her dreams in her dreams.

Find *Fated* and more at: www.sarahready.com.

JOIN SARAH READY'S NEWSLETTER

Want more *Switched*? Get an exclusive bonus epilogue! When you join the Sarah Ready Newsletter you get access to sneak peaks, insider updates, exclusive bonus scenes and more.

Join today for an exclusive *Switched* epilogue: www.sarahready.com/newsletter

ABOUT THE AUTHOR

Multi award-winning author Sarah Ready writes women's fiction, contemporary romance and romantic comedy. Her books have been described as "euphoric", "heartwarming" and "laugh out loud".

Sarah writes stand-alone romances, including *Josh and Gemma Make a Baby*, *Josh and Gemma the Second Time Around*, *French Holiday*, *The Space Between*, and series romcoms including *Ghosted*, *Switched*, *Fated*, and romcoms in the Soul Mates in Romeo series, all of which can be found at her website: www.sarahready.com.

You can learn more and find upcoming titles at: www.sarahready.com.

Stay up to date, get exclusive epilogues and bonus content. Join Sarah's newsletter at www.sarahready.com/newsletter.

ALSO BY SARAH READY

Stand Alone Romances:

The Fall in Love Checklist

Hero Ever After

Once Upon an Island

French Holiday

The Space Between

The Ghosted Series:

Ghosted

Switched

Fated

Josh and Gemma:

Josh and Gemma Make a Baby

Josh and Gemma the Second Time Around

Soul Mates in Romeo Romance Series:

Chasing Romeo

Love Not at First Sight

Romance by the Book

Love, Artifacts, and You

Married by Sunday

My Better Life

Scrooging Christmas

Dear Christmas

Stand Alone Novella:

Love Letters

Find these books and more by Sarah Ready at:

www.sarahready.com/romance-books

Printed in the USA
CPSIA information can be obtained
at www.ICGtesting.com
JSHW020343030124
54555JS00003B/12